Outstanding Praise for the Movie *Legally Blonde*
Based on the novel by Amanda Brown

"In *Legally Blonde*, Perry Mason meets Miss Clairol. The verdict? Guilty of inciting a near laugh-riot."

—*USA Today*

"One of those rare comic gems that makes you laugh yourself silly."

—Rex Reed, *The New York Observer*

"Two thumbs up!" —*Ebert & Roeper and the Movies*

"This movie is a guilty pleasure and a half . . . Blondes may or may not have more fun, but in this case, they certainly provide more fun."

—Stephen Hunter, *The Washington Post*

"This movie is full of good humor. Based on the novel of the same name by Amanda Brown, *Legally Blonde* is a sassy satire that retains a message: Believe in yourself and follow your dreams. Besides being funny, it's an ode to self-empowerment—especially girl power—and its target audience of young women everywhere will gobble it up like the latest glossy edition of *Cosmopolitan* magazine."

—CNN.com

Amanda Brown based *Legally Blonde* on her experiences as a law student at Stanford. She is blonde, and at work on her next novel. She lives in San Francisco.

LEGALLY BLONDE

AMANDA BROWN

A PLUME BOOK

PLUME
Published by the Penguin Group
Penguin Putnam Inc., 375 Hudson Street, New York, New York 10014, U.S.A.
Penguin Books Ltd, 80 Strand, London WC2R 0RL, England
Penguin Books Australia Ltd, 250 Camberwell Road,
Camberwell, Victoria 3124, Australia
Penguin Books Canada Ltd, 10 Alcorn Avenue,
Toronto, Ontario, Canada M4V 3B2
Penguin Books (N.Z.) Ltd, Cnr Rosedale and Airborne Roads,
Albany, Auckland 1310, New Zealand

Penguin Books Ltd, Registered Offices: Harmondsworth, Middlesex, England

First published by Plume, a member of Penguin Putnam Inc.

First Printing, January 2003
1   3   5   7   9   10   8   6   4   2

Grateful acknowledgment is made to American Broadcasting Companies, Inc. for
the use of lyrics from the song "Conjunction Junction."

 REGISTERED TRADEMARK—MARCA REGISTRADA

LIBRARY OF CONGRESS CATALOGING-IN-PUBLICATION DATA
Brown, Amanda.
Legally blonde / Amanda Brown.
p.   cm.
ISBN 0-452-28373-6
1. Women law students—Fiction.   2. Stanford University—Fiction.
3. Stanford (Calif.)—Fiction.   I. Title.
PS3602.R65 L45 2003
813'.6—dc21   2002034559

Printed in the United States of America
Set in Garamond
Designed by Eve Kirch

LEGALLY BLONDE

CHAPTER ONE

ELLE Woods glanced at the reflections of her bickering sorority sisters Margot and Serena in her vanity mirror. She sat on a pink-skirted stool with faux fur trim that matched the comforter on her bed, where her Chihuahua, Underdog, was comfortably resting.

"At least mine won't sag!" Serena pointed to her saline-enhanced chest. "My boobs are as perky as the day I put them on my credit card!"

"So what if they'll never sag," Margot said, unimpressed. "They're as hard as rocks."

"They're also blocking the only natural light in this room," Elle whispered to Underdog, who looked up sympathetically. Both Underdog and Elle had heard Serena and Margot's argument countless times before. Elle refused to get involved, because her father, the trendy Beverly Hills plastic surgeon Dr. Wyatt Woods, known among the nip and tuck crowd as "the Best for Breasts," had done Serena's work. Anyhow, Elle had a more pressing concern.

"They're not hard. They're firm!" Serena said, and stamped her foot. There wasn't half an inch between Serena and Margot, squared off chest to chest.

Margot's lips, pouty from last year's lip injections, were

set in a glossy purple smile that matched the Nike swoosh on her little-used cross-trainers. Despite the fact that Margot had undergone enough plastic surgery to be on a frequent-slicer plan, she told Elle that she prided herself on the fact that she had never let a doctor touch her boobs. Clinically, anyway.

"Have you guys totally forgotten? Tonight could be the night!" Elle shouted to get Serena's and Margot's attention. "I need to look *perfect*. I want everything to be exactly right tonight!"

"Of course I didn't forget," Serena said, turning her back on Margot. "I even have a *Cosmo* tip for you. I read that you can totally put someone at ease by matching their body language. The article said that Jennifer did that with Brad and it made it a lot easier for him to pop the question, since he was kind of nervous beforehand."

"Warner *has* to propose to you tonight, Elle," Margot chimed in. "Not only is tonight your third anniversary, but I checked your chart and masterful Saturn has begun a long transit through Taurus. It's your time to make life-altering decisions."

Elle appraised her appearance once again in the mirror and decided she needed a bit more blush. Her long blonde hair gleamed and framed her heart-shaped face. Her flaw-less fair complexion was set off by huge deep blue eyes that shone with kindness, and her size 2 figure was poured perfectly into her red slip-dress.

"In fact, I'm way ahead of you, Elle," Serena said. "Look what I picked up today!" She held up a copy of *In Style Weddings* with a shot of J-Lo on the cover.

"Oh my God!" Margot shrieked. "Not that one. Don't you know anything? J-Lo never should have done that cover! There's an *In Style Weddings* curse. Like three of their cover

brides, including Courtney Thorne-Smith, were divorced before the issue hit the stand!"

"That's true," Elle said, "but that was totally sweet of you,
Serena."

A voice over the sorority house intercom suddenly interrupted them just as Margot pulled out the latest issue of
Brides magazine: "Warner's here, Elle."

"Keep your fingers crossed!" Elle said to Serena and Margot as she checked her reflection again, still unsure about
the dress she had chosen. "Are you *sure* this is it?" she
asked her friends for the fourth time.

"Maybe you should go with pink. It is your signature
color," Serena said. "Ow!" Margot had given her a sharp elbow to the ribs.

Elle stood frozen, suddenly unsure of her choice. Would it
be the dress she would want to tell her great-grandchildren
about when she regaled them with stories about the night
Warner proposed? What if it looked dated and stupid by
then?

"No, Elle, that's it," Margot said. "I'm positive! Red is the
color of confidence and it matches your aura."

"Well, I don't want to look like I expect anything." Elle
tucked her smooth golden blonde hair behind her ears,
checking that the diamond earrings Warner had given her
for her birthday were securely in place.

"He'll ask. You *know* it's coming, Elle," Serena said, sounding mildly annoyed. "Anyway, Margot's right. Red is better."

"Group hug!" Margot announced, and suddenly Elle was
sandwiched between the biggest and most expensive boobs
in the Delta Gamma house.

Warner stood waiting in the foyer. His tall, blonde, and
handsome looks never failed to leave all of Elle's sorority
sisters in a stunned silence. As Elle approached him, he

pulled her close to him with one arm while smoothly holding a dozen long-stemmed shell pink roses in the other.

Elle snuggled against him; her smile lit up the room as
her delight to be with him radiated from her. She was completely absorbed in the moment. "Mar, will you put these
in a vase for me?" she absently asked her friend, who was
standing at the bottom of the stairs with the rest of the Delta
Gamma house, all trying to look casual while inspecting the
couple with magnified intensity and not a little envy.

"I'll do it," Serena said, stepping in front of Margot and
making an obvious show for her sorority sisters of tucking
In Style Weddings under her arm before she reached for
the flowers. "Warner, you look fantastic. Anything special
planned for tonight?"

Warner looked slightly amused by Serena's comment
and gave her a devastating smile.

"Every night with Elle is special," he said. He gave Elle a
smile, and squeezed her hand. "C'mon, Elle. I don't want to
be late."

As Warner guided her through the Delta Gamma front
door, Elle looked back over her shoulder at Serena and
Margot, who were giving her a big thumbs-up.

CHAPTER TWO

WARNER held the door of his black Mercedes convertible for Elle, and she slid into the plush oyster-colored leather seat. She gazed up at the sky to make sure the stars were in alignment, as *Cosmo* had promised they would be. They were. Suddenly she felt completely sure that tonight was *the* night. They drove for a while in contented silence, the cool air of a California October night blowing the golden blow-dried strands of her hair.

"I hope you won't be disappointed, Elle," Warner said as he exited the freeway. "I know you wanted to go to our favorite place, the Beach House, but I thought we should go to the Ivy tonight, since it's the place where this all began." He smiled at Elle in all his perfection and placed his hand high on her thigh.

"You could never disappoint me," Elle purred back. She glowed as she placed her unadorned left hand on top of his. "Our first date was one of the most amazing nights of my life."

They were stuck in Los Angeles traffic under a Calvin Klein billboard. The model loomed over them, a bronzed work of art. Elle stared at Warner's golden profile with adoration and thought how lucky she was and how she'd be even luckier by the end of this glorious night. There could be nothing better than spending the rest of her life with Warner Huntington III.

Elle's entrance into the Ivy caused a stir. Even here, where every night the restaurant was filled with long-legged blondes and movie stars, her radiant beauty and sweet smile made her stand out. Several men tried to get her attention as she and Warner made their way to their table. Warner wore a look of satisfaction as he observed the other men admiring Elle.

A waiter of the L.A. variety, who really considered himself an actor, came to take their order with an annoying dramatic flair. "Hi, I'm Zach and I've gotta tell ya, we've got some fresh fish tonight so good it oughta be against the law!"

"Actually, we're ready to order," Warner said abruptly without looking at the menu or the waiter. Elle and the waiter exchanged puzzled glances, and she began to protest, but was silenced when Warner ordered a bottle of Cristal. He must be so nervous, she thought, and immediately felt sorry for him as he got ready to ask the biggest question of his life. She lowered her head and looked up through her Chanel-enhanced lashes.

"Tonight is so wonderful, Warner, and you should know, I plan to keep the celebration going *all night*." She leaned forward seductively, expecting Warner's ice blue eyes to meet her smoky stare, but to her amazement, he was gazing distractedly around the room.

"Is something wrong, lovebug?" Elle asked as the waiter headed toward their table with the champagne.

"Nothing at all, Elle," Warner replied, patting her hand as his attention returned to her. He motioned the waiter to pour the champagne. "In fact, things couldn't be better." He smiled and took a deep breath.

Elle just knew this was it. Maybe it was a little odd that Warner wasn't waiting until after dinner, when the ring could be nestled in crème brûlée, but, she reasoned, he must be too overcome with nerves to wait.

"Elle," he began in a low, confident voice, "the last three years with you have been perfect." Elle sighed in agreement. "Tonight, I want to share the best possible news with you."

Elle's heart skipped a beat, and she took a deep breath to control the urge to blurt out, "Yes! Yes I will marry you!" Warner paused and waited until the waiter finished filling their glasses and left them alone again. "Well first, darling, I have something I want to give to you."

Elle closed her eyes and tremulously extended her left hand to Warner, hoping this would help him slip that "something" on her finger. She could hear the pealing of wedding bells in her head and was wondering if she should go with Vera Wang or a completely unknown but soon-to-be-famous dress designer when Warner's voice invaded her reverie. "I want to give you this reminder of our time together," he said gently.

Elle frowned, somewhat disconcerted by the use of the word "reminder." Why would he call an engagement ring a "reminder"? she wondered. Then she remembered what Serena said *Cosmo* said about how nervous Brad Pitt had been when he asked Jennifer to marry him, and she smiled at his clumsy word choice. It was so adorable! She closed her eyes again, only to open them again in confusion as she felt Warner turn her left hand over so the palm faced up.

"Warner, what are you doing?" Elle demanded as she stared at the Cartier ID bracelet she had given to him on their second anniversary. It had been engraved *Elle and Warner forever.*

"I thought you'd want me to return it," he replied sweetly as he closed her palm and brought it to his lips.

"Return it?" Elle said, jerking her hand back. "Why would you do that?"

"Well, I knew when you gave it to me that I could never *return* your feelings, so I thought . . ." He let his words trail off and licked his lips as he looked around. Elle stared at him in disbelief. His words began to blur and she shook her head to clear her thoughts.

"What I mean is, I thought now would be a good time to give it back. We're not going to be together forever, Elle. You know that. It was a sweet thought, but I've decided to turn my life around and get serious. I think we should make a clean break before I leave for Stanford Law School." He paused, waiting for her to respond. When she didn't and just stared at him he continued quickly. "Oh, right, did I forgot to tell you I've decided to go to law school next year? That's the good news I wanted to tell you."

Elle's mouth was dry. She reached for the champagne flute, but realized her hands were shaking and she couldn't safely hold the glass without risk of spilling it on her dress.

"What are you *talking* about?" Elle's voice was louder than she intended. Warner looked around the restaurant nervously.

"When you said you'd always love me were you just being *optimistic*? And when you said you'd never felt this way about anyone before were you lying? And how could you make a decision about your life, *our lives,* like law school without telling me? How long have you known?" Her voice was shaky and suddenly her sobbing was uncontrollable.

"I didn't lie, Elle," Warner whispered, trying to make sure Will Smith and Jada Pinkett, seated two tables away, couldn't hear them. "I never told you that I felt the same way *you* did, did I? Think about it." Before Elle could respond he took her hands in his. "Listen, honeybun, this is really hard on me. Can't you see that? You know how much my family expects of me and the high standards I have for myself—"

Elle interrupted him by yanking her hands away from him. She glared at him in anger and disbelief, but Warner continued on.

"I had to ask myself, 'Warner, is it worth it to go through any more of my life with a girl who will never be *serious* enough to be my wife or the mother of my children?' Do you know the courage this took, Elle? How hard it was for me?" He paused for a moment and appraised her cleavage. "*Really* hard," he added. He looked down, apparently wounded by his own high standards.

Elle left the table and turned angrily on her heel, leaving Warner fumbling for his wallet so he could escape the restaurant without any further embarrassment. He threw some money on the table and hurried after her.

Outside, the valet looked up from the screenplay he was writing long enough to give Elle an appreciative once-over in spite of her tear-blotched face. She was about to ask him to call a cab for her when Warner cleared his throat audibly behind them, and the valet jumped up and ran to get the car.

"C'mon, Elle," Warner said. "Let me take you home." At that moment home was just where she wanted to be, and the faster she could get there, the better. Sullenly, she agreed.

After what seemed like an eternity to Elle, the car screeched up. Warner barely gave Elle time to close her door before he turned up the volume on the radio and merged into the Friday night traffic on Robertson.

Elle could not believe what had happened. She stared at Warner's perfect profile. "This is not happening," she said to herself. "It's 2002. It's the time of *Buffy*, *Charmed*, and *Charlie's Angels*. Be strong." Elle imagined Warner meeting up with Buffy in a dark alley and felt a tiny bit better until the violence of the image was shattered by a glimpse of her still-unadorned left hand. She felt trapped in an Aaron Spelling drama where bad things happen to good-looking people.

Warner had pulled up in front of the Delta Gamma house. When he noticed Elle waiting for him to come around and open her car door as he always had before, he leaned across her, opened the door, and gave her a quick kiss on the cheek.

"See ya, Elle," he said with his hand resting on the shift already in first gear.

Elle stumbled out of the car and into the house entirely devastated, completely un-Buffy, and resoundingly un-Elle.

CHAPTER THREE

TRYING hard to hide her devastation, Elle Woods entered the spacious TV room of the University of Southern California Delta Gamma house. Not expecting Elle to come home for at least a few more hours, Margot and Serena were completely engrossed in *The Osbournes*.

"I heard Kelly Osbourne has an MTV veejay who is seriously into her," Serena said.

"Hmmm . . . that's cool," Margot responded, pursing her lips the way she did when she was thinking really hard.

Glued to the television, they didn't even hear Elle's sniffling noises or see her tear-stained face until finally Elle blurted out, "Some sisterhood . . . you're supposed to be my best friends. Maybe I should have been a Theta."

Serena and Margot looked at their friend and gasped. Mascara streaked Elle's blotchy, anguished face as she fell onto the couch.

"Warner . . . broke . . . up . . . with . . . me!" Elle shouted, her words broken by uncontrollable sobs.

"You didn't get the rock?" Margot asked, astonished. She looked as if she might start crying too.

"It's not a Kappa, is it?" Serena shrieked, falling to Elle's side. "I'll kill them!"

"No, no." Elle shook her head. "It's not another girl . . . it couldn't be."

As the Delta Gamma social chair, Margot vigorously agreed. "I hereby cancel our annual mixer with Sigma Chi."

Elle smiled at Margot, but shook her head sadly. "Margot, forget it. It's too late." She sank deeper into the floral chintz couch, resting her chin on her knees, her eyes brimming with tears. "It's o-o-o-over."

Serena and Margot stared at Elle, then at each other in genuine disbelief. If Elle and Warner weren't getting married, what would become of the rest of them? Everyone knew Elle and Warner were perfect together. They went together like shampoo and conditioner.

CHAPTER FOUR

Elle, Serena, and Margot went upstairs to Elle's room, which only a few hours before had been filled with bridal expectations. The room's cotton-candy-pink walls were almost covered by photos of smiling blonde Delta Gammas at sorority yacht trips and black-tie formals. Tonight, however, the girls looked nothing like their upbeat, glamorous counterparts in the photos.

"Everything was normal, at first," Elle began after Margot served them her famous pink Margotitas with a pink crazy straw. "We were at the Ivy and the mood was perfect. The Cristal had just been poured when Warner basically told me: 'Elle, when I start law school, I think we should stop seeing each other.' Boom! Moving off to Stanford Law School, and he told me he needs to find someone more 'serious.' "

" 'More serious!' " Margot huffed with her pouty MAC Glaze lips. "What's that supposed to mean? Serious about what?" she asked.

"I don't know what it means!" Elle said angrily. "That's what he told me. He said, 'Elle, I'm ready for someone more serious.' Just like that. I think maybe he's grown out of this"—she motioned around the room—"this scene . . .

and out of me!" Elle wiped a stray tear as Margot poured more pink slush from the blender.

"Who the hell does he think he is?" Margot demanded. "There is no better girl, no better Delta Gamma, no better wife for Warner Huntington III."

"Right!" agreed Serena. "When did he decide that he was too good for Miss June?" Serena mocked. "You were certainly fine for him at his all-important Sigma Chi rat-frat parties."

Elle had been Miss June on the USC calendar for three consecutive years. She was president of Delta Gamma and of the Intersorority Council. She had practically *invented* her major in sociopolitical jewelry design by merging technical classes at the architecture school with sociological research on tribal ornamentation and feminist critiques of beauty myths.

She remembered Warner's pride when she won homecoming queen last October. She was driven around the stadium in her own BMW convertible, the white car glittering with freshly painted USC war stripes, draped in crimson and gold as Elle and homecoming king Warner Huntington waved from the car.

"There are way better guys around here than Warner, Elle," Serena said. "You know how Javier is dying to date you." Serena's ex-boyfriend Javier was moneyed through his family's investment firm, which had wisely bought California's largest cement manufacturer and celebrated enthusiastically after every earthquake.

Thinking about Serena's sloppy seconds made Elle cry harder. Her perfectly tanned shoulders shook with every sob. "I was just positive Warner was going to propose to me tonight! I feel so humiliated!" She looked sadly at her left hand. "I thought the Huntington Rock of Gibraltar was mine for sure. You remember the Rock? The family six-carat?" Margot and Serena nodded solemnly. "Why would he tell me about that ring if he wasn't going to marry me?"

"Elle, he's such an operator," Serena said. "I don't mean to say I told you so, but he doesn't care about anything other than himself and his résumé." Warner was president of the student senate and had been a first boat rower in prep school and a pitcher on USC's baseball team, which had played in the College World Series the previous spring. Warner often joked about how impressive his college résumé would sound when he ran for president, but he was only half joking.

In fact, Elle remembered, when she wanted to bring Warner down a peg, she would gently mock his political ambitions. "Oh, Warner," she would coo, "you have the makings of a great vice president." This would infuriate him. The second son in his family, he had come west primarily because he didn't want to follow his older brother to Harvard. He was tired of running second.

"Wasn't his grandfather a senator or something?" Margot asked.

Elle nodded, sipping her drink. "Mmm-hmm, from Connecticut. For like fifty years or something." Warner had often told Elle that family tradition would lead him into politics and that public service was a Huntington family legacy. His Grandmummy Huntington was DAR Newport, Rhode Island, a grande dame with tremendous influence over her family since the death of Warner's grandfather three decades earlier. She never let Warner forget that his blood ran blue.

"I should have seen it coming when Grandmummy Huntington came to L.A. for Warner's birthday last month," Elle conceded. "Warner hasn't been the same since. Grandmummy ignored me through the entire dinner and then, as she was leaving, told me that I reminded her of Pamela Anderson!"

"Ewww! Pamela Anderson!" Serena and Margot said in unison. That was the ultimate insult.

Underdog hopped up on the couch, and Elle tugged his soft ears and stared into his devoted deep brown eyes. "You still love me, Underdog," she cooed to him as she fixed the pink satin bow attached to his rhinestone collar.

CHAPTER FIVE

Elle's tears gave way to resolve as she and her two best friends worked late into the evening devising plans to bring Warner to his senses.

Elle decided around 3:00 A.M. that she would go to law school and beat Warner at his own game. Decided, maybe, after one too many pink Margotitas. Tequila-induced or not, the idea stuck. If Warner was going to Stanford Law School to find someone "serious," he was going to find one serious Elle Woods.

Elle spent the rest of the fall semester in hibernation, studying for the Law School Aptitude Test, which she had scheduled to take in January. Everyone attributed her social disappearance to her breakup with Warner.

Three months later, Elle was positively beaming as she emerged from the LSAT. Not only were the required sections a breeze, but the extra section, "Logic Games," allowed her to use what she considered to be one of her greatest strengths: abstract organization. Ever since high school Elle had been a whiz at seating arrangements for parties, saving events that could have been diversity disasters without her strategic social skills. She was famous for the dinner parties to which she would invite sorority sisters with open rivalries or roommates on the outs. She partnered talkers with listeners and athletes with beauties, with dazzling success.

So when she encountered the silly time-zone puzzles in the "Logic Games" section she finished four minutes ahead of the clock. Nothing on the exam came close to approaching the subtleties and entanglements of Elle's social world.

Days after the exam, Elle sauntered into her mother's contemporary Los Angeles art gallery on La Brea. The walls had been sponged in rich vegetable-dye pigments and covered with deep brushed metal. The redwood-stained floor shone, and the lighting in the gallery was set to flatter her mother more than the art.

"Kiss noise!" Elle's mother said when she saw her. Elle leaned across her mother's desk and they exchanged air kisses to avoid smudging each other's artfully applied makeup.

"Mother, I've got some news that may surprise you," Elle announced nervously as she settled into a comfortless straight-backed chair.

"Oh, darling! You're finally marrying Warner!" Eva guessed. Elle had always told her mother everything, but hadn't had the guts to tell her about the awful October night when Warner dumped her. She knew her mother would be devastated. Although her mother ran one of L.A.'s most successful galleries, she had always told Elle that a woman's most exalted achievement was in landing a moneyed husband and maintaining a successful marriage.

"No, Mother," Elle said, "um, not yet. The news is, I've decided not to work in the gallery this fall. I'm, uh, well, I've decided to go back to school."

Eva smiled and turned stiffly back to her work looking at slide submissions from new artists. Elle could sense her disappointment. "Design or film, dear?" she asked.

"I'm going to law school."

Eva bolted out of her chair. She was teetering from shock in her Gucci stilettos and was afraid she might faint. She quickly reached for her chair, and once she was seated, she stared at Elle for several moments before she could speak. "Law school? What are you talking about? Darling, one must pass tests for that sort of nonsense and—"

Elle interrupted. "Oh, I know," she said, and giggled nervously, tugging at the quilted Chanel fabric of her pale-pink-and-white checked micromini. "I've already taken the test and I think I aced it. It may seem sudden, I know, Mother, but I just totally want to be a lawyer." She shuffled her perfectly coordinated pink-and-white spectator pumps on the gleaming floor and tried to think of a reason that would satisfy her mother.

"I see," Eva said. "Have you applied to schools already?"

"Well, of course! I applied to Harvard, and Pepperdine as a backup. And, um, Stanford too, I think." She paused. "Yes, those three, definitely," Elle lied. She had only applied to Stanford. After all why would she set foot on a campus that didn't have Warner on it?

"Well, your father will be devastated!" Eva said. "Do you have any idea how much his medical malpractice insurance was last year?"

Elle thought about telling her about the nobler pursuits of the law that she had recently brushed up on to help her write her personal-essay part of the Stanford application, but decided it would be a waste of time. Ultimately, she would get Warner back and both of her parents would be happy.

* * *

In late April, while standing in the foyer of the Delta Gamma house leafing through her mail, Elle found a very thin envelope from Stanford. As was typical for a sunny day, the house was empty. Elle ran up the winding green carpeted staircase to her room, gripping the white railing painted with delicate gold anchors with one hand and holding the letter in the other, praying it was a letter of acceptance. She listed all of her credentials in her head before she opened the letter to try to calm her nerves. She had a 4.0 grade point average, a perfect LSAT score, and tons of extracurricular activities. She just hoped that Stanford had liked her personal statement.

Leaning against the inside of her bedroom door, Elle opened the letter with trembling hands and began to read aloud. Her eyes began to fill with tears of joy after she read the letter's first sentence. "Dear Ms. Woods, we are pleased to extend a spot to you in our first-year class."

After graduation Elle moved back to her parents', and from that day on, with Underdog faithfully at her side, she began the project of becoming someone she was sure Warner would regard as "serious."

Her first instinct, as always, was to turn to *Cosmo* for advice. The magazine, ripe with articles with titles such as "How to Make Sure He's Ga-Ga for You!," had been virtually foolproof in the past. However, when Serena found Warner's brother and his bride featured in *Town & Country*, Elle knew that that was her new bible.

With *Glamour* and *Allure* tucked safely under her bed, and *Town & Country* under her arm, Elle shopped at Laura Ashley, traded in her BMW convertible for a Range Rover, and bought a pair of Oliver Peoples wire-rim glasses (without prescription lenses of course). She began wearing pearls.

In August, after a month of daily six-hour shopping excursions, Elle Woods was ready. She packed her flowery sundresses, tartan headbands, and pink furry slippers, zipped her Louis Vuittons, and headed north with Underdog.

CHAPTER SIX

ELLE couldn't believe how demoralizing the Crothers Dormitory was. Her dorm room was less than half the size of her walk-in closet at home and had a low ceiling, dingy gray walls, and a tile floor of an undeterminable color. A solitary window provided the only light.

Elle looked at her watch and realized she was already late. She left her dorm room and the moving men who were grappling with how to wedge in at least three times the amount of clothing and personal items as the room was meant to hold, and drove hurriedly to orientation. She parked the Range Rover and considered what to do with Underdog.

"Sorry, precious," Elle said, rubbing the dog's head. "I'll take care of this really fast and you can guard the car." She poured Evian into his pink inflatable travel dish, cracked the windows, turned on his favorite Cole Porter CD, and blew him a kiss as she darted off.

The melee in the courtyard in front of Stanford Law School reminded her of the first day of summer camp. Groups of proud parents stood around cooing to their embarking prodigies, who brandished dreadful "Hello My Name Is" tags on their chests. Elle thought about her parents, who couldn't bear to see her "wasting her talents at law school." Second-year law students worked at tables hawking Stanford Law bumper stickers, T-shirts, sweatshirts, coffee mugs, pens, notebooks, backpacks, and shoelaces to eager buyers. Elle declined the opportunity to purchase Stanford Law paraphernalia and looked for an alphabetical line to guide her, but Stanford had a markedly different organization than civilized activities like sorority rush.

"If you went to Harvard, pick up your name tag here," read the sign in front of a crowded table of students pushing each other to get their tags. "If you went to Brown," a busy table of Euro wanna-bes beckoned, "pick up your name tag here." The MIT/Cal Tech table was teeming with PowerBook-flourishing techies and Trekkies. The Smith table resembled a NOW convention of "Before" candidates for beauty makeovers. Elle approached the "State Schools, except Penn, which really is Ivy" table with a nervous glance, uncertain whether the University of Southern California actually counted as a state school. There was no name tag for her there.

Drifting past the sign for "Cornell, which is not really an Ivy," Elle felt a creeping sense of horror. Maybe the acceptance letter had been a joke, a terrible mistake. At the far end of the swarm stood a single card table with the sign that she knew was meant for her alone.

"If you went to Santa Monica Community College for summer school, pick up your name tag here," read a sign at a table so distant it was the equivalent of being seated by the kitchen at Lutece. Nobody was staffing this table, on which lay Elle's lone sticker with her name and an orientation schedule anchored by a rock. "Very funny," Elle said, blushing. She had passed her math requirement at Santa Monica but certainly didn't count it as her alma mater. She shoved the hideous name tag into her Prada bag and departed quickly for a second row of tables.

Pushing past people from among whom Blackwell would have found it impossible to pick out the ten worst dressed, she found a relatively calm-looking woman who wasn't accompanied by her parents or carrying a Power-Book, and asked her if she knew where she was supposed to go next.

"I don't know." The woman looked her up and down and gave an uninterested shrug. "I'm waiting for my fiancé."

"Thanks." Elle moved to a nearby table and surveyed its collection of pamphlets on date rape, drug and alcohol abuse, and sexual harassment. The table workers were also aggressively distributing brochures for psychiatric care at Stanford. A lengthy pamphlet on substance abuse among graduate students was shoved into Elle's hand from the unmanicured clutches of a do-gooder.

Finally, making her way to an unoccupied wooden bench, Elle sat down to read her orientation schedule for the following day.

Tuesday:

9:00 A.M.—10:00 A.M.	Registration
10:00 A.M.—12:00 P.M.	Book Purchase
12:00 P.M.— 1:30 P.M.	Westward-Ho "Bar"-b-que
1:30 P.M.— 3:00 P.M.	Campus Tour (including Law Library)
3:00 P.M.— 5:00 P.M.	You and Others: Meet and Greet
5:00 P.M.— 7:00 P.M.	Dean's Welcome
7:00 P.M.	Pizza Party, followed by "Bar" Revue

"*Bar*baric," Elle said and groaned. As if greasy pizza and a "Bar"-b-que, where they were likely to serve Sloppy Joes, weren't bad enough, the schedule covered every minute of the day with law-themed activities. How could she even begin to color-code her closet (pinks first, of course) before classes began on Thursday? She thought of Underdog and decided to beat the scheduled book-purchase rush the next day and go straight to the bookstore.

Elle returned to the Range Rover, grabbed Underdog, and hurried to the bookstore. She located the Law section by approaching the already familiar crowd of beaming, chattering parents. While Stanford med students and engineers had their own bookstore on University Avenue, law books were sold on the bottom level of the campus bookstore, a dingy dungeon with a gray-lit stairwell and linoleum floors. Elle had naively thought that she would beat the long lines by arriving ahead of the preprinted schedule for book buying. No such luck: dozens of law students, eager to get an edge on their classmates, were staring lustfully at the casebooks they would soon own.

Elle gathered her unwieldy casebooks, twelve in all, thinking how inconvenient they would make vacation travel, and took her place behind yet another set of proud parents and a law student whose stiff demeanor and signature J. Press uniform of khakis, a white shirt, and a navy blazer left no doubt that he had gone to Yale and had never ventured outside of New Haven for shopping trips.

An MP3 player and sunglasses would have been a good call, thought Elle as she tried to ignore the student's father loudly reminiscing about his days at Harvard Law. An MP3's volume couldn't have gone high enough to drown him out, not even if she had played Kid Rock. Elle soon learned that his name was actually Mr. Daniel Baxter III. Tripp, to his friends, as he was greeted by an old Princeton classmate whose pants were sprinkled with alligators and whose belt was embroidered with tiny Princeton crests. His daughter was starting Stanford undergrad, he told Mr. Baxter, with a hearty pat on the back and a quick mention of what he had shot at the club last week.

Baxter's son, a poor imitation of his father and probably his grandfather before him, smiled and nodded at appropriate times as his father boomed his thoughts like a drill sergeant. "Anne, doesn't this remind you of when we took Edward to Choate? And then Yale? A heavyweight rower and an all-American squash player!" Tripp Baxter broadcast, punching Edward on the shoulder. Elle's classmate must not have been the first son, since his mother addressed him not as "Daniel" or even "Dan" but "Edward."

Mr. and Mrs. Baxter weren't buying sweatshirts or bumper stickers, and their haughty expressions revealed that they had as little in common with the sweatshirt buyers as with the linoleum floor beneath Mrs. Baxter's bright yellow espadrilles.

Mrs. Baxter smiled at Edward and pushed him along, her eyes twinkling amid crow's-feet and wrinkles that came from too much time on the tennis court without a visor. Elle realized with horror that Anne Baxter's dress was a Lily Pulitzer almost exactly like the one Elle had purchased at Barneys after seeing it in the "What's Hot" column in *Allure*. Squinting at the flamingo pink print, Elle made a mental note to start a Goodwill pile immediately.

"Edward," his father began, "did I ever tell you about John Kaplan, a Harvard Law classmate of mine?" Tripp glanced down at his green-and-blue happy whale pants, a color eruption thankfully ending at his brown L.L. Bean shoes.

Ed's mouth hung open and silent in what Elle saw as an indication that his thoughts were as dishwater-bland as his hair. But he didn't have time to answer before his father regaled all but the deaf with the tale of the illustrious John Kaplan.

"He was brilliant! Or at least he used to be," Mr. Baxter

said after a pause, "before he left the East to teach at *Stanford*, if you can imagine," he said between eruptions of laughter. "Well, anyway, you should have seen him at *Harvard*. We'd sit there in Professor Gluck's class; boy, he could shake you up. And Kaplan . . . when he bothered to show up to class . . . would take absolutely no notes. Not a word! He just turned his back to the professor and stared at the wall. He never even bought his books, the rascal. But when he was called on, he'd give the correct answer along with such keen insight that even the professor was stunned. What a genius, that Kaplan!"

"Terrible what happened to him," Anne said as she arranged her headband.

"Yes, terrible." Ed's father nodded sadly.

"What happened?" Ed asked, his voice tremulous.

"Terrible," Elle said under her breath. And sadder still that with all of these casebooks, all of the reading she would have ahead of her, she would probably have to miss Conan O'Brien.

Elle pulled out *Allure*'s September issue and noisily turned the pages in an attempt to let Tripp Baxter know that he was interrupting important reading. Her annoyance went unnoticed, so there was no choice but to find out what tragic event had happened to John Kaplan.

"Well, one tragedy for you, Edward, is that he wrote your Criminal Law text," his father said, laughing. Ed looked down over his overdeveloped chest at the enormous book with such tiny print that it should have come with a magnifying glass.

Elle glanced at Kaplan's name on the red Criminal Law text that she was holding.

"He died at a very young age. Around fifty, I think," Anne answered sadly, shooting a nasty look in her husband's direction.

"If he never studied, how could he teach?" Edward said.

"Well, he found a way, I tell you," Daniel Baxter III answered with a resounding boom.

Elle stepped out of line, deciding the moral of Kaplan's story was that if he never even bought his books and still managed to become a professor, there was no need for her to worry about missing her regular manicure time, which would fall during Criminal Law.

CHAPTER SEVEN

AT nine o'clock the following morning, Elle was back at the law school for registration. "Elle!" Warner exclaimed with what was clearly surprise. Elle noticed that his yellow shirt matched his sun-bleached hair. He pulled a pale, frowning brunette standing beside him closer. "What are *you* doing here?" He looked with curiosity at Elle's Laura Ashley pastel sundress and sensible string of pearls.

She hadn't seen Warner approaching, and his simple question caught her off guard. "I'm registering. Like everybody else." Elle had thought of a million lines to say to Warner alone, but the sight of him with another woman evaporated her confidence and repertoire of snappy Warner witticisms.

"Registering for what? This *isn't* the textiles department, Elle." Warner laughed.

"Really? I'm thrilled to hear that! Otherwise I would have been standing in the wrong line for hours to register for, like, fashion design when I came all the way here to enter *law* school," Elle answered, smiling. She glanced at the preppie woman who was pulling Warner's sleeve, anxious for his attention.

"This is . . . Sarah," Warner said, turning toward his companion. Her mousy brown hair was bobbed and cemented in place by a navy blue headband with appliquéd daisies. Elle stared at Sarah through the pink tinted lenses of her Oliver Peoples sunglasses and managed a weak smile.

"We prepped together," Warner said, in a pathetic attempt to break the tension. Elle remembered pictures of Sarah from Warner's Groton yearbook. She had to admit, Warner had landed a prize preppie. Her grandfather was immortalized on a postage stamp. Grandmummy Huntington must already be selecting the paper stock for the wedding invitations.

Elle extended her hand toward Sarah. "I'm sure Warner's told you about me."

Sarah reached out tentatively and shook Elle's hand limply as she surveyed Elle with contempt, deciding that Warner must have been blinded by Elle's lustrous blonde hair. She was certainly nothing like the decent friends he'd had at Groton.

Warner had told Sarah about Elle, but he hadn't needed to. Sarah would have found out at any number of events, such as Harriman Cup or Far Hills. Everyone they prepped with knew about Warner's foolish college fling, the unsuitability of which was his grandmother's favorite topic of conversation.

"Mark my words, that . . . that woman will never, *never* call herself a Huntington," she would often tell her friends when they gathered at her beach club in Newport.

In theory, before she had seen her, Sarah had accepted Elle as within the tolerable bounds of Warner's youthful randiness. A college fling. Now, gawking at what Sarah surmised to be a Barbie doll with a pulse, in her flower-print sundress, she realized she had underestimated the depths to which Warner had sunk since he left Groton. Wrenching her hand from Elle's, Sarah adjusted her headband to display the massive diamond on her left hand.

"I'm Sarah Knottingham. Warner's fiancée," she stated pointedly in her best Groton drawl.

Elle couldn't believe it. She stared openmouthed as Sarah, the Rock, and Warner spun around in her head while she tried to process what had just happened. She thought she might be having a nightmare and shut her eyes tightly, hoping that when she opened them, the whole scene would disappear. But it didn't.

Elle went back to her dorm room, plopped on the bed, and patted it so Underdog would jump up. "Underdog, you've got to keep quiet," Elle warned, clamping his tiny mouth to stifle a bark. "You're not allowed, but I need a friend here." She pulled her dog's soft ears affectionately.

Elle sighed. Casting aside the dress she would never have worn a year ago, she slid into her more comfortable Delta Gamma Anchorsplash T-shirt to begin unpacking. She glared at the chipper dress where it lay on her bed and scowled at its floral explosion as if the dress were at fault.

"What am I doing here?" Elle sighed, sinking to the floor, her life scattered amid the boxes. A narrow twin bed, a desk, and a chair were the only furniture in her gloomy new room. A year ago, she had pictured her life after college so differently.

Elle had been sure that at this very time, her world would revolve around planning her wedding. She had thought that deciding whether she should have tulle or silk organza for the skirt of her wedding dress would be her biggest concern.

Instead, she found herself in a law school dorm. Elle trembled. "What have I done?" she moaned again as she dropped her head into her hands. She sobbed, remembering Sarah's brunette bob and her pale hand brandishing the

Rock of Gibraltar, the family jewel that should have been Elle's.

"Well, I'm here now," Elle decided, forcing her agony into resolve. "Warner, Sarah, and for that matter, my parents better not write me off just yet." She stood up to search for the telephone.

CHAPTER EIGHT

AFTER finally locating her fuzzy pink Princess-style phone in a box labeled "Lifelines," Elle sank into her bed and held Underdog tight. Looking for solace, she decided to call Margot and Serena. She knew they would be home, as they never missed an episode of their favorite soap, *Passions*. Margot was convinced every week that something was actually going to happen. The fact that nothing had changed in the story line since the show's beginning didn't bother her, eternal soap optimist that she was. Elle smiled as she thought of her friends.

Margot picked up right away. "It's Elle," she called out to Serena, putting the phone on speaker.

"Hi, you guys!" Elle was so happy to hear their friendly and familiar voices.

"Elle! How are you? We miss you already!" Serena said.

"I miss you guys too! You can't imagine—" Elle began, but was cut off by Margot.

"How is the Neiman's up there?" Margot asked. "Is it as good as the one down here?"

Elle started to say that she hadn't had a chance to set foot inside a store, much less to make comparisons, when Serena burst in.

"Elle! How's Warner? Was he surprised to see you? Did you get the Rock yet?" she asked in rapid succession.

Elle didn't know where to begin, and it was just too demoralizing to repeat the horrible turn of events over a speakerphone. "Warner's fine, but no Rock just yet," Elle lied. "I'm getting ready for classes though and you wouldn't believe how many books I have." She sighed heavily.

"Oh, you poor thing!" the girls cooed together. "We are so glad to be out of school," Margot added, speaking for both of them.

"Well, we're dying to hear more, but we're late for a meeting."

"Meeting?" Elle was skeptical.

"Jesus is the Weigh!" the girls chimed together.

"It's a new spiritual weight-loss program," Serena said.

"You have to come with us next time you are in L.A. We've only been once and already we feel thinner and more at peace with the universe," Margot said.

"Gotta go! Much love and send Warner a kiss!" they said in unison.

Elle hung up feeling worse than ever. Serena and Margot had found Jesus and Sarah had the Rock. She collapsed into a heap of pink silk pillows and cried until she had to get ready for her first law school event.

Elle tried to think of something positive as she walked across the Stanford campus on her way to the Dean's Welcome. She noticed that a few political tables had been set up, and Elle approached one with interest. The table's sign read "Burn Your Bra," and though Elle was worried that the woman with the frizzy brown bandanna-tied hair clutching a clipboard was a movie extra for a sixties movie, she was still glad to see something she thought she recognized.

She smiled as she remembered the bra-burning party

she'd given for Serena after her augmentation. An L.A. post-surgery tradition, all of the guests brought lingerie for the guest of honor in her new cup size.

As Elle neared the table, the table worker jumped up to yell at a couple of fraternity pledges who had dropped a few *Playboy* magazines on her table and then run away laughing. Elle noticed with distaste that the woman definitely hadn't replaced the bra that she had burned.

"Bra burning is a political statement!" the gender warrior exploded.

Elle squinted, puzzled. "Are you talking to me?" she asked her.

"Liberate womyn from the dominance of male-imposed body image, force-fed by capitalists! Boycott the Wonderbra!"

Elle left quickly, deciding that her first overture to Stanford activists would be her last.

Students and parents filled the law school's auditorium in giddy anticipation of the dean's speech. Dean Haus was known around campus as "Great Haus," a compliment to his warm personality and sense of humor, as well as his fabulous ten-bedroom, six bath residence, courtesy of Stanford.

Dean Haus himself looked the part of a next-door neighbor on a sitcom: fiftyish, tall, thin, and kindly looking, with faded blue eyes behind horn-rims that were perched on his long, thin nose. But Elle didn't find the Dean's Welcome was welcoming for long.

Dean Haus began by touting the achievements of the 180 students chosen from thousands of applicants for an exalted place in Stanford's first-year class. Expressing his pride in the tremendous diversity of his students, Dean Haus treated the audience to a brief description of the law school's new shining stars, pointing out a special few.

First a member of the Joffrey Ballet was recognized.

Then two surgeons, one cardiac and one orthopedic, stood up to take their bows. Next, the dean introduced a Rhodes scholar, a Harvard English professor, a cellist from the Boston Symphony Orchestra, and two Pulitzer Prize winners. A mechanical engineer who held twenty-six patents was booed by the four electrical engineers as he stood up. Elle was intrigued by this evidence of engineer snobbery, similar, she mused, to the way San Franciscans felt about Los Angeles. After the world record holder in pole vaulting stretched his spider arms in a victory cheer, the dean paused dramatically.

Elle's gaze had searched out Warner somewhere between the introductions of the English professor and the patent collector. He was seated with Sarah two rows in front and to the left of her. She cringed when she saw they were wearing matching cardigans. Elle watched him to see if he would look in her direction, and she was so involved in trying to catch his eye that she was astounded by the dean's next introduction.

"And now, ladies and gentleman, what class would be complete without a sorority president?" the dean smirked to a scattering of boos and laughter. Even Warner was among them. "Ms. Elle Woods"—he gestured for her to stand— "also has the distinction of being, among thousands of applicants, our only *homecoming queen!*"

Elle reddened as Dean Haus continued. "Appropriate to Silicon Valley, our own Pentium blonde!"

Elle had never heard of a shade called pentium but suspected it must be a horrible color from the outburst of laughs. Declining the opportunity to take a bow, she gathered her things and exited with hasty steps.

CHAPTER NINE

ELLE'S first day. was a disaster. When she arrived at Criminal Law, the first class on her preprinted schedule, Elle realized she had forgotten to bring her name card. Each seat had a special desktop slot that was designed for the display of these large cardboard cards, which enabled professors to humiliate you by name. Elle was alone in her anonymity: all her fellow students were impeccably labeled. Elle groaned as Sarah walked into the room and sat down behind a card that read "Knottingham, S."

"At least it doesn't say Huntington yet," Elle mumbled to herself.

Sarah was chatting with Claire Caldwell-Boulaine, whose card was printed "Caldwell, C." but had been crossed out and changed in angry Magic Marker to the appropriate hyphenated form. A white cotton cardigan hung neatly from the back of her chair.

"Like a talking *Barbie*," Elle overheard Sarah whisper. Claire shushed her friend, tapping her pearl-studded ear and indicating Elle. She flipped open her monogrammed Bermuda Bag to scribble notes instead. She passed a note to Sarah on which the words *HOMECOMING QUEEN!* could easily be read by Elle.

"Wait and see!" promised Sarah.

The prematurely balding boy next to Elle, labeled "Garney, T.," busily tapped away on his laptop computer. Elle wondered what he could possibly be taking notes about already as she looked around the PowerBook-filled room.

Her neighbor paused to check the time on his enormous twenty-four–function digital watch and glanced around the room. A perturbed scowl emerged on his face when he found that no professor had yet arrived. Unnerved, he compared his watch with the wall clock. Four HiLiters in a rainbow of neon hues were lined up next to his open casebook.

Out of the corner of his eye, he caught sight of Elle's pink legal pad and fuzzy pink pen topped with a feather. Shocked, he asked her, "Where is your PowerBook?"

Ignoring Garney, T., Elle glanced again at her schedule, hoping it would show she was in the wrong room, in the way people irrationally look twice into an empty refrigerator on the chance that chocolate mousse has appeared. "Nope," she said. "This is the right room." Looks like I'll be seeing a lot of Sarah, she thought as she watched Sarah pass the folded note back to Claire.

After four years of arranging her college schedule in a creative, now-and-then pattern, Elle had been crushed to learn three things about her law school classes: they were prescheduled, mandatory, and daily, five days a week. "Warner could walk in any minute," she reminded herself, glad she had taken the time to dry her hair. She glanced back hopefully when the door swung open.

Her heart plunged when Sidney Ugman rushed through the entryway. Elle had known and avoided Sidney Ugman for years. He was her next-door neighbor in Bel Air and they had attended the same grade school. Sidney had circled her for years, returning like a bad dream, an evil Weeble who could not be knocked down.

Sidney's father, Lee Ugman, was a major client of Eva's gallery. He decorated every office of his sixty-lawyer law firm with paintings and sculptures Eva had sold him. Sidney long ago took advantage of this business relationship by being more intimate with Elle at dinners and gallery events than she ever, ever would have tolerated in public.

His parents often boasted at social events where Sidney and Elle were both present that Sidney and Elle had a "special relationship," which is why Lee Ugman bought so loyally from Eva's gallery. "Might as well keep it in the family," he speculated. Of course, the idea of this "special relationship" was created by Sidney alone. Recognizing his friend the digital watch–wearer tap-tapping his keyboard next to Elle, Sidney took the other open seat in the row.

"What's on your PowerBook?" Elle heard Sidney joke with the watch-wearer. They exchanged some sort of Trekkie handshake.

Finally, Professor Kiki "Slaughter-Haus" made her entrance. Catherine "Kiki" Haus was a package deal, a Stanford Law School professor by virtue of the fact that she was the wife of the dean, whom Stanford had wooed away from Harvard. While her husband was known around Stanford as Professor Great Haus, Kiki had been tagged "Slaughter-Haus" years ago, when she taught Constitutional Law, after the infamous Supreme Court *Slaughterhouse* cases.

Even after Kiki switched to teaching Criminal Law, the "Slaughter-Haus" nickname stuck because her class was reputed to be unendurable. Especially among the male students. The professor was also nicknamed "Three-C Kiki" because of rumors that at grade time she evened out her perceived social injustices by giving three Cs, always to three men, especially golden-boy fraternity types.

When Elle heard this "Three-C" rumor from Bianca, a sorority sister whose boyfriend, John Brooks, had graduated from Stanford the year before, she imagined Stanford Law would be full of interesting, golden John Brooks types; but looking around, Elle couldn't figure out who would get the Cs in this crowd.

Kiki's class represented in a particularly blunt manner what Elle was just learning about law school: everything was upside-down from her previous life. Sidney had a whole gaggle of pasty-faced twenty-four–function digital watch-wearers jabbering about *Deep Space Nine* with him. Claire and Sarah were already chummy with the exclusive East Coast preppies in Add-a-Bead necklaces. The Ben & Jerry's herd had more left-wing causes than it knew what to do with, though the revolutionary tables would be certain to disappear when law firms came to interview. Humanities Ph.D.'s met at coffeehouses to fill out crossword puzzles in foreign languages. Science Ph.D.'s compared the merits of researching on Westlaw versus Lexis and encrypted their phone numbers. But Elle had no one. She was arriving at the harsh realization that she, Elle Woods, was unpopular.

CHAPTER TEN

KIKI Slaughter-Haus, wide-faced, fortyish, and sturdily built, began circling the podium with her eyes anchored to her notes. She spouted a stale stream of Gloria Steinem–era feminism interrupted with a lengthy "uh" between every few words. "All law . . . uh . . . is biased. Um . . . against women. Uh . . . institutionally," she droned.

This was Criminal Law? Elle had looked forward to this class as compared to the others. She thought they'd talk about lawyers, guns, and money, like the Warren Zevon song.

Kiki called only on women. In her introductory monotone she was making the point that women have to balance work and family life, whereas men, presumably like her husband, are free from this dual responsibility. Nobody had any idea what this had to do with criminal law, but the tap-tap-tapping keyboards took down every word.

"Uh, you, without the, uh, name card." Slaughter-Haus pointed at Elle. "Uh, what's your name?"

"Elle Woods."

"Uh, Ms. Woods, why did you, uh, come to law school?"

First question, first day. A softball.

Sarah turned around with interest. The room grew quiet.

"To be a lawyer?" Elle guessed.

Kiki went in for the slaughter.

"And, uh, why do *you*, uh, want to be a lawyer?"

"So I can do my own divorce," Elle answered candidly, smiling. "Without getting taken to the bank."

She shot a glance in the direction of Sarah and Claire, to see if her casual mention of divorce had any effect on them. She caught Claire's eye and added a cool shrug.

"I see," Kiki said. "You all want to be lawyers, but first you have to pass my class. And last year only half of the students who sat in these seats made it out alive."

Kiki turned her back to write on the board. Sarah stuck her tongue out at Elle, at which Claire giggled. "I told you so," Sarah said.

Elle was picked out again in Torts class for a question based on the reading. There was no settling into law school, Elle discovered. Reading was actually assigned before the first class, but Elle hadn't gotten to it yet, and didn't even have her books with her. With no name card and no books, Elle was an easy target.

Torts was the class of basic personal-injury law. A "tort" described not a cream-filled dessert wheeled in on a cart, but an injury over which you could sue somebody. Any sob story with a price tag was a tort. The class focused on everyday grievances like car accidents or harassing phone calls, the stuff of daytime talk shows.

The basic rule was one you might see behind a cash register: "You break it, you pay for it." But law school had a way of complicating even the simplest rule. "Actionable tortious infliction of emotional distress," for example, meant "being mean enough to get sued for it." The point of torts, Elle decided, was to learn how petty squabbles can be dressed up multisyllabically.

Today's word, which Elle might have known had she read the assigned chapter, was "subrogation," a neat way for the bad guy to escape paying damages by suing somebody else. Insurance companies are quite fond of the concept.

"You, without the PowerBook or a name card . . ." Professor Glenn, a white-haired red-nosed Harvard lion tortiously inflicting a terrible mix of plaids with a brown tie, pointed at Elle. "What do you think of subrogation?"

Elle wondered if this professor had a feminist theme too, like Kiki Slaughter-Haus. "Well," she attempted, "it's endemic in our society. Especially the subjugation of women."

The class fell apart in laughter, leaving Elle to wonder alone what was so funny. Professor Glenn, whom the wags had renamed Professor Glenn-Fiddich in recognition of the obvious difference between his lucid morning classes and his rambling, red-nosed afternoons, shook his head sadly. He was sober today and appeared to regret it.

"Thank you, Ms. Woods. Let's turn to somebody who's done the reading."

An arm shot up. It was impossible to tell whether the arm belonged to a man or a woman. Elle now realized that the time she had spent reading *Cosmopolitan's Life After College* issue had been a total waste of time. The "Law School Revue" article hadn't mentioned anything remotely resembling the law school life she was experiencing. She acknowledged she might need a new source of advice.

Elle suspected she might learn more by staying home and watching Oprah anyway. She began daydreaming.

If I were president, I'd put Oprah on the Supreme Court. Phil's too liberal, Geraldo's too insensitive. Larry King wouldn't take the pay cut. Ricki Lake? She paused, considering. *No. Wouldn't get confirmed. But Oprah . . . everyone knows she's fair. She's got enough cash to retire from TV. And maybe the tabloids would lay off her weight fluctuations if they only saw her in the black robe.* Elle smiled. Definitely Oprah.

She gasped and drew back as if shocked when Sidney's clammy hand gripped her arm. "C'mon Elle, beam yourself back down," he said. "Class is over."

"Beam yourself someplace else, Sidney," Elle snapped. Turning to leave the room, Elle heard whispers behind her back. Sidney zipped his black vinyl PowerBook pack and followed her out.

"Elle"—he caught her arm in the hall, gloating—"this isn't Bel Air. You're not so popular here, you know. People don't even like you." He tightened his grip as she twisted to get away.

Sidney held on to her arm as Elle moved down the hall, still trying to shake him. "I have soooo many friends here already, Elle. You should be nicer to me. . . . I *might* let you into my study group," Sidney snarled.

Elle spun around and faced Sidney, finally yanking her arm free. "Sidney, don't make this worse than it already is for me," she said. "Please." Sidney's laugh was her answer.

Elle tensed. "Do me a favor, Sidney? You and your whole study group?"

"What?"

Though she knew her efforts would be futile, she looked at him. "Please, Sidney, just leave me alone."

She regretted her words as soon as the grin crossed Sidney's face. The tables had turned and he relished her misery. He was the king and she was a standing joke. Law school was his chance to make her pay, and he was going to enjoy every minute of it.

Hating herself for having attempted to appeal to his better nature, Elle turned on her heel and stormed off.

CHAPTER ELEVEN

ELLE went immediately after class to Savoir-Vivre, the salon she had found during orientation week when she skipped the Westward-Ho Bar-b-que. The salon was located in the Stanford Shopping Center, and she found a darling French manicurist who served as her link to a saner world, the world that read *W* and never gave a thought to subrogation or the writing of briefs.

Sighing deeply, Elle leaned back into the soft black-and-white raw silk pillows and put her left hand under the air dryer. "Josette, it got even worse."

Josette went to work on Elle's right hand, shaping her thumbnail with short, rapid strokes of the file. Her shiny black corkscrew curls bounced as she worked. "Worse? Elle, what you told me before . . . it was already horrible!" Her delicate features scrunched up at the thought, making her look like a perplexed Kewpie doll. Josette said "horrible" in a Frenchified way, "hor-*ree*-bil." It was fun to hear her talk. Elle had booked enough time for a pedicure as well as a manicure; she was starved to talk to someone with discerning taste, and would have stayed longer if she could.

Elle glanced around the salon, noting that the only

woman within hearing distance had her hair wrapped in foil and was sitting under a noisy hair dryer. "See, I *have* to go to class because I don't have any friends and I don't know who would take notes for me if I took 'vacations' now and then," she admitted in an embarrassed manner.

"You should make a friend then," Josette advised.

"No, Josette, wait till you hear what these people are like! This one guy from MIT, the Gummi Bear Man . . ." Elle shuddered as the vision of his computer-lab pallor, orange hair, and long, pimply neck invaded her thoughts. "He sits behind me in Civil Procedure and he claims to be doing some kind of scientific experiment about congestion or combustion . . . whatever. Anyway, this scientific experiment involves his utterly disgusting habit of sucking on Gummi bears all through class. When the professor turns his back, he spits them out and flicks them up so they stick on the ceiling."

"Eeeeew!" Josette exclaimed. "And you must sit in front of thees, thees *man*?"

"Not only that, Josette, but in the line of fire! See, Gummy Bear Man's plan is for the Gummi bears to turn into downward missiles in the spring, when it gets warm, so they'll drip down on somebody in that seat second semester. But since it's Indian summer, his Gummi bears have been melting already!"

"Eeeeeew," Josette repeated. "Do they dreep on you?"

"Josette, I can't even attend class when the temperature is over seventy-five degrees. I would be pelted by chewed-up Gummi bears!"

"Do you want me to do a design?" Josette asked, nodding in reference to Elle's nails.

Please, how tacky. "No thanks, I always do pinks. I've brought a bottle of my favorite Chanel pink to keep here."

"What about the other students?"

"Well, there's Gramm Hallman. He wastes everyone's time by somehow managing to turn every class discussion into a whiny explanation of the Spanish Succession, blow by blow. It was his thesis topic at Yale, which he'll inform you within the first fifteen seconds of meeting him."

"He sounds very boring."

"Boring? He's not half as bad as Ben! Ben *lives* for law school. He watches Court TV when he's not reading the *Legal Times* or briefing cases. He reads the *Stanford Law Review* in the library when we have an hour break between classes. He looks like he's going to collapse under the pile of casebooks he carries around. He loves law school so much, he wants to stick around for more! He told me that ever since he was seven years old he wanted to be a law *professor!*"

"I think I wanted to be a ballerina when I was a little girl," Josette mused. "Or a princess. What about you?"

"I wanted to be one of Charlie's Angels! Chris, of course."

"What about zee women in your school?" Josette asked.

Elle examined her fingernails and put both hands under the air dryer. Stretching out her feet for the finishing touches, she sighed wearily. "Josette, if they are any indication, the future of America looks bleak and poorly dressed."

Josette giggled. "Why are *you* in law school, Elle?"

Elle thought about it and wondered if she should tell her. "I followed my college boyfriend, Warner, here," Elle admitted. "He broke up with me before he came to Stanford, and I thought I'd go to law school too, you know, to win him back. But now he's engaged to this awful woman named Sarah and I'm stuck here and I'm going to have to finish. To show him, at least, that a woman doesn't have to be a mousy brown-haired headband wearer in frumpy Lanz nightgowns to be serious." She stopped and looked at

Josette, then continued shyly. "And smart and competent. I'm sure as soon as he figures that out, Sarah will be history."

"Maybe you should see another man?" Josette suggested.

"I know, I'm pathetic."

Josette needed to get to another client. She tapped Elle's hand, directing her to move to the front of the salon by the window.

"Do you want the same time next week?" Josette said.

"What? Sorry," Elle answered. "I was zoning there for a minute. Yes, please, the same time next week." She slipped on her sandals without smudging her polish and headed toward a career-counseling seminar. The seminars were offered once a week after classes, from the very beginning of the semester. Elle had signed up to see what the future promised. She also hoped to run into Warner there, but neither he nor Sarah was anywhere to be seen.

Judging from the lecture, her future boded nothing promising. The career counselor advised a solid diet of alienation from the outside world during the quest called "résumé building." As if it weren't bad enough that law students scorned direct contact with life in three years of ostrichlike submersion. No wonder nonlawyers peeled away from law students like a sunburn.

The prize for law school success was this: an opportunity to slave away in a law firm library researching obscure legal issues, perfecting a nervous twitch, and checking the clock in obsessive fixation on billable hours in order to make money for someone else, more specifically, a partner. This was called the "partnership track." You sold your right to light and freedom for seven to eight good years, all in the name of an equity share and free time for golf.

Upon returning from the lecture, Elle found an official-looking note taped to her door at Crothers. The Housing Office had been notified that she was keeping a dog in her room, which was not permitted by the regulations. Elle was requested to find a new home for the dog, or find a new home for herself and the dog. Her rent would be prorated if she chose to vacate student housing altogether.

"So much for animal rights," Elle sighed. "Guess we've got to find a new home, Underdog." She collared her exuberant pet and took him outside.

CHAPTER TWELVE

Most classes in law school were an exercise in intellectual torture. Civil Procedure laid out the ground rules for litigating cases in court. Anyone who could read and follow directions could understand Civil Procedure. You had to memorize concepts in order to bandy them around with other law insiders or spit them back on exams, but beyond that, Elle reasoned, there was no reason to know the law by heart. Also, it would be malpractice to practice off the top of your head.

Elle was engrossed in a magazine and winced when Professor Erie called on Ben to answer a procedural question. They would be in for another marathon of "Ben Unplugged." Elle was glad she'd brought the new *Vogue*.

Ben earned a wide chorus of laughs when he changed the names in the casebook from A, B, and C to D, E, and F, "to pro-*tect* the *in*-no-cent." It was a matter of lawyer-client confidentiality, he explained to a smiling Professor Erie.

Ben's "abstract legal problem solving" involved applying what *he* saw as a "categorical benchmark" from one class to another. As if sitting through Civil Procedure weren't bad enough, Ben wanted to concentrate all five law school classes into every hour.

Elle noticed that Ben was wearing a bulky digital watch. She glanced at the ceiling, worried that all his hot air would melt the Gummi bears. They appeared to be holding their position.

The woman next to her offered her a piece of gum. "It's Snappin' Apple," the woman whispered, "my favorite."

"No thanks," Elle said, smiling. The woman wasn't a headband wearer, and unlike most of her classmates, didn't carry a coffee Thermos with the emblem of her Ivy League alma mater. She was J. Crew fresh-faced pretty with ivory skin and clear blue eyes. Plus she was sort of blonde, or could be, with some better highlights.

"It all sounds like alphabet soup to me!" she whispered again with a grin.

Elle looked at her neighbor curiously.

"A can serve process on B, but not on C; A can implead D, but has no personal jurisdiction over F. What the hell is *quasi in rem* jurisdiction?" She scribbled this note on a paper, which she passed to Elle.

"I don't know, sorry," Elle scribbled back. "I skip this class a lot to avoid falling Gummi bears." She slid the paper over tentatively.

"Isn't that GROSS? I think I'll come early and stick a piece of GUM on his seat!" came back the response. "By the way, my name is Eugenia."

Elle laughed. She not only knew about the Gummi Bear Man, she was fighting back! This girl was all right.

"Miss Iliakis?" The note passing was interrupted. "Is Miss Iliakis here today?"

Eugenia gulped, sliding the piece of Snappin' Apple to her cheek, causing it to bulge slightly. "Uh, yes." She waved her hand. "Back here."

"Miss Iliakis, here in the second problem, A"—Professor Erie turned to Ben—"you don't mind if I call him A, do

you, Counsel?" This attempt at humor was smashingly successful with Ben and his watch-wearing pals.

"No, that will be fine, Your Hon-or," Ben played along.
Tittering giggles could be heard around the room.

"Good. Now that we've got our dramatis personae down,
Miss Iliakis, let's see if we can help them get into court."

Eugenia looked helplessly at Elle.

Professor Erie turned to his favored "counsel," Ben, who
happily demonstrated his civil procedure acumen for the
benefit of his growing law student following. His twenty-
four–function digital watch, which looked as if it also func-
tioned as a data bank, showed 11:45. Another peak tanning
hour wasted.

In the hall, Eugenia caught up with Elle. "Do you want
to grab some lunch with me before Torts?"

"If we can leave this dungeon," Elle answered, shocked
that someone was actually speaking to her, much less asking her to lunch.

"Sure," Eugenia agreed. "Wherever."

The margaritas at lunch were irresistible. Eugenia suggested they call it a day. "I can get the notes from Claire or
somebody."

"Cool." Elle had lucked out.

Over lunch Eugenia told Elle she was from a Greek
neighborhood in Pittsburgh, grew up among Eastern Rite
Catholics, in particular the Warhola family. Elle listened
with interest. "My mother used to see Andy Warhol at church
when she was a little girl, before he went to New York and
produced the Velvet Underground and all that."

"At church?" Elle imagined an improbable entourage of
transvestites in kimonos.

"Growing up in Pittsburgh, and then going to Yale, I

thought once I'd landed in California I'd hit the creative world, you know? The art scene: air kisses and egos."

Elle laughed. "You're like Christopher Columbus. Right direction, but you landed about five hundred miles too far north!"

Eugenia was impressed when Elle told her that her mother ran an art gallery in L.A. and even more intrigued that Elle wanted to be a jewelry designer, not a lawyer. She didn't even ask why Elle was at Stanford Law.

Elle marveled. Had she actually found a friend in law school?

CHAPTER THIRTEEN

IT was early October and Elle was confined within the gray walls of her Crothers Dorm studying when the phone rang. She glanced idly at the ringing phone. She decided to let her machine pick up, the safest strategy to pursue in a hostile environment.

She froze when Warner's voice began speaking. Of course, he didn't identify himself. He didn't need to.

"Elle, uh, I meant to call you earlier to see how things were going for you at law school. I've got to say I still can't get over the fact that you're here! Especially *Stanford*! As you probably know, Sarah, my fiancée, is in your section and from what she tells me, you're still the same old Elle!"

Elle glared at the machine. I'll bet Sarah has plenty to say, she thought.

"Anyway, I should have called before, but listen, Daniel's coming to visit and I promised I'd show him our videotape from Vegas. If you can lend it to me, I can make a copy, or just borrow it. Okay, honey?"

Elle warmed at his use of the word "honey."

There was a pause in Warner's voice, which stiffened momentarily. "Thanks, Elle. 854-STUD." He cracked up. "Really, that's the number. I thought you'd prefer the acronym. Call me soon."

Elle collapsed into her pillow. "Oh, God, the Vegas tape!" She rolled over, laughing, and stared dreamily up at the ceiling.

Unbeknownst to his upper-crust family, and probably to Sarah, Warner's secret, persistent ambition was to direct films. He was an adulator of Martin Scorsese. For three years he had dragged Elle to film after film, and when he got a camcorder of his own, he began "directing documentaries" of their adventures.

Warner was plagued with his East Coast conviction that the film industry was flaky, disreputable work. Elle encouraged Warner's creative spirit, arguing that film was the art medium of their generation. Nonetheless, Warner never applied to film school or advanced beyond filming a few weekend sprees.

The videotape he asked about was a hilarious, bumpy ride through the high-rolling weekend expedition of Elle, Warner, and Warner's old prep-school friend, Daniel, on the streets and in the casinos of Las Vegas. With only Daniel and Elle in the picture most of the time, except when Warner turned the camera on himself, the eyewitness camera traveled from Siegfried & Roy's white tigers prowling their Mirage jungle to a lost kid crying in front of the Treasure Island ship; from a zoom-in on the $100,000 minimum poker table, interrupted by an unidentified hand and some shuffling bodies, to a sorry pile of ignored porn leaflets littering the dirty street; from Elle, suggestively exposing her cleavage across the blackjack table in a Badgley Mischka dress, luminescent with Stoli and cash and the glow of winning after hitting on eighteen; to Daniel, arching one eyebrow, doubling down and betting smart.

The video wrapped up with a panorama of the gamblers' erstwhile home in the Imperial Palace, an inelegant "love suite" with tacky faux-shogun decor. The room was, in fact, creatively engineered. The grand bed with its counterfeit bamboo posts was raised on a tremendous platform off to the side of the room, graced overtop with a massive ceiling mirror. Adjoining the bed was a Jacuzzi, also up a step, surrounded by glass doors because, as an investigation of the bathroom revealed, the Jacuzzi was the room's only shower. The camera traveled up to the shower nozzle installed in the bedroom wall, and finally to the mirror over the Jacuzzi, which reflected either the Jacuzzi or the bed, depending on your seat.

The "documentary" ended with the Jacuzzi mirror reproducing upside down three wobbly revelers: Warner, his shirt undone, with the camcorder over his eye; Elle, leaning sleepily on Daniel; and Daniel, winking, supporting Elle's drowsy blonde head on his shoulder.

Elle picked up the phone, immediately reproached herself, and hung up. A smile reasserted itself across her face as she beat the urge to call Warner back. "I'll make him wait awhile. I'll make him wait until Daniel's in town."

Instead, Elle returned the call from her new landlord. He'd left a message approving her request to move in immediately. The crazy old man didn't seem to recognize her, though she had met with him in the past two days.

"Mr. Hopson, Elle Woods. I'm moving into the unit . . . with the carpet . . . problem . . . today?"

The only decent condominium development Elle could find that allowed pets was mysteriously named "the Mediterranean." It had a vacancy because of some bizarre flying-carpet occurrence. Adjoining construction had interfered with water pressure to the Jacuzzi bath in the master bedroom, resulting in air jets that broke the carpet loose from

its tacks and blew it, together with several pieces of furniture, in billowing surges across the room. Lacking better
options for immediate occupancy, Elle took her chances
with carpet surfing.

"The jeweler?" the crackly old voice finally recognized
Elle. She had thought it best to describe herself as a jewelry
designer, since it was most proprietors' unwritten policy
not to rent to litigation-prone law students. A good policy,
in general.

"Right, right, sir, exactly. The jewelry designer. I just
wanted to make sure you know I'm bringing my dog."

"Dog? You have to pay an extra deposit for pets!"

"Yes, we discussed that before, Mr. Hopson. I wrote you
a check."

"You did?"

"Yes I did. Yesterday."

The voice on the other end grumbled. "When do you
want to move in?"

"Mr. Hopson, I picked up the key yesterday. You said
you'd skip the repainting so I could move in today. I just
wanted to tell you I'm coming this afternoon, so you can
tell the man at the security gate."

"What? You're coming today?"

"Yes," Elle repeated, frustrated. "Tell him to let in Elle
Woods. W-o-o-d-s. Thank you."

CHAPTER FOURTEEN

ELLE glanced around her dorm room at the clutter of her remaining possessions. She had packed most of her things the previous night. She had sent home boxes of china, glassware, and framed paintings with the movers in September, when she discovered the shoebox size of the dorm room, but nevertheless, Elle never quite achieved minimalism.

She sighed, exhausted at the prospect of heavy lifting, which she *never* would have had to do herself at chivalric USC, where sorority girls had fraternity boys who had pledges for just this sort of activity. Warner and his various pledge-serfs had carried his share of Elle's furniture and boxes in the past.

What an idea! Elle smiled and picked up the phone. She had absolutely nothing to lose and freedom from broken nails to gain. 854-STUD.

She frowned when Sarah's voice chirped a message on Warner's behalf. "Answering-machine possessiveness," Elle sighed, "the mark of a threatened woman."

"Warner, honey," Elle cooed, drawing out her voice intentionally. "So darling of you to call. I have that videotape of us . . . in Las Vegas . . . right here with me at school. I think it's your best documentary!"

She shifted her tone to serious. "The problem, Warner, is that I'm moving, and all my things are packed in boxes; it's in a box around here, I'm just not sure which one. I'll try to get them moved soon enough to dig out the videotape for Daniel, but it takes so long . . . doing this by myself . . ." Elle thought quickly. "Maybe you could give me a hand, if you need the tape right away.

"Anyway, sweetie, give me a call; you have my number already!"

Elle opened her desk drawer and pulled out the video-tape labeled "Vegas." She held the tape cradled against her chest. *This is my ticket.* She began to pack the tape in a box within boxes, like the precious doll-within-dolls she was given as a child. "Nobody'll find this box for a while."

Within the hour, Sarah's white Volvo station wagon pulled into the Crothers parking lot next to Elle's Range Rover, the back of which was overflowing with boxes and garment bags.

Elle looked suspiciously at the Connecticut-tagged Volvo as she labored toward her car, balancing a lamp in one hand and a mirror in the other. She recognized flowery Sarah climbing out of the driver's seat.

"Come to help me move?" Elle said.

Sarah crossed her arms, staring at Elle without speaking.

"I'd invite you in, but I didn't invite you over," Elle said. "Besides, I'm busy moving."

"I heard a little message from you on Warner's machine. What videotape are you talking about?"

"Ah, how little you know about your fiancé." Elle relished the jealousy that consumed Sarah's serious face. She lifted a garment bag to make room for more belongings, ignoring Sarah, who paced impatiently behind her.

With the mirror safely packed, Elle stepped away from

the Range Rover and turned the palm of her hand out to check her fingernails for chips or smudges. "Moving can pose *such* a threat to your manicure," Elle observed momentously, remembering the first day of class when she overheard Sarah call her a "talking Barbie." Satisfied that her manicure was holding up, Elle sauntered back inside, pursued all the way to her room by a flustered, furious Sarah.

Elle grinned. "Be a sport and grab a box on your way out, would ya, Sarah?"

Sarah turned viciously. "No, I will not be . . . a sport! And I will not carry your boxes. Listen, I have just one thing to say to you, Elle Woods, and I'll make it as painless as I can."

Elle flopped on her bed and pulled Underdog onto her lap. "Ooooh, Underdog, Sarah's here to make a threat." She pulled Underdog's ears up like a bunny rabbit's. "Listen up!" She and rabbit-eared Underdog looked expectantly at Sarah.

Sarah reddened with anger, then proceeded in a low, snarling voice. "It is rather obvious, Elle, to anyone with half a brain at Stanford Law School, that you are having some trouble adjusting." Elle gasped in mock amazement, parting Underdog's jaws with her hands so the dog, too, peered at Sarah with openmouthed surprise.

"We're having trouble adjusting!" Elle said to her dog.

"Basically, Elle, you're the laughingstock of this school. I think there's a betting pool already with odds out on whether you make it through finals. Considering you have no friends, and absolutely no chance of success as a law student, you might be looking for a shoulder to cry on right about now. So I came over to tell you one thing: *Don't let it be Warner's.*"

It sounded to Elle like Sarah had rehearsed this speech on the drive over, more or less, and the smug look on her face revealed that it had come out sounding better than she had expected. She turned to exit grandly.

"Don't worry, Sarah. I'm not interested in Warner's shoulder at all."

Sarah turned around tentatively. "You're not?"

"No, I'm not. Not at all." Elle smiled and stood up from the bed with Underdog cradled in her arms. "Not one bit." Then she slammed the door in Sarah's face.

CHAPTER FIFTEEN

WARNER hadn't called back. Elle checked her watch. Criminal Law was dragging on. The professor had turned to the board, drawing another worthless map to illustrate federal court jurisdiction based on diversity of citizenship.

Elle glanced around the room at the two or three hands raised already, in advance of a question. The twins in the class, Jeremy and Halley, were waving fitfully, as usual. These irrepressible class volunteers impressed and competed with each other by firing instant half-brained speeches before anyone could suggest a thoughtful answer, a practice they referred to as "clutch thinking."

"Miss Caldwell-Boulaine," Professor Erie said. Elle looked up from her copy of *Vanity Fair*. She had read the cases for today's class, but found them so boring that she had a whisper of hope that Claire, too, might be confused.

"The corporation being sued does business in Arizona, which is where the plaintiff bought his car. But the car exploded in California, injuring only California residents. Since the subject matter of the lawsuit is a tort, how would the parties get into federal court?"

"On diversity jurisdiction, Professor Erie," Claire said

with confidence. Claire was not only correct, she was chipper, and Elle didn't know which she found more annoying.

"Correct." The professor smiled, turning again to the board. "In which state would the defendant be served with a subpoena?"

Before Claire could answer, Fran interrupted.

"Professor," she said, waving, "I have an objection."

Her voice startled Elle. It was a hoarse whiskey voice that should have belonged to an elegant woman who chain-smoked with an ivory cigarette holder rather than to a frizzy-haired brunette feminist with unshaved legs, a scrawny body, a unibrow, and huge, rough hands.

"An objection." Professor Erie arched an eyebrow, playing along. "Okay, Counselor. Proceed."

Fran shifted uncomfortably in her seat and tugged nervously at her skirt, which looked like the "Indian" bedspreads sold at Pier 1. "It's just that . . . I wish you'd stop using that word."

"What word is that, Miss Anthony?"

"Mizzz," Fran corrected, scowling. "The word sub-*poena*. It has no place in an emancipated society."

"I think she's suffering from subpoena envy," Aaron said as he elbowed Tim.

Doug overheard Aaron's comment and snorted with laughter. "She *wishes* she had a subpoena!" He poked Sidney, who gave him a high-five. The Trekkies were in an uproar, and Fran spun around angrily.

"See?" Fran shrieked.

Pointing at Doug, Fran accused, "That's *exactly* the testosterone oppression that women have to fight! Look! He has pornographic materials in class!"

Doug had a color printer in his dorm room and provided the Trekkies with erotic pictures he downloaded from the Internet. He shoved a "Starship Intercourse" file into his notebook, reddening like a beet. "I don't know what you're talking about," Doug sputtered. The Trekkies turned guilty stares to the floor.

Professor Erie raised his voice with exasperation. He finally asked a question that Elle liked. "When does this nonsense stop?" It was getting to the point where men at Stanford couldn't speak an unobjectionable word. "Class, enough! Mizzz Anthony," he drew the word out with irony, "what would you prefer I call the subpoena? After all, that's what the *courts* call it."

Fran shrugged. "Call it a writ. That's what they call it in England, where they have some sensitivity about these things."

Leslie nodded vigorously.

"Fine, Ms. Anthony. A writ."

He turned back to Claire, who seemed a little shaken by the commotion. She answered correctly that the "writ" should be served in Arizona, and Elle crossed the word "subpoena" out of her notes.

Elle was hurrying out of class when a hand on her shoulder spun her around. Warner stood before her, out of breath, in a great show of the effort.

"Elle, wait a minute! I tried to call you back last night, but I got your machine."

Elle looked doubtfully at him. He hadn't left a message. "I was home most of the night," she said, "packing."

"Okay, I didn't leave a message," he admitted.

"Oh, yeah, I forgot." Elle brightened. "I drove a couple of boxes over to my new condo. My mondo condo," she laughed. "It's cool. You should come see it."

"I'd like to," Warner offered. "Have you moved your stuff completely in yet?"

She had moved almost all of the boxes already.

"No, no, I've got a lot left to move," Elle lied. "I couldn't lift the heavy boxes by myself and I'm sure you remember how heavy my trunks are. I'd love some help, Warner. If you can get away," she added in a lower tone, checking behind her in case Sarah was nearby. She could bring some boxes back to the dorm this afternoon, while everyone was in class, she thought quickly to herself. That way he'd have a lot to carry.

They started walking toward the front door of the building and Warner paused and cracked a smile. "Great. I'd be happy to help you," he said.

Elle shrugged and walked ahead of him knowing the effect her pale pink cashmere sweater and tight silk skirt would have on him.

He followed her outside. "Listen, I'd love to get away, Elle," he said quietly, "but not for lunch." Elle laughed.

He glanced back over his shoulder to the law school. "I've got plans. Sarah, you know."

Elle grinned and pulled on her sunglasses. "I didn't mean for lunch, Warner, sweetie. I simply need some good Sigma Chi muscle. Call me when you can come over tonight." Impulsively, she kissed Warner on the cheek, then spun around and walked away.

Elle had no doubt that he was looking forward to helping her move, even if Sarah would be furious.

CHAPTER SIXTEEN

"THANKS for taking me, Josette." Elle looked around at the empty salon. "I know it's late. I don't need a full manicure, just a couple of silk wraps to fix these." She indicated two broken nails on her right hand. "You don't even have to paint the others. I mean, you just gave me a manicure, what, Tuesday?"

Josette's ringlets shook briskly. "No pwob-wem, no pwob-wem. But we must do the whole hand. Painting coats over these two only," she explained, "ees no good. It will be uneven. Ter-*ree*-ble! Here"—she tapped the table— "thees hand."

Elle, relieved, dropped her hand down on the table. Josette looked disapprovingly at Elle's ragged nails.

"I know, they're a mess," Elle said, following Josette's stare. "I had to move over twenty boxes today. This afternoon. That's why I couldn't get in until so late."

"Again?" Josette interjected. "Just a few days ago . . . you were almost done with your move." Elle nodded, but wasn't sure how to explain.

"So you're moving again?"

Elle blushed. "Josette," she began, looking anxiously around her. The only other person in the salon was the receptionist, who, as usual, was excitably occupied on the phone. "Remember that guy, my old boyfriend, who I told you I followed up to this place they call a law school?"

"Yes, hees name was Warner, I think. Right?"

"Right. Warner." Elle smiled. "Ow!" Her fingernails burned under Josette's vigorous filing.

Josette let up on the filing and brushed Elle's nail with a purplish oil, which tingled pleasantly. "Warner, with the fiancée?"

"Sarah Knottingham." The smile died from Elle's face.

"Is thees"—Josette glanced at Elle's bottle of pink nail polish meaningfully—"for Sarah . . . or for Warner?"

Elle looked puzzled.

Josette gripped Elle's hand and held it up for emphasis. "Why do we make your nails beautiful?" She lowered Elle's hand into a dish of moisturizing lotion and began massaging her fingers as she unraveled the mystery she had posed. "For him? Does he like zee pretty hands? Or to show her, maybe?"

How French, Elle thought. "No, it's not to show up Sarah. But I am seeing Warner tonight. He's coming over to help me move."

"Move!" Josette rolled her eyes. "You will break zees all again!"

"I don't think so. This time I'll have some help. See, Josette"—Elle glanced around again surreptitiously—"I called Warner. I wanted to see him, so I told him I was moving, and I sort of hinted that I could use his help."

"You'll never get him back with nails like that!" Josette wrinkled her brow and indicated Elle's broken nails. "Don't worry. I will fix them."

"Thanks, Josette." Elle blushed. "You won't believe this. I'm just going to stop saying 'This is the most idiotic thing

I've ever done,' because every time I say that, I run out and get myself into something worse."

"Yes, yes, what is it? What did you do?" Josette motioned impatiently with the brush for Elle to get to the point.

Elle grinned sheepishly. "Okay, okay, this is pretty embarrassing. Today I skipped my afternoon classes and moved some boxes and furniture out of my new condo. The stuff I just moved yesterday. I moved it right back into my dorm room. It took a few hours; that's why I couldn't get here till late. Tonight I have to move it back to the condo all over again, but now Warner will help me!"

Elle couldn't see the broad smile breaking across Josette's face as she worked to keep the nail-polish brush steady. Josette whipped the brush up above Elle's hand to avoid smudging the polish as she shook with laughter. A pink stripe drew itself across the table underneath the arc of the flying nail polish. "You must be very much in love," she said.

Elle, face-to-face with her own desperate romantic ploy, gave herself over to the giddy truth. She tossed her head back against the manicurist's chair and laughed openly, feeling a gleeful absence of shame. She was in love. The bulb-framed mirrors, Amber Valleta wall prints, and Kiehl's products swirled together with her pink nail polish into one preposterous joke, with herself as the punch line.

"You're right!" Elle said. "Josette, I'm a mess. I'm a lovesick fool!"

CHAPTER SEVENTEEN

Elle collapsed on the couch in her new condo, surrounded by a multitude of thrice-moved boxes.

"Warner, my arms and legs are aching! Whatever's left, I don't even want it. I'm exhausted. Please, let's call it a day."

She lifted her hand to let Warner examine the damage. "See? I've already broken a fingernail."

Warner took the examination of Elle's fingernail as an opportunity to hold her hand.

"Elle, this place looks like the basement of a museum! I can't believe all these things ever fit into your dorm room." After a pause, he said, "I don't guess we'll dig out that videotape tonight."

"No." Elle smiled. "Not tonight." The Vegas tape was the one string she still had tied to Warner. "Warner, it's going to kill me to part with that videotape," she said dreamily. Her head tilted back and she let her eyes travel over the ceiling. Then she began to reminisce. "That tacky Imperial Palace. I'll always love it, all of it, the ceiling mirrors and plastic bamboo. Las Vegas, of all places. Still, it was our palace." Her eyes sparkled with the memory. He was still her prince.

The time had passed when it still made sense for Warner

to be holding Elle's hand. He dropped to his knees, level with the couch, interrupting her words with a long kiss. She looked into his half-closed eyes with wide, adoring delight. And then, suddenly, to her surprise, she giggled.

All of her pointed yearning for this moment, all the tension of waiting, evaporated into dizzy girlishness. Covering her mouth with her hands, Elle brushed Warner's face accidentally.

"I'm sorry," she gasped as she watched him draw back, looking perplexed and slightly angry.

Warner stood up brusquely and moved to the door, trying not to show his anger and embarrassment. Elle had *never* laughed at him before. "I should have left when we finished moving. Just leave the videotape in my mailbox at school, okay? Sarah would kill me if she knew I was here."

At the mention of Sarah's name, Elle's mood changed abruptly. She shook her head in self-reproach. "What was I thinking, Warner? You don't want to be here, you've got a life, practically a wife! All you want from me is that tape. Well, you don't have to kiss me for it."

"Elle," Warner protested, moving back to her, his eyes slowly traveling up her body. "It's not like that at all. I'm not here just for the tape. I wanted to see you." She quieted, but stared at him suspiciously.

"Elle," Warner explained, holding her shoulders, "I have a lot to lose. Sarah's very sensitive about this. She doesn't want me to have anything to do with you."

Elle backed out of Warner's grip. "Please just go, Warner," she said. She crossed her arms and stared miserably at the door, avoiding his eyes, humiliated by her own tears and the fact that she thought about him every day.

Elle choked back quiet sobs until she heard the door close, then listened intently to Warner's footsteps departing in a hurry outside. Once certain he had left, she dropped her head into her hands, confused.

What a disaster. Underdog jumped playfully up on the couch. "Hey there, Underdog," Elle said, scratching his head. "I'd better start getting serious about all of this reading for Contracts. I think I just blew my marriage chances." She had chased Warner to law school, she hated law school, law school hated her, and Warner was hog-tied by his fiancée. On top of that, she had become romantically challenged, reacting like a giddy teenager when Warner made his move.

Her boxes were packed, and she considered moving them all the way back to L.A., escaping and saving herself while she could. She didn't know what she wanted anymore. Yes, she still loved Warner, but she wanted him to love her and only her. If she couldn't tear him away from Sarah, she'd have to think of something else.

Elle imagined how satisfied Sarah and her friends would be to see her parachuting out of law school, scared and beaten. The Barbie doll who couldn't take it. Elle scowled, recalling Sarah and Claire's whispered joke on the first day of class, remembering Dean Haus's mockery of her homecoming queen crown. They would all love to see her fail. And oh, wouldn't it kill them to see her graduate.

Setting her jaw with renewed determination, Elle tousled Underdog's fur. "We'll both be underdogs," she said, encouraged by her dog's calm, devoted eyes.

CHAPTER EIGHTEEN

BALANCING the empty coffee mug that she had drained during Contracts class, Elle did her once-a-week law school mailbox check, prepared to throw away all of the law-related flyers. In the nearly two months that Elle had been at Stanford, she hadn't found anything more in her mailbox than notices of student meetings or the occasional Barbie doll ripped from an ad to tease her. But today her mailbox was stuffed with an enormous stack of papers tied with a red ribbon. A small envelope addressed "Elle" lay at the top of the papers.

She peeled the envelope open and withdrew a single page of white bond stationery. A poem, marked with calligraphy, done in strange scrawls of fountain-pen ink, caused her to gasp.

> *I'm staring at your picture now,*
> *Don't be alarmed or nervous.*
> *I'm not some weirdo off the street—*
> *I plan to do you service.*
>
> *I am your Secret Angel*
> *And I'm sure you will agree*

That as I stare into your eyes
The pressure is on me
To give you gifts of cunning
To give you gifts of grace
To give you presents worthy
Of the beauty in your face.

What better way to win your heart
Than with a simple rhyme?
What better way to keep you here
Than with a class outline!

Don't leave law school, Elle. You are one of a kind.

Your Secret Angel.

Elle leaned against the row of mailboxes, stunned by the cryptic offering. With an astonished quiver, she untied the stack of papers and read the thick black type on the top page. "Criminal Law, Slaughter-haus, Fall '01." Set apart by a cardboard divider was a second title page atop a separate stack. "Torts, Glenn [Fiddich], Fall '01." A quick peek at the pages confirmed what the poem had promised. Someone had given her class outlines, the key to law school success!

Week one discussed subrogation, the same topic Professor Glenn had led with this semester. The outline followed the same format as her class. At that Elle grinned broadly, tucking the papers into her Prada bag with confidence. Elle wondered who could have sent her such a gift.

"Take that, Sarah," Elle said defiantly. "You haven't beaten me yet."

Mr. Heigh had brought his wife to Criminal Law again today, Elle noticed, as she stared at the woman who was poking through her cooler to grab a snack before the lecture began. A late-in-life achiever, Mr. Heigh decided while running a health food store in Berkeley that he was "smarter than any of the damn lawyers I deal with." Smart enough, of course, to become what he despised.

A marketing genius, Mr. Heigh dressed frequently in promotional items from his store, which was called, imaginatively, Heigh on Health. When he was low on laundry, he also fancied running shorts about two sizes too small and vulgar tank tops, expressing sentiments like "How do you spell relief? S-E-X" or, Elle's personal favorite, "Sexy Grandpa."

Mr. Heigh brought his wife to class because they believed in "sharing their experiences." Mrs. Heigh seemed to enjoy the field trips, packing bean-sprout pita pockets with carrot or prune juice in a Heigh on Health cooler that never left her side.

Professor Kiki Slaughter-Haus sputtered through another episode of Criminal Law. Elle was relieved to see that at least today Kiki had the sense to work with a visual aid, in the form of a diagram on the chalkboard:

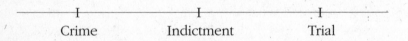

| Crime | Indictment | Trial |

"Another day in the slaughterhouse," Eugenia said, prompting a shushing noise from fixated Gummi Bear Man. As usual, he had Gummi bears and a *New Republic* lying highlighted in front of him, ready to cite.

"Uh . . . the uh . . . Speedy Trial Act, has what as its goal?" Kiki trailed off, and Halley, always trigger-happy, piped up, "A speedy trial!" Her twin nodded in agreement.

This *would* be their issue, thought Elle, glancing at the speed demons. The Speedy Trial Act directed prosecutors to bring defendants to trial within a fixed amount of time from indictment.

"There are . . . uh . . . different incentives that operate at different times in the process." Professor Salughter-Haus moved her pointer to the word "Crime." "To require a speedy trial from the time of the crime would put pressure on the investigation. The incentives would be on the police to work quickly. Why might we not want a trial . . . uh, to start up that soon?"

Professor Slaughter-Haus turned to Cari, who answered promptly. "The incentive might make prosecutors' charge the defendant too quickly. We don't want to put that kind of pressure on prosecutors; we don't want them to prosecute until their case is solid. Right after the crime, if they had to bring a speedy trial, it might trigger premature prosecution."

Eugenia poked Elle in the shoulder and said, "Premature prosecution! I hear with love and understanding you can work together and make it last long enough for both of you."

· Elle burst out laughing, then whispered back: "I think you can get counseling for that." Kiki glared but ignored them.

"Yes, Cari, but . . . um, there is also delay to consider. The defendant wants a prosecution to be triggered so it will be over sooner. As the delay gets longer and longer, the defendant will object. The innocent defendant might want a speedy prosecution."

"The poor prosecutor," Eugenia whispered, "maybe he just has performance anxiety." Elle hid her face in her hands, shaking with held-in giggles.

Jeremy butted in, unable to attract Kiki's call with his jumping-frog routine. "The prosecutor doesn't have forever," he declared. "The defendant's in jail all this time, okay, while the prosecutor gets his case ready to go. Nobody wants to trigger premature prosecution, but sooner or later the defendant will start objecting and the prosecutor will have to pull out."

Elle exploded when she caught Eugenia's flashing eyes, and her laughter echoed through the quiet room.

"Ms. um . . . Woods, do you have something to add, uh, about the, um . . . the problem of delay? We have time for one more comment."

Elle noticed Jeremy's scowl and imagined it was because she had stolen his limelight.

"It's not just the length of the delay," Elle said, "it's what the prosecution does with it that counts."

Elle glanced at Eugenia, who looked as if she could hold out no longer. They grabbed their books to make a speedy exit.

CHAPTER NINETEEN

"**I** don't know if I can take it anymore," Elle said, turning her hand over so Josette could massage the silky cream into her palm. "I'm getting calluses from writing so much." She pointed to the nail-polish bottle on the end of a row of bottles.

"Not zee black?"

Elle shrugged. "It's Halloween, Josette. I've got a costume party tonight. You're an angel for taking me on your lunch hour."

"Ees it a school party?"

"Well, maybe. There's a law school costume party I was thinking about stopping by." Warner might be there, and Elle wanted to show him she was unscathed, beautifully cool, and over him.

"You are sure you want zee black?" Josette repeated. "Are you dressing up like a weetch?"

"No, I'll leave that to Sarah," Elle sniped. "I'll dress in this ultratight black getup that I actually used to wear to parties, back when all that techno-industrial music was hip."

Josette smiled. "You zee boss." She applied a single coat of heavy tar-colored polish, and within an hour Elle was hurrying back to school.

Looking around at her classmates in Torts, Elle realized that any day could have been Halloween at Stanford Law School. If anyone had showed up at her sorority house wearing a polyester undershirt with iron-on dragons, she'd have handed them a piece of candy and closed the door.

Layer-dressing was also popular, maybe because the school's central heating system was so out of whack. The temperature du jour was a warm one, yielding a panorama of T-shirts even beyond the standard Ben & Jerry's selection. T-shirts with a message, like twenty-four–function digital watches, were a trendy Stanford Law School item. The point was often to display some grand devotion to a worthy cause or fabulous accomplishment like a summer in Guatemala building "infrastructure," whatever that meant. Gramm Hallman, devotee of the Spanish Succession, had today opted for "Yale, Bored of Education."

Fran paraded her "Peace Corps Sarajevo '99" gear for maybe the third time in as many weeks.

Andrew Walton, the Harvard M.B.A. who carried a Motorola flip phone that never rang, wore "Harvard Business School . . . There's Nothing Quite Like It." For that, Elle decided Andrew Walton got the Honesty Award of the day.

Professor Glenn-Fiddich arrived a full fifteen minutes late. Elle sniffed a strong odor of scotch as the professor wobbled down the steps to the front of the room.

"Another lengthy liquid lunch," Eugenia whispered, nodding at Glenn as he fumbled through his lecture notes.

"If I taught Torts, I'd drink too," Elle said.

"Sorry I'm late, class." Professor Glenn stood gazing aimlessly in front of him. His white hair was plastered against his forehead, as if he had been sweating. His olive-and-brown plaid jacket seemed hastily thrown on. The collar was raised in the back, causing one lapel to turn inside out. He seemed to have grown thinner since the previous class, so his eyes appeared large in his rosy face. A fly woke him from his haze, and he swatted the air around his head. "Damn fly."

Suddenly Professor Glenn announced the class topic. *"Palsgraf!"* His eyes darted around the room as if someone would challenge him. Satisfied, he continued. *"Palsgraf*'s the case for today, class." He laughed, shaking his head. "This one's a beauty. The kind of tort you just won't see every day. My compliments to the lawyer who had the guts to bring this one, I tell you."

Having neglected to bring his seating chart, Glenn looked around the room for a student he recognized and could call on. "You," he pointed at Ben. "Tell me what Judge Cardozo says in this case."

"Car-*do*-zo?" Ben scowled at the professor, who was proceeding out of cherished law school order. Facts were always supposed to come first. "Don't you want me to describe the *facts* first, before the *leg*-al *iss*-ue?"

"What the hell, you read it. Some idiot had a package with explosives in it, and the train stopped, and this lady bumped into somebody, and ten other things happened, and then all the minks Miss Palsgraf raised on her mink farm went crazy and ate their young."

Ben couldn't take it. "The *mink* farm was in the *Madsen* case, Professor," he corrected. "Palsgraf—"

"I was speaking hypothetically!" Professor Glenn snapped. "Whatever happened, the important thing is what Cardozo held. What did the judge say in this case? How about you?" He pointed to Jeremy, snubbing Ben.

"Cardozo said Ms. Palsgraf was out of the zone of danger, and so he denied recovery. He said her damages were unforeseeable. He said the railroad has a duty of care only to people within a foreseeable zone of danger." Elle scribbled "no money for the plaintiff."

"Duty of care," Professor Glenn repeated, staggering to the chalkboard. He drew two wiggly lines across the board, then crossed them with a series of tracks. "This is the Long Island Rail Road." he stepped back, observing his picture. "The zone of danger describes the limit of people who are within the railroad's duty of care."

"Like passengers," Halley interjected. "And passersby, too, people at the crossings, maybe in the station."

"Right," Professor Glenn started, forgetting what he meant to ask. "So we understand *Palsgraf*, then. Any questions, see me during my office hours. I've got an appointment." The sodden professor collected his papers and teetered out the door.

CHAPTER TWENTY

ELLE parked her Range Rover on the quiet street and pulled down the vanity mirror. Scary. Underneath a kinked blonde mop stared vicious circles of heavy black eyeliner and two cruel streaks arching from her eyelids upward in a Cleopatra motif. Elle pulled out the cheap Wet 'n' Wild lipstick found only in lesser drugstores and traced a shocking black smile. She grinned devilishly.

Adjusting the metal-spiked dog collar, Elle surveyed her extreme getup. Not to be toyed with, she laughed, feeling bold. She kept the light on long enough to read the directions she had scribbled on the back of a class syllabus. Warner had called her early that morning while she was out walking Underdog, leaving a message on her machine that tempted her to believe she still had a chance.

"Elle, come to the party tonight," he had said. "I'll get away if I can. I know you hate the law school stuff, but I'd love to see you there." It was then that she decided to go to the party, although she wasn't sure what to say to him. Her costume, at least, would remind him of what he was missing.

Confidently Elle and Underdog strolled across the lawn.

Underdog was dressed as Dogzilla in a green-scaled one-piece costume. She wore hip-length vinyl boots, a peek of fishnet on the inch of her thigh still visible beneath the leather micromini. Studded skulls and crossbones on Elle's plunging leather vest gleamed in the porchlight. Although she hadn't written down the address, she knew the party was in the third house from the corner. It was awfully quiet. The partyers were probably in the basement. Anyway—she shrugged—she didn't expect a wild crowd.

After she rang the doorbell a second time, the porch door creaked open. A gray-haired man holding a *TV Guide* and a remote control stepped from the dark foyer.

"Can I help you?" The middle-aged man peered with great interest at the chain that attached Elle's dog collar to her waist.

Elle froze, dumbstruck. Then, looking down at her costume, she faltered, afraid he would call the police.

"Oh my God!" Elle said, horrified. "This must be . . . the wrong house." She shifted nervously and held her directions up for him to see. "I, uh . . . I must have gotten the address wrong. I'm looking for some . . . for some law students?" Underdog shifted nervously at her feet.

The man smiled at Elle. He strolled out onto the porch and stood facing her.

"I like your outfit," he smiled. He made no move to return to his TV dinner. "Maybe I can be your party?"

Elle flushed crimson when she realized this creepy old man assumed she was for hire. "Oh no . . . it's no . . . it's not what you think. It's Halloween!"

"Of course not," he said, playing along.

Elle backed up with Underdog under her arm and scurried toward her car.

* * *

After her humiliating brush with the solitary TV watcher, Elle was actually relieved to get to the party. As it happened, the house was the third from the next intersection with Oxford Street. Following directions had never been Elle's forte. She was still blushing when she approached the open front door and headed for the noisy blend of music and chatter inside.

She and Underdog clanked down the stairs in a racket of chains and boot heels, and grimaced when the fever-pitched whine of yammering law students assured her that she had found the right house. Immediately she stood face-to-face with Sidney: or a head above Sidney, whose frame appeared even more dwarfed than usual in a costume of flowing black robes.

Had she been behind him, Elle would have noticed that Sidney's old graduation robe was emblazoned in gold lamé with the name "Chief Justice Rehnquist."

Too familiar as always, Sidney reached out to grab hold of Elle's spiked leather wrist-cuff. From the orange stains around his mouth, Elle surmised that he had been at the punch bowl frequently that evening. She yanked her hand free from his grasp.

"You look sooooo hot," Sidney whimpered. "You drive me bananas." He gawked at Elle, swaying, a bit off balance, almost stepping on Underdog's front left paw.

"Save it, Sidney."

"Beam yourself into the chamber." Sidney pointed inside. "But I'm not going back in until my brother Justice Scalia arrives."

"Thank God." Elle had no interest in who was dressed as Scalia. She surveyed the room for a sign of Warner.

Cari barged by in a severe navy suit and wig of tight black poodle curls, briefcase in hand. Marcia Clark. Elle looked critically at Cari's imitation of the avenging prosecutor, certain that O.J. would have been convicted if Cari had been at the helm.

Sidney was groping again for Elle's arm. "I can't believe you didn't come as one of your *Star Trek* . . . figures," Elle remarked, stepping safely beyond his reach.

Sidney's glassy eyes lit up. "Well I am. I'm Captain Kirk, you know." He stood proudly in his graduation robe.

"Of course." Elle wouldn't recognize Captain Kirk anyway.

"Not tonight, Elle. I mean in the great enterprise of life, I am the captain. Aaron said he was coming as Captain Kirk," Sidney blurted, "and he insisted I would have to be Scotty. Scotty!" he spat, insulted. Elle walked away fast. Braving the rest of her law school peers seemed the better option.

"I am greater than Captain Kirk," she heard him slur behind her. "The only man greater than the captain of the *Enterprise* . . . Rehnquist!"

At least I should shake things up a little bit, Elle figured, turning the corner to make her entrance. Striding through orange and black streamers that draped the doorway, she did look out of place. Two *Star Trek*–clad figures stared noticeably.

Fran, dressed as Gloria Steinem with a hippie-middle-parted wig and an "ERA Now!" button, dropped her drink. "Look who graced us with her presence," she hissed, typically talking about Elle, but not to her. Picking up the empty plastic cup, Fran scowled at Elle's cleavage spilling out of the leathery bra beneath her studded vest. "I can't believe that *even* you, Elle, would wear an outfit like that. It is *so* degrading to womyn."

Claire, who seemed to have taken up with Fran, stared with wide-eyed amazement at Elle's costume.

"If I wanted to degrade myself, Fran darling, I'd have come as a brunette," Elle shot back in Claire's direction.

Claire was outfitted in a poor copy of Elle's favorite pink quilted Chanel suit as "Lawyer Barbie." Claire pushed the play button and smiled victoriously at Elle. A recording played from her Dictaphone, repeating in falsetto the phrase "Law school is really hard!"

Brushing by her toward the punch bowl, Elle tugged on Claire's fake blonde wig. "Don't you wish," she laughed without turning around.

If Elle had been making predictions, she would have assumed Michael would come as Count Dracula or some such hero of gore. Instead, she was amazed to encounter Michael at the punch bowl dressed as Andy Warhol. His typically slicked-back hair was powdered into a gray mop, and he had somewhere found a black wool turtleneck and tight Studio 54–era jeans. He peered through round-eyed spectacles approvingly at Elle's dark getup, and silently offered her the drink he had poured.

Elle took the cup gratefully. Maybe some people around here do have a little imagination, she thought. But the appearance of Dastardly Dr. Dan shattered her charitable mood.

Dr. Dan, formerly a cardiac surgeon, had come to law school to launch a second career. He attended class in his scrubs as if he had just left the operating room, claiming not only that they were "comfortable," but that he had a lot of old scrubs that he didn't think should go to waste. He often paired his scrubs with too tight T-shirts that he believed showed off his overdeveloped chest and disguised his short stature. He ran his fingers through his too black to be real and obviously blow-dried hair constantly, as if he couldn't get over his own beauty. Elle suspected that Dan was picking up premeds over at the main campus. Even after losing his medical license for malpractice, Dan could not rid himself of that personality trait of self-intoxication peculiar to doctors. The insufferable doctor of ego headed straight in Elle's direction.

Elle almost giggled when she realized that Dr. Dan, draped front and back with posterboard playing cards, was dressed as the King of Hearts. He eyed Elle through his tinted contact lenses. "Good thing there's a cardiac surgeon here, Elle," Dan joked. "Your outfit might give someone a heart attack."

"An ex–cardiac surgeon," Elle pointed out. She looked dismally around the crowd for Warner.

Another Trekkie approached. "Captain Kirk here," Aaron introduced himself, sticking out his hand to greet Elle. She sighed and managed a half-smile, scrutinizing Aaron's bizarre neon stretch suit with the mark of the starship *Enterprise*. She offered her free hand. "I heard."

Sidney, ever possessive, rushed over.

"You know, Sidney," Aaron began, "I think it is just splendid that you have come as the Chief. Rehnquist."

"Well," Sidney whined, "you should not have tried to be the Captain. Kirk. You are much more a Scotty figure."

Aaron cocked his head but didn't respond.

"Scotty is not the leader," Sidney continued, "and not terribly eloquent. But he works harder, and in the end he knows how the *Enterprise* operates."

Not to be one-upped by Sidney's taunt, Aaron rejoined, "Well, you are well suited to be Chief Justice Rehnquist. The reason is because he is Darth Vader: an evil, dark force of power used to destroy the constitutional enterprise."

A. Lawrence Hesterton, who had been staring over Aaron's shoulder waiting for a lull in the conversation to compare Elle to a harlot in *The Canterbury Tales*, was not entertained by the lowbrow discussion. Also known as Literary Larry, A. Lawrence was like a soft-voiced teddy bear with wavy brown hair and warm brown eyes so deeply set behind his round spectacles that they appeared almost sunken. A two-time Pulitzer Prize nominee, Larry had left his English professorship at Harvard when his tenure was denied. He considered himself superior to any conversational allusions that derived from nonliterary sources. Aaron, still chortling at his joke, turned to Larry. "What would you wear if you were a justice?" he challenged.

Larry arched his bushy left eyebrow superciliously. "I am precisely as amused by this conversation as Queen Victoria by peasants."

Elle took this as her cue to leave, since the conversation was taking a turn for the worse. She departed amid a chorus of "May the force be with you"s from the Trekkie Admiration Society. Ben, greeting Elle with a surprised stare, was dressed in suit and tie, white socks poking out underneath the high-water hems of his ill-fitting pants.

"Why aren't you dressed up?" she asked.

Ben had been waiting for the question. "I am," he cackled, pointing at his outfit: "I'm a *law suit*!" He erupted into another fit of laughs.

Distraught, Elle looked at the unromantic downbeat setting. She noticed that Mr. Heigh and his wife were dressed like Lyle and Erik Menendez. She had the toupee; they were both in tennis clothes, and he carried a plastic gun. Heather, complete with frizzy blonde wig, scribbled notes on a yellow legal pad and introduced herself as the brothers' lawyer, Leslie Abramson.

"How witty," Elle addressed no one in particular. She glanced around again with mounting despair. Of course Warner's not here, she thought. I don't even see Sarah. They probably have a date. She sniffed. And here I am, flanked by the entire starship *Enterprise*, Lawyer Barbie, half the

Supreme Court, Gloria Steinem, Marcia Clark, and even the Menendez brothers. Everybody but Warner Huntington.

As Elle turned to leave she noticed Fran launching another offended tirade near the door. "O.J.! What an outrage! You *would* sympathize with that wife-beating murderer!"

"It's a good thing Sarah's not here to see this," Claire chimed in.

Elle's ears perked up. Warner, in a USC football uniform, number 32, was dragging a ball and chain on his foot as he headed for the punch bowl. O.J.! He had not strayed too far from L.A. after all. He smiled at the insulted women and pacified Claire with a kiss on the cheek. "He was acquitted," he pointed out, silencing even Fran, who stared agitated at the floor.

Elle, obvious in her excitement, rushed to the punch bowl. "Warner!" she exclaimed.

"Jesus, Elle," Warner gasped, looking her outlandish costume up and down several times.

"Well"—she shrugged—"I don't have you to monitor my wardrobe anymore."

"You look really hot," he whispered, motioning with his head for Elle to join him away from the crowd. A keg out on the back patio was spent and unoccupied. Elle and Underdog walked out and were joined quickly by Warner. Underdog greeted him as enthusiastically as his costume would allow. He couldn't jump as high as usual in his Dogzilla costume.

"What are you supposed to be?" he asked, pulling gently on Elle's dog collar.

"Whatever you want me to be," she whispered back in her smokiest 1-900 voice.

Warner smiled. "Did you get my message?"

Elle nodded. "Where's your other ball and chain?" she said, pointing at the shackle on his leg.

"Home."

Elle smiled wide like a child. "Home?" She paused thoughtfully. "Postparty at my mondo condo," she offered, thinking that this time Warner wouldn't leave her apartment until the morning. "This one goes all night."

"It's a little dicey, Elle. Sarah's feeling kind of sick. She has a cold, and I don't know, I've been sort of tending to her."

"Nursing a *cold?*" Elle asked, amazed. "*You?*" That was so un-Warner. It really was all over. She turned to leave.

"It's not really the cold that's got her down." Warner stopped her, grabbing her arm. "See, her dog . . . back in Greenwich, the one she's had since she was a kid . . . well, her parents finally put it to sleep. I mean, it was really old, I don't know, I swear it's been in and out of the vet every weekend since I've known her. But she's bummed out. That's why she didn't come to the party."

"Oh that's terrible," Elle replied, dejected. "Postmortem dog blues." She looked at Underdog and felt sympathetic. "But you came here anyway?" she asked more hopefully.

"Yeah. I needed some new faces. See, Sarah doesn't think I need to go out anymore. Since we're getting married and all." He paused, a little exasperated. "But I wanted to see you tonight."

Elle glanced back at the party and saw Claire glaring at them. "We probably shouldn't stay here together much longer."

"You're right." He looked inside at the motley assortment of gossiping law students.

Elle shook her head, reminding herself she had planned to act cool. "Anyway, I need to go, Warner. I've got another party in the city," she lied. "Unless you're coming over. It's your call."

"I'll be fifteen minutes behind you," he whispered quickly. "If you promise not to behave like a laughing hyena."

She beamed and fought the urge to wrap her arms around him. "Oh, Warner, I promise! I'll tell the doorman."

CHAPTER TWENTY-ONE

WARNER was true to his word. And Elle was true to hers. He had not stepped even a foot inside the doorway to Elle's apartment when she smothered him with kisses.

Underdog hopped sideways to avoid being pummeled by the flurry of clothes that fell in a trail from the door to the couch. Elle had tears in her eyes as Warner's lips traveled down her neck to her bare shoulder. Suddenly he paused, laid his head on Elle's chest, and sighed deeply.

"Elle," he murmured. "Elle, what am I doing with Sarah?" He raised his head and stared into her eyes.

Annoyed that Sarah's name had intruded so quickly, Elle pushed his hand away from her cheek. "I don't know, Warner. You tell me. What does she want from you?"

"She has what she wants from me."

"Which is?"

"A ring."

The Rock, of course. "Almost," he said. "She has almost everything she wants. I guess she wants my name, too. Soon."

Huntington. Elle Huntington. How many times had she whispered it to herself, even practiced her new signature?

She gazed at Warner, feeling the poison rivalry with Sarah seeping in.

"Well? Do you love her?"

"Yes, I love Sarah," he responded mechanically. Elle was doubtful. After all, Warner's credibility was a little low given where he lay cradled in her chest.

"Sarah loves *me*, Elle. We'll be happy in Greenwich or Newport. Her father wants me in his firm, of course, or I could work for my father's firm. Until I run for office. Sarah supports anything I do. Well, I mean, *either* thing. I don't know, Elle, I'm just so confused. You know I really want to direct . . . my documentaries, you know. She'd never understand that."

Warner stroked Elle's soft hair, seeking solace from his trauma.

"Let me get this straight, Warner." She sat up, pulling a blanket around her shoulders and sliding away from him across the couch. "Your *darling* fiancée, who loves you more than anything, and is flexible about whether you work for her family or yours, doesn't let you go out anymore because she simply adores being with you alone. Right? She will support whatever is best for you, work around your decisions, as long as they merge with the life she wants, correct? Your education and family connections have poised you for work in a white-shoe firm or a Fortune 100 corporation, either of which will pay you obscene amounts of money. But this life doesn't fulfill your artistic ambitions."

"Elle, I knew you would be the one to understand." Warner reached for her. "You're the only one who really gets me. I—"

Only minutes before, she had been overwhelmed with long-awaited joy. Now, Elle could barely hold back her newfound wrath and disgust.

"Warner, I do understand!" she said emotionally. "God do I understand! How can you struggle from day to day? The jobs, the loving wife, the political career . . . it's lined up for you, sure, but you deserve more out of life, don't you? Money, prestige . . . that's not enough. Oh no. You should also be a director, make movies, create. As long as you can maintain a solid reputation in Newport, Rhode Island, and stay securely in Grandmummy's will."

Warner's blonde head bent toward the floor, beaten. "Okay, okay, point well taken. Are you done yet?"

Her voice softened. "Yes, Warner. I am." With that she looked up at him. "Until you are true to yourself, you won't be able to love anyone. I think you better leave."

He looked up into her eyes. "Can I kiss you before I leave, Elle?"

"No," Elle replied sadly.

After Warner left, Elle wrapped herself in her favorite blanket and went to bed, but she didn't sleep very well. Instead she and Underdog watched *When Harry Met Sally* on TV. Convinced by the movie that Warner would figure things out just like Harry did, Elle finally fell asleep dreaming of that day.

For the first time since September Elle couldn't wait to get to class. She backed into the curb with a thud that she didn't even hear, her gleeful voice-over of the very un-November Bob Marley filling the world sealed inside the Range Rover. "Let's get together and feel all . . . right!" she finished in her best Rasta, hopping out of the heated front cushion with first-day-of-school enthusiasm. She was actually early, ready to take on classes that now seemed a small hurdle in the path to a possible reunited bliss with Warner.

Checking her mailbox, she found a second package,

ribbon-tied by her Secret Angel. Another poem, she guessed, opening the envelope curiously.

An exhale empties out the heart
An inhale fills the soul
Of all the dreams that I hold dear
To kiss her is my goal

A loving theft, a pilfering
A joining of the lips
A trade of moisture, warmth and breath
In soft and tiny sips

How slim my chances for this dream
I'll blindly roll the dice
And if she will not have me
Then a handshake will suffice

One time she'll fill her chest with air
A trifle, just to say
"Nice meeting you," and with this breeze
She'd blow my heart away.

I belong to you, mon cherie.

S.A.

Elle fought a chill at her Secret Angel's intimacy. Too bad he didn't introduce himself today, she thought with a shrug. I feel like kissing the world!

Elle tossed her mailbox's week-old mélange of flyers and student notices into the "Paper Only" wastebasket. She hesitated, smiling despite herself at the painstaking swirls of her Angel's fountain-pen ink. After a moment she folded the letter and returned it to its envelope, which she tucked into a casebook. She flipped open the outline hopefully. "Professional Responsibility, Pfisak, Fall '01."

He's gonna help me beat this place. Elle tingled with relief. Impulsively, she planted her coveted kiss on the title page, leaving a pink heart-shaped imprint on the top margin. Fate had returned to fight in her corner.

CHAPTER TWENTY-TWO

IN the bathroom, where Elle ducked to check her Chanel "Pink-Alert" lipstick between classes, she was surprised to encounter a crowd of mirror-peerers. Typically, while there were lines for the Xerox machine and the laser printers, the path to the bathroom mirror was always free of law students.

Claire was struggling with her headband. Elle watched her tuck an errant strand of hair behind her ear, noting that the headband did nothing to disguise the fact that Claire had hair the texture of a Brillo pad. Once she conquered the headband, Claire pulled her white turtleneck snug and fixed her glasses.

Elle tried to muscle into a space in front of the mirror to apply lip liner. Meanwhile, Claire complained to an unidentified person in the bathroom stall.

"Today is yearbook picture day. I can't believe I forgot! This is the picture that follows you *forever*," Claire whined to the stall dweller.

Dissatisfied with the work she had done on her headband, Claire finally announced that she "simply was not ready." She was going to ask the registrar if she could make a special trip over to the studio and be photographed there.

"Why don't you just send over your portfolio?" Elle couldn't help but inquire.

"Portfolio?"

"*Everybody* in California has a portfolio, Claire." Elle smacked her lips and blotted her pink smile against the back of her hand.

Claire rolled her eyes. Elle had once overheard Claire tell Sarah that it was a "constant torment" to her that while she had sat up nights amid a dozen coffee cups reworking her honors thesis "to satisfy some crusty, pedantic old adviser, Elle had been waving at the homecoming crowd from the back of a convertible with a crown on her head."

The way Claire saw it, Elle figured, was that it was just simply unfair that she had worked for a prestigious degree from Harvard only to wind up with the same post-grad credentials as a fruity bimbo from The University of Spoiled Children. So every Monday, just to annoy Claire, Elle waited until halfway through class to tap Claire on the shoulder and announce: "Only seven and a half hours until *Ally McBeal*!"

"Do they want a full body or a head shot?" she now asked Claire's worried reflection. "Because if it's full body, I'll just send my ad series for Perfect Tan." Elle grinned and shrugged at Claire.

"Perfect Tan. Perfect Barbie," Elle heard Claire mutter venomously.

CHAPTER TWENTY-THREE

LAW school put a stranglehold on Elle's social life that Jesse Ventura would have envied. Feeling as if she had no life to speak of or about, she decided that she should get out more at night and read the Angel's outlines during the day.

She picked up the cordless phone to call Margot. With finals approaching, her classmates had become the Typhoid Marys of stress, and she needed a break. She had pored over the outlines from her Secret Angel, and had picked up Emanuel outlines on a tip. Still she was nervous. She needed to talk to someone outside the law world.

Elle dialed Margot, but before she could even say hello Margot was practically shrieking her good news.

"Wedding bells are ringing, Elle! And they're ringing in my condo!"

Elle pictured Margot's latest boyfriend and tried to see them growing old together. A romantic at heart, she loved the vision, funny as it was to think of Margot or Snuff mature and married.

"So Cupid struck in Malibu?"

Margot had moved into a Malibu condo after graduation, and had thrown a BYOK party in the fall. Bring your own karma. Elle had skipped the party. She had just started law school, and all she'd had to bring was negative energy.

"You got it, Elle," Margot cried. "I'll be a bride by next year!"

"Marg, that is absolutely fabulous." Elle tried to disguise the note of discouragement that she felt, having expected to beat Margot to the altar. "I couldn't be happier for you," she added. "When's the big day for you and Snuff?" She smiled more easily at the vision of Snuff, a twice-divorced record producer who was Margot's whirlwind summer lover and now fiancé.

"Well, you know Snuff's gotten me really into Zen," Margot chirped. "I have to figure out how they do the whole wedding thing. I was thinking we could have it at that church in Sedona that overlooks the Arizona Vortex."

"Funky!" Elle applauded the choice. "Barefoot like Cindy Crawford?"

"Oh God no," Margot protested immediately. "I mean, I want a real dress and everything. And one for you too, beautiful. Of course I insist you be my maiden of honor."

Elle flinched at the word "maiden." Always the brides-maid, never the bride. It was still a compliment. "Thanks, Marg," she sighed.

As if reading her mind, Margot softened. "I never thought I'd get married before you, Elle. Not in a million years."

Elle shrugged. "It's not a race, silly."

"I hear Bebe's divorcing already, after only six weeks!" Margot giggled, referring to the first of their sorority sisters to tie the knot. "Not Snuff and me. We're totally in love," she crooned.

"I'm honored, Marg. Really. Maiden of honor in the Zen Vortex, who could ask for more?"

"Can you come home this weekend? I know it's a rush,

but I want you and Serena to get fitted for dresses. Plus I haven't seen you since you left for law school."

"Sure." Elle knew she should probably study, but with her tapes she'd be set.

She turned the stereo on to check out her first install-ment of *Torts on Tape* while she began to pack. "Welcome to *Torts on Tape*," mumbled the professor's voice from Elle's stereo speakers. Underdog whined, dropping his head beneath his paws.

"I know, Underdog." Elle consoled her pet with a vigor-ous rub. "But I'll try anything." She dug through a heap of flashcards she had emptied on the couch, locating the stereo remote where she had used it to mark her place in a *Cosmo* quiz. "Somebody has to keep Emanuel outlines in business," she laughed, gazing at two enormous shopping bags bursting with commercial study guides.

Smoothing out a hanging bag, she tried to focus on the tort du jour, "negligent infliction of emotional distress." The gory tale involved a man suing the hospital that had sent him an amputated leg in the mail, rather than the personal belongings of his deceased father, which he had requested.

Elle cringed, imagining the UPS package. *This tape should have a warning label.*

CHAPTER TWENTY-FOUR

"**W**ELCOME . . . to *Torts on Tape*," the now familiar voice began as Elle buzzed along the freeway on the five hour drive from Palo Alto to L.A. She had heard the story about the amputated leg so many times that she had developed a definite fear of delivery men by the time she pulled into the driveway of her parents' house.

Elle greeted her parents and then called Serena and Margot. They arrived as she was unpacking the books she had brought home with her. They hugged her, but quickly exchanged glances at the sight of their pale, tired friend.

"We haven't seen you once since you left for law school," Margot said. She gave Elle a circumspect look. "And look! You have black rings under your eyes."

Serena nodded. "Elle, what are you doing to yourself?"

"You try amusing yourself with flash cards for sixteen hours," Elle said.

"Tell us. You've been out partying with some gorgeous Stanford man, I know it. Come on, don't keep secrets." Obviously Serena hadn't seen the Stanford face book.

"I don't believe you brought books with you," Serena said, looking at Elle's bedroom turned library.

"Well, leave them here," Margot directed. "We've got shopping to do."

Elle agreed and the three girls squeezed into Margot's tiny Carrera parked outside.

The valet took their keys at the Valentino boutique. "Isn't a Valentino wedding the best?" Margot poked Elle.

Elle laughed. "Explain to me again how this works with the Zen theme."

"Okay." Margot cleared her throat. "It all makes total sense. See, the wedding's in the Vortex, right?"

"Right."

"Well, Vortex and Valentino both begin with V! It's so harmonious! I had this fully positive rush the moment it hit me!"

Serena held the door and Margot hurried inside. "She's over the edge," Serena whispered to Elle. "Wait till you see what she dreamed up for the bridesmaids."

Margot rushed to a hanging rack behind the counter and slid it across the floor. A row of black dresses swung together as Margot pulled the rack to a halt.

"Black?" Elle looked at Margot with confusion.

"It's Zen, black and white . . . yin and yang!" Margot exclaimed, mixing her metaphors. "See, I was watching MTV, and I saw the Robert Palmer video 'Addicted to Love.' And since I'm addicted to love, and it's so romantic, you know . . . I had this idea. You, and Serena, and all of my bridesmaids . . . you're going to be the Robert Palmer girls. Skintight black dresses, red lips, and guitars."

"Guitars?"

Serena mouthed the words "I told you so."

"Yeah, Snuff knows a zillion bands. We'll just borrow some guitars. Anyway, it'll be just like the video, except you guys will be all tan and blonde," Margot piped over the shutter door where Elle was changing into her dress.

"The *rest* of us will, anyway." Serena folded her arms and stared at Elle, who hopped out of the dressing room pulling a sock off her foot.

Margot's animated expression disappeared instantly. "Morticia!" she shrieked, covering her face with her hands. Elle leaned against the wall, kicking her sock across the floor. She glanced at her reflection in the harsh light. "What? Is this too tight?"

Margot started to cry. "Elle, you just can't look like that at my wedding. Oh, no, forget it." She shooed away the seamstress who had begun to pin the hem of Elle's dress.

"Look like what?" Elle glanced from the mirror and the reflection she had grown used to seeing to the horrified faces of her friends.

"Your skin! Oh my God, she does look like Morticia," Serena observed sadly.

"If you were a plant you would die!" Margot wiped her eyes. "Elle, your skin has become so . . . so shallow."

"Shallow?" Elle didn't bother to correct Margot.

"Totally shallow," Serena agreed. "It's disgusting."

Serena put an arm around Margot to comfort her. "Don't worry, we won't let her go like that. She can fake bake or something."

Margot was somewhat consoled. "Maybe since you'll be so busy with law school you could even use tan-in-a-can and look decent for my wedding."

"I'm sure," Serena said, directing her words at Elle. "She'll be studying, or whatever, but she'll still be tan one way or another."

They compromised: she would sit in the tanning booth while listening to her school outlines on the MP3. It was unspoken but also decided that Serena would replace Elle as the maiden of honor. Elle's appearance wouldn't be so

noticed if she were just another guitar-swinging brides-
maid. Hopefully she'd be able to find a Wolff tanning bed
within the city limits of Palo Alto.

Margot called her at school frequently to make sure she
wasn't skipping her appointments in the tanning room. In
December Margot told Elle she was worried that she might
be studying and fading into a paler tone, and came to visit
her at Stanford.

Margot approved of Elle's living arrangement. Still, she
frowned to see the books and papers that littered her
condo. Elle admitted she had been working hard to catch
up in school, and really hadn't done much else since she
last saw her friends in L.A.

"So what's going on in LA-LA land?" Elle said, joining
Margot on the couch. "How's Malibu? Still the valley of
other people's rumors?"

"Totally," Margot announced. "Well, you know all about
Holly Finch."

"Who's Holly Finch?" Elle asked, staring listlessly at the
ceiling.

"*Who* is Holly Finch? Elle, tell me you're kidding."

Elle breathed "No" quietly and didn't make an excuse
for herself. Margot was perpetually the victim of her last
conversation. Something new, something five minutes ago,
must have been rumored over cocktails at one of Snuff's
promotions.

"Elle! She's topic numero uno in L.A., baby. The *virtual
vixen*. She's caused a total cyber-uproar."

"Are you into computers now?" Elle asked skeptically.
She needed an AP wire to keep up with Margot's fads.

"Well, no. Not me, but a lot of industry people are on-
line. It's all the rage. It's not like they're Trekkie types
or something. They're keyed into a whole virtual world.
Multimedia."

Margot was speaking a language she had obviously overheard in some Viacom hospitality suite.

"So what's the 'cyber-uproar'?" Elle asked, a touch
sarcastically.

"Well, Holly Finch's dad owns this big multimedia firm
and a record distributorship. He had a database of *major*
industry connections and Holly got a hold of it. She set up
this totally shady, all anonymous electronic bulletin board
so people could sign on with false names. It was totally
L.A. exclusive. You could only join if someone died or
quit . . . or if your net worth added up to the right numbers."

"So why is the, uh, virtual vixen in trouble?"

"Well, it seems she used her network to zap around
more than just *information*." Margot paused for a moment
to let her hint sink in. "Everyone was on-line in fantasy
mode, you know, talking about *how they like it*." She lowered her voice to a conspiratorial hush. "Elle, from what I
hear, they had some major perversions. A totally mangy
scene."

"So what?" Elle yawned.

"No," Margot insisted, "that's not all. See, the on-line
routine was just, like, an opener to get hooked up to the
real thing. S-E-X, whatever kinky way they wrote about in
their network profiles. Drugs, too. It was like mail order
from fantasyland! Key your dream girl into the computer,
and tomorrow she's ribbon-tied on your doorstep."

"But I thought everyone used pseudonyms." Elle hesitated, confused.

"Totally. They used everything. Heroin, acid, X."

"What?" Elle interrupted. "What are you talking about?"

Margot paused, reconsidering. "Well, not so much X.
That's passé. But I'm sure you're right. They must have had
a lot of orders for the one you just said."

"No, Marg," Elle laughed. "Pseudonyms . . . uh, false names."

"Oh." Margot quieted. She paused for a second to absorb the new word. "Pseudonyms." Then she continued. "The thing is, Holly kept a master list. For every fake name, she has the real identity, plus a practical *directory* of their sick turn-ons. *Highly placed* industry people, and she's threatening to publish the list if she goes to trial."

"What's she charged with?"

Margot laughed shrilly. "Holly Finch won't see the light of day for years when the feds get through with her. She's up on distribution charges for every drug under the sun, and even something about sex with *panda bears*!"

"Panda bears?"

"Yeah, pandering, I think it's called. I'm telling you, Elle, these people are sick cookies."

Elle walked to the kitchen, offering to get Margot an iced tea rather than chance laughing out loud at her friend.

"And then, even I still can't *believe* the most major crime happened right near my condo. It wasn't random, or anything, it was a total hit. Chutney *Vandermark's* father is dead and her stepmonster did it. If you were already a Malibu lawyer, you'd be really busy!"

Elle had long since ceased reading the newspaper or even *People*, but the name did strike her as familiar. "Who?"

Margot kicked a pile of Elle's casebooks aside, ignoring her question and looking for the remote control. She approached the TV set and poked a few buttons in vain. "How do you do this without the remote?"

"Uh, I don't know," Elle admitted. "Wait, here it is."

Margot grabbed the device out of her hand and flipped the channels until she found *Hard Copy*. "God, Elle, it's all over the major media."

The voice-over told a grim tale as a dramatic reenactment of the crime scene appeared on the screen. "Heyworth Vandermark, seventy-four-year-old tycoon. His life taken not by his heart condition, but by a cold-blooded assassin." An actress portraying the dead man's daughter wailed to police investigators, "I found his body, right here—" she pointed to a chalk outline—"and his wife was bent over the body, trying to move it!"

The narrator continued. "Twenty-three-year-old Brooke Vandermark, sixth wife of the slain multimillionaire, stands accused of the chilling . . . Murder in Malibu. An exclusive eyewitness interview with Heyworth Vandermark's only daughter, Chutney Vandermark, on this week's *Hard Copy*."

"Oh, Margot, turn that trash off," Elle complained. "I can't fill my head with this stuff before exams."

"Well, while your head is full of that *Tarts on Tape*, the rest of Southern California is filling up with the Vandermark murder," Margot snapped. "It even made *Vogue*." Margot muted the TV show. "Chutney went to USC, Elle."

"Wait, I remember a Chutney from rush. Wasn't she a Theta?"

"Delta Gamma," Margot said. "But get this, her stepmother, the murderer . . . *she* was a Theta. Typical."

Elle giggled. "That's a little strong, don't you think, Marg?"

"I don't know. The whole scene is so gnarly. Did you know that the stepmonster, Brooke, is a year *younger* than Chutney? Twenty-three. Shot the old geezer point-blank."

"That's so awful," Elle gasped.

"I know. I would just die if my father married somebody younger than I am."

Elle shook her head. "No, I mean, it's awful about her father being killed."

Margot looked puzzled. "Oh, that. If you think that's bad, I hear he left all his money to his wife."

CHAPTER TWENTY-FIVE

Before she left, Margot told Elle about a "darling plastic surgeon" who was living in the Palo Alto area. His name was Austin. Serena had met him in Aspen, and was anxious to get him together with Elle. "Serena says he's gorgeous," she promised. "Can we give him your number?" Looking critically at Elle's book-littered condo, she added, "You really should get out more."

Elle shrugged, a bit embarrassed, since things weren't working out with Warner. "But I haven't been on a date for ages. I'm totally out of practice."

"All the more reason," Margot said, turning to leave. "He'll call you soon. He's dying to meet you."

From Margot's brief description, Elle couldn't tell if a date with Austin would violate any of her rules about dating. There were three types of men she would not date: men with pinkie rings, men with more than one alimony obligation, and men with children older than she was. She figured she'd give Austin a try.

And he did call quickly, before the week's end. Whether he was dying to meet her or just plain hard up, she couldn't tell. They agreed to meet for drinks.

* * *

Elle wasn't sure at first how she was going to pick out Austin at the restaurant. All she had to go on was what Margot had told her, he was a "darling plastic surgeon"; but it didn't take a minute for her to recognize the "status doc" sitting at the bar. He wore a big Breitling watch around a dark, hairy wrist, and a snug Prada suit. His Porsche keys were prominently displayed next to his cellular phone, and he was drinking Campari and soda. His complexion was dark and he swam in hair gel: just the type Serena would swoon over.

"Austin," Elle said as she approached him and offered her hand. He nodded, looking slightly surprised, but extended his hand in return. "Elle?"

She nodded. The doctor looked approvingly at her little black dress and the figure that filled it. "Nice to meet you, Elle. Allow me to say that you are *great* raw material."

"Raw material," Elle muttered under her breath, dreading the time she would have to spend with him.

The flashy couple drew stares as they headed together for a table. The waiter scowled when Elle announced she could only stay for drinks. She was actually glad that she had a twenty-page memo due the next day. She explained this to Austin, saying she'd have a late night ahead.

He nodded, understanding a busy schedule.

When Austin was seated, Elle excused herself to "powder her nose." In the ladies' room Elle glanced at her Wolff-bed tan, which looked a bit yellowish in the light. Hurriedly she whipped the Chanel compact from her bag and dotted powder on her cheeks, smoothing it across her face to even her flesh tone. In her rush the narrow, almond-shaped nail on her ring finger caught the tip of her nose with a sting.

"Ow." Elle drew back sharply, and the bathroom attendant, who had been sitting quietly, leaped up with a hand towel to lend her assistance. That was when Elle realized her nose had started bleeding.

"Oh, God," Elle gasped in the mirror as a thin red line trickled above her lip. She grabbed the towel thankfully and pressed it against the cut.

"Use cold water," the attendant advised. Elle nodded and dipped one end of the towel in the sink. She replaced the chilly corner against her nose and held it there, peeking every so often until the bleeding stopped.

"Thanks," she said, tipping the attendant, whose job, she thought, might possibly be more boring than law school. With an anxious glance in the mirror, she dashed nervously back to the table. She had been in the bathroom about ten minutes, and Austin had finished his drink. He looked at her with curiosity, but resumed conversation easily when she asked him about himself.

Elle learned that Austin, though never married, was being stalked by a woman who had offered herself under his surgeon's knife after sending to his home a card signed, "Your canvas." At the time, he considered her formalities to be a little weird, but he decided to perform the operation anyway. He changed his mind when the woman ripped off her hospital gown and threw herself on the operating table, declaring: "My love, cut anywhere! This will prove that I trust you completely!"

"Business took the backseat," Austin laughed, "after that exhibition." He had his nurse escort the humiliated patient to a changing room, with orders not to return.

Elle threw her hands to her mouth and laughed. "Oh, Austin, how terrible," she said. She reached for her drink and noticed a small red streak on her index finger. Austin noticed it also.

"Oh no," she said, reaching into her purse for her compact. She opened it quickly and confirmed that her small bathroom gash had reopened. Her eyes darted up to Austin.

"Excuse me," she said, and hurried back to the "powder" room. The attendant rolled her eyes but obligingly provided Elle with a fresh towel.

Elle returned to the table thankful to see Austin standing, claiming his beeper had gone off. "I know you'll be up late tonight anyway," he said. Elle blushed. She was sure he had a certain suspicion about her sudden nosebleeds, but she didn't feel the need to explain she had merely injured herself in spastic application of face powder. He wouldn't believe her anyway.

In the lull before the waiter returned with his credit card slip, Austin reached out his hand and held Elle's arm gently. "Elle," he smiled, "are you seeing anyone right now?"

Elle knew she didn't want to date Austin again, but didn't want to admit to her life as a law school hermit. "Yes, Austin, I'm seeing a few people."

He looked puzzled but interested. Gripping her arm with fatherly concern, he asked, "Why do you see more than one therapist at a time?"

"Oh," she said, realizing that Austin had been asking about psychiatrists. She shrugged her shoulders. "I'm more complicated than I look."

"I see," he said. From the tone of his voice, Austin seemed doubtful.

"Two heads are better than one?" she tried again.

"Sure," he said. Clearly she'd need to add a new rule to her dating commandments: Never date men named after cities in Texas.

CHAPTER TWENTY-SIX

ONE rule Elle was learning fast was this: Blondes do not have more fun in law school. Her unsuccessful day in Professional Responsibility was a prime example of Stanford's antiblonde snobbery.

Professor Pfisak had asked the students to write a two-page "miniessay" in which they were to invent a legal organization that would serve the public interest. They could choose any cause they felt was neglected in the "corporate capitalistic status quo." In the context of this imaginary group, Pfisak asked the class to discuss the Model Rules of Professional Responsibility governing formation of the attorney-client relationship.

Elle turned in a miniessay describing her public interest vision: the Blonde Legal Defense Fund (BLDF). Its mission would be to combat antiblonde discrimination in all its forms. At the same time it would be a full-service law firm by and for blondes, providing positive blonde role models, focusing on community outreach in high-blonde areas like beaches. The BLDF would be particularly aggressive vindicating claims of hair salon malpractice.

The firm's decor would memorialize great strides in blonde history. It would feature sizzling Jean Harlow and

Marilyn prints and an exhibit of Christie Brinkley's magazine covers through the years. The BLDF would have an
ongoing display of the artwork of famous blondes, starting
with one of Princess Grace's pressed-flower arrangements.
Absolutely nothing by Madonna, though, since she could
not be considered a true blonde.

Elle went to some trouble in her miniessay to explain
the distinction between a true blonde and a natural blonde.
The BLDF would take cases of brunettes who had been
discriminated against, but only those who could be considered blonde at heart. True blondes, whether natural or not,
could be identified by their inner light of buoyant, charmed
confidence. Andre Agassi, for example, had the beacon of
a true blond despite the atrocious things he had done to his
hair. On the other hand, Madonna's light was snuffed out
for good when she turned her platinum hair to that icky
black color. The change meant Madonna wasn't blonde at
heart, since no true blonde would ever go back. Billy Idol
would still be okay.

Elle discussed the difficulty of finding blondes who are
established intellectual role models, one effect of antiblonde
discrimination. Male blonde intellectuals seemed particularly scarce. She could invite Robert Redford to serve on
the BLDF board of directors, or maybe get an endorsement
from Andrew McCarthy, but Elle was having trouble coming up with famous blonde men who weren't actors or
surfers. Dan Quayle was the highest-ranking blond Elle
could think of, but he might have to be disqualified for
making fun of Candice Bergen, another blonde.

The scarcity of respected blonde business leaders would
be evidence to use in workplace discrimination claims of
BLDF clients. Elle could just see squirming employers justifying the promotion of a brunette over an equally competent blonde: "But, Your Honor, it's only fair—blondes have

more fun." And herself, lead counsel, fighting on: "Objection. Irrelevant and prejudicial."

When Professor Pfisak began reading Elle's essay to the class, it was clear that his idea of reforming the capitalist status quo did not start with the Blonde Legal Defense Fund. Voice heavy with sarcasm, the professor paused several times to shake his head in apparent disbelief. He repeated phrases that especially struck him: "Did you get that, class? Madonna is not a true blonde because she turned her platinum hair to that icky black color. *Icky* black."

Amid her classmate's jeers and her professor's ridicule of the Blonde Legal Defense Fund, Elle held steadily to her vision.

CHAPTER TWENTY-SEVEN

STANFORD sadistically scheduled its exams after the winter vacation, stealing Christmas and New Year in one fell swoop. Even the Grinch stopped after Christmas. Elle parked the Range Rover in the driveway of her Bel Air home, then dragged heavy casebooks and Emanuel study guides to the doorstep.

Underdog had jumped from the passenger seat, overjoyed to be home. "Well, it's good to be back, even if I have to study over vacation," Elle said, the yipping dog lifting her spirits.

Elle's mother, Eva, was a holiday fanatic. She always went to extra lengths during the Christmas season, spoiling Elle wonderfully. The year that Tori Spelling's "White Christmas" was the talk of the town, Eva became irritated every time she heard it mentioned. *She* should have thought of flying in enough snow to blanket their yard, she rebuked herself. The truth was that Eva, a native Angeleno, associated snow with skiing and not Christmas.

Elle didn't have to wonder for long what gimmick her mother would think up this year. As soon as she entered the front hallway she was greeted by a preposterous "Elle Tree" that dwarfed the diminutive Eva and even Elle's lanky father, Wyatt. He beamed at Elle in his place beside his wife. His bland club-tennis-pro-blonde good looks and agreeable ways were a perfect counterpoint to Eva's wacky and vivacious personality.

A twenty-five-foot fir tree, twinkling with elaborate five-by-seven ornaments, stood in the foyer. Elle gasped as Eva led her excitedly to the tree.

"Oh, Mother," Elle said, and laughed. She hugged her giggling mother and gazed dumbfounded at the unique tree trimmings. Each was a reproduction of a famous painting, copied by artists from Eva's gallery. Each featured Elle's own face in the most unlikely of settings.

"Look, look, darling," Eva said, reaching out to one of the images. "My favorite is the *Birth of Elle!*"

"Mother." Elle blushed, mortified to see her face on the plump, naked body of Botticelli's Venus. "Oh my God! That's *me*, and she's so fat!"

The *Mona Elsa* wasn't so bad, since only the shoulders gave away the grande dame of da Vinci, and the artist had been nice enough to leave Elle's hair blonde on the reproduction. Elle's sky blue eyes replaced the art-book gazes of women from the imaginations of painters of centuries. She smiled flawlessly from Matisse to Modigliani, Rubens to Renoir, Gainsborough to Gauguin to Goya. "Mother," Elle said as she embraced Eva warmly, "you are without doubt the craziest Santa on the block."

"Never boring!" Eva exclaimed.

"Never boring," Wyatt said, winking at Eva. "Here, Elle, my favorite is the *American Gothic*. I think it suits you."

Grant Wood's famous pitchfork-wielding couple had been transformed, with Elle's face atop the matronly dress of the midwesterness, and a simple question mark on the blank face of the man standing beside her.

"You answer the question mark any way you want."

"Daddy, you know whose face *I'd* like to see there!" Elle hugged her father gleefully.

She retired to her room, leaving word with her parents that she wasn't taking calls, not even from Serena or Margot. "They'll just report the party schedule. I don't even want to be tempted. Tell them I'm sick or something, okay?"

Eva sighed and glanced worriedly at Wyatt.

"Please, Mom. I don't want to fail my exams."

"All right, honey," Eva said. "I'll call you for dinner."

Stress meters were running high the week of final exams, the library packed to capacity with students trying to make sense of a four-month blur of rules and procedures in a not-English not-Latin vocabulary called legalese. The Secret Angel had kept Elle, and through her Eugenia, supplied with accurate outlines, but the wear of living in a pressure cooker made exams almost welcome.

Reading furiously through byzantine Civil Procedure cases, Elle actually happened upon a useful bit of information. When creditors sue a debtor, they cannot take things that are "essential to everyday life." So Elle was consoled that if she ever hit rock bottom, she would be spared her wardrobe, make-up, telephone, and standing manicure appointment.

CHAPTER TWENTY-EIGHT

EUGENIA pressed her face against the screen of the window next to Elle's door and rang the bell a third time. She detected the muffled sound of a hair dryer blowing in the bathroom.

"Well, at least she's up," she said. Eugenia shifted the package that was making her arm tired. The blow-dryer stopped for a minute, and Eugenia gave the doorbell a long ring. "Elle!"

Elle peeked around the corner in her pink-and-white-striped terry-cloth robe. "Genie?"

"Hey, Elle, I came to make sure you got to your first exam on time. I'll drive you over if you want."

"Oh, great," Elle said, opening the front door. "Coffee's on in the kitchen. French roast."

"Thanks," said Eugenia. "Can't get enough of the stuff."

Elle hurried back to the bathroom. "Come talk to me while I get ready. I'm totally nervous."

Eugenia sank down Indian-style on the floor in the hallway and set her coffee cup down. "The doorman asked me to bring this in to you." She indicated the package. "Here." Eugenia carried the box to the kitchen with Elle trailing behind her. "You might want to open it. It's from Warner."

"That's so sweet!" Elle exclaimed. "It's probably a good-luck present. I should have sent him something, too. I was thinking about it." She cut through the masking tape eagerly with a steak knife.

A note was taped to a second box inside. Elle read it aloud as Eugenia sipped her coffee.

"Dear Elle,

I guess I should have sent these to you a while ago. Sarah finally insisted that I get rid of them. She doesn't like to be reminded of you, and I guess it's not right for me to have them anymore. How many married men do you know who keep pictures of their ex-girlfriends? I can remember you without pictures anyway. Whenever I go to the beach I think of you doing the ad for Perfect Tan. (Even sometimes when I see you at school!) Good luck on your exams.

Love, Warner."

Eugenia put her cup down slowly. "Pictures?"

Elle opened the box, stunned, and spilled a pile of photographs across the kitchen counter. She picked them up one by one, growing increasingly shaky. Eugenia walked over and didn't speak.

"Delta Gamma Crush party, 1999. Homecoming, 1999. Sigma Chi Bahamas party, 2000." She paused. "God, we kept Chuck Lane photography in business. Derby Days. I don't believe it, here's us in Aspen. On Valentine's Day." She smiled sadly, tears welling up in her eyes. "Some good-luck present."

"What a cretin." Eugenia cursed harsher words in a low voice. "Elle, come here." She put her arms around Elle, who sank her head on Eugenia's shoulder.

Elle shook weakly, leaning on the counter. "Why did he

have to send them back? I've got copies of all these." She
stared at the images of her face and Warner's, fanned
across the white countertop like so many playing cards.
"Why now? How could Warner do this to me? Oh, God, Eugenia, I can't go to the exam today. I just can't do it."

Eugenia shook her head angrily. "Warner? He's as sensitive as a block of wood. It's Sarah who sent these."

"What do you mean, Sarah?" Elle gulped, her eyes dull,
morose and unfocused. She hadn't even thought to blame
Sarah for Warner's ill-timed delivery. What good was all this
studying? Night after night spent poring over Emanuel outlines was supposed to have taught her how to spot a hidden legal issue when it snuck up on the exam. Had she
destroyed her own mind in the process? Chasing after elu-
sive subtleties, missing the obvious culprit? "Of course, it
must be Sarah," Elle realized with a sigh of misery. Sarah
was behind everything Warner did wrong. But still, "Warner
wrote the letter, didn't he? Those were his words."

"Elle, don't you get it?" Eugenia persisted. "It's no coinci-
dence that you got these pictures now. Sarah 'insisted,' did
she? I'll bet she insisted. Damn it, she's got him jumping
through hoops."

"Eugenia," Elle began, but Eugenia waved her off.

"I'll say this for Sarah, she plays hardball. Elle, she doesn't
want you to make it. You've been working your heart out
for these exams, and you're ready. I know you are. She's
just trying to shake you up. She wants to get you out of law
school. Don't let her win."

Shivering, Elle pulled her robe tight around her.

"Elle, I mean it." Eugenia grabbed Elle's shoulders, straightening her with a vigorous shake. "You go get dressed and
put this out of your head. Don't let Sarah or Warner . . .
don't let either of them ruin what you've worked all semester for."

Elle dropped her head and stared at the floor. "I don't care if Sarah made him do it or not. I came here for Warner, Eugenia. He's who I've worked all semester for! Nobody else. I only wanted to show him that I could finish. . . ." Elle's quivering voice broke into a sob.

Eugenia released Elle's arms and collected the pictures on the counter. She shoved them back into the package and glared at Elle without speaking. Elle hid her face, unable to stand the black reflection of her own weakness in Eugenia's withering stare. Eugenia sighed, seeming to soften, but when she spoke again she spoke gravely.

"Warner and Sarah won't be thinking about you today, Elle. They'll be thinking about Contracts. Before your memory is five minutes old, they'll be framing their law degrees. Do whatever you want, leave if you feel like it, but don't forget: at least one of them will be thrilled to see you fail."

Elle bristled. "Try to see what I see, Eugenia. I made an incredible mistake coming here." She reached for the letter, an anxious flush coloring her pale face, spotting her neck with crimson patches. "Look, for every single case I read, for every class outline I fell asleep with my face on top of, what does Warner think when he sees me at school? Does he care that I've got a brain, that I can do anything his fiancée can do? That I'm as serious as any preppie from Groton? No, he thinks Perfect Tan! My bikini shot!" Elle restrained her voice with an effort, wiping a tear angrily from her burning scarlet cheek. "What difference will passing an exam make? Warner doesn't care and he never will. It won't change the fact that I'm not from Greenwich. I'll never be a Knottingham. I'll never be what he wants. And its just become clear to me that I'll never be a Huntington! What's the point of keeping this up anymore?"

"Finish because you can, Elle," Eugenia answered in a firm tone. "Leave on your terms, not theirs. Not *hers*."

Elle peered sheepishly at Eugenia, then shook her head in the negative. "Who are you kidding, Eugenia? I can't even remember what a contract is anymore."

"Offer and acceptance," fired Eugenia.

"Don't forget consideration." Elle smiled meekly, and Eugenia laughed out loud.

"See? You know this stuff better than I do. Come on, Elle, don't flake out now."

Elle gave an uncertain glance at the clock over the stove. "There's still time."

Eugenia smiled. "I'll drive. You can read the outline in the car, if it won't make you sick. Elle, it will *kill* Sarah if this little stunt doesn't faze you."

"Warner, too, huh?" Elle looked mischievous.

"Definitely." Eugenia opened the cupboard. "Want a Pop-Tart?"

"Gross!" Elle giggled. "Those are left over from the ones you bought before. I don't know how you can eat that stuff."

"Fine, have a rice cake. But get ready. This is your day."

The first exam, Contracts, began at 9:00 A.M. Elle finished the four-hour test a full hour early because, in her panic, she misread the clock.

Having raced under the pressure of her own deadline, Elle realized that with a full hour to go she had nothing to add to the thoughts scribbled in her test book. In fact, a weird postexam amnesia erased whatever random ideas she had just assembled into arguments.

One down, Elle thought with relief, floating happily down the aisle to drop her exam with a smack on the front desk. As she turned to leave, Elle caught a glimpse of dozens of hapless, furtive eyes shooting to the wall clock in fear that they were behind schedule. Watching her classmates' nervous heads and shaky hands jerk to work faster was so delightful that Elle decided she would try to finish all her exams first.

Civil Procedure was the only exam that Elle didn't finish an hour early. One question involving jurisdiction reminded Elle of the Secret Angel's outline, which was sixty pages in rhyming verse on the Federal Rules of Civil Procedure. The verse, called "Jurisdiction Diction," was a takeoff on "Schoolhouse Rock" 's "Conjunction Junction," a mnemonic approach to memorizing that turned out to hurt more than it helped.

While trying to remember the difference between *in rem* and *in personam* jurisdiction, Elle visualized the "Conjunction Junction" episode instead. "Hmm hmm hmm hmm, phrases and clauses," she sang to herself, annoyed that she couldn't remember the first line. She mixed the episode up with "Lolly lolly lolly get your adverbs here," and in the next minute remembered her favorite, "Interplanet Janet." As precious minutes ticked by, Elle, worlds away, was humming "She went to the sun, it's a lot of fun—it's a hot spot, it's a gas. Hydrogen and helium, in a big bright glowing mass."

She had to fight to get the tune to "I'm Just a Bill" cleared from her head as she stared dismally at the blank page in her test book. Indecisively, Elle settled on an argument that the plaintiff had *quasi-in-rem* jurisdiction, which she thought was iffy enough for half credit.

What was worse, Elle noticed as she glanced back over her essay that she had written "queasy" instead of "quasi" every time she used the key phrase. "Freudian slip," she muttered, scratching out each offending word. Serena was in Aspen and Margot was comparing wedding dresses in the Valentino boutique; Elle was rushing to eke out a miserable essay on jurisdiction amid a sweaty throng of grademongers. She felt queasy, all right. Elle paused and left the word "queasy" uncorrected once, on principle.

The week after finals might have been some measure of vacation, since classes didn't begin for another ten days, at any place other than Stanford Law. But here "vacation" defined time to study or write papers. The law school scheduled interviews for spring internships and summer jobs during that hiatus, just to ensure that its captives lived and breathed law school stress constantly.

Eugenia had made plans to spend half of the time at home and then meet her college boyfriend, Kenneth, and some other friends from Yale in Vermont to go skiing. "These early interviews are a waste of time," Eugenia explained. "Grades aren't even out. The first round is just where they weed out severe social misfits."

Elle laughed. "Who's left?"

Eugenia was admirably unconcerned with the pressures of job hunting. Her thesis adviser wanted her to do research for him in New Haven over the summer, still trying to encourage her to pursue a Ph.D. in literature. She had a safety net, so she walked on the employment tightrope with casual grace.

Elle noticed with interest that Christopher Miles, a well-known defense attorney in San Francisco, was interviewing first-year students for spring semester internships. The January issue of *Architectural Digest* had named his firm, Miles & Slocum, among the top ten law firms in the country for its office design. It was the only California firm to have made the list.

Naturally, Elle's first instinct had been to drop by the offices with business cards from her mother's art gallery. But when Eugenia told her that Christopher Miles was interviewing for research assistants on the Vandermark case, Elle developed a keen interest in getting the job; and when she saw Warner's name among the forty-odd students on the interview list, she made the internship her first priority.

Elle was eager to talk to Eugenia about the interview. So far, the only interview advice she had came from a *Cosmopolitan* quiz, "Are You a Savvy Job Interviewee?" She thought advice from someone who had actually held a few jobs might prove more helpful. Eugenia's tips proved her right.

Seeing Elle's name on the interview sheet for the coveted internship, Sidney added his name in bold print and then hunted Elle down. When he spotted her coming out of the law lounge with Eugenia, he was characteristically armed and ready with an insult.

"Elle, *why* don't you just get married and go play tennis at the club like you are *supposed* to?" His snide comment drew thundering laughter from the other Trekkies standing with him.

Sidney broke into a new set of hysterics, appreciating his own witticism. Even Sidney knew of Elle's desperation to break up Sarah and Warner, a topic that had apparently become common knowledge at the law school.

Less bothered than she would have expected to be by Sidney's comment, she walked right past him.

"What luck," she said to her mother on the phone that evening. The "Murder in Malibu!" Margot would flip if she heard Elle might be working on the hottest case in L.A. She might even forgive her for going to law school, Elle ventured optimistically. But when Serena called, Elle realized that even a stylish lawyerly debut would play to no applause from the roving bons vivants she called her friends. Law school was still an unacceptable alternative lifestyle.

Serena had invited Elle to join her in Aspen during the week of Elle's interview, and couldn't believe it when Elle turned her down. "Come on, Elle, has that sickhouse poisoned you? Do you hear what I'm saying? Absolutely everybody is here this week. I mean, it's a practical *reunion*. Davis asked about you, and Vince is here. And Charles . . . Charles still *adores* you. He's always asking about you."

"Serena, it's not just any interview," Elle protested, playing the card she thought would win Serena over. "Listen, you heard about the Vandermark murder. I mean, it made *Vogue*. It was all Margot could talk about when she came up here to visit."

"Yeah, of course." Serena recognized the hot topic. "Everybody's talking about Brooke 'the Blonde Butcher' Vandermark. Her picture's been on the front of every tabloid. You know she was a Theta? Typical."

Serena was beginning to sound more and more like Margot.

"Right," Elle said. "Well, this big-deal defense lawyer took Brooke's case, and he's here, see? I have a chance at an internship on the 'Murder in Malibu.' Isn't that exciting? He's interviewing here to get some law students to help him do research or something. Or get him coffee. I don't care, I think Brooke Vandermark is getting a bad rap. I want to help her."

"A Theta?" Serena sneered. "What are you all concerned about a Theta for? Don't you remember when they beat us in the swimsuit competition at Derby Days? Jesus, Elle, I mean, it would be one thing if she were one of *our* sorority sisters. Then maybe I'd get it. But a Theta?"

"Who cares, Serena. It's a great opportunity."

"Elle, what's up? Are you totally gone?" She tried to reason with her friend. "I'm in a hot tub right now, chiquita." Elle visualized Serena's parents' eighteen-thousand-square-foot "log cabin" and sighed. "You could be here too, babe. What's with you?"

"Okay, okay, Serena, don't make this harder than it is. Would the interview make more sense if I told you it had to do with Warner?" Elle heard Serena burst into laughter.

"Oh God, Elle, I almost dropped the phone," Serena giggled. "I could get electrocuted!" Elle heard a man's voice explaining how cordless phones work. "What? No, Nathan, it has electricity. Shut up." Elle heard splashing. "It doesn't run on air. Hee-hee-hee. Cut it out! You'll zap us!"

"Serena. Serena," Elle said. "Warner's interviewing too. I hardly ever see him. We don't have classes together. We could work together on this, you know. If I get the job. Then I could talk to him, talk some sense into him."

Serena quieted. "Oh, you poor thing. Elle, there are so many other fish . . . on the slopes."

"Fish on the slopes?" Serena sounded drunk.

"Hee-hee. On the slopes. Elle, what about Charles? He's just dying to see you again." One man was as good as another to Serena.

"Serena, listen. I'm all the way up here in this hellhole. I came here for Warner. I might as well give it the old college try."

"Will you *please* come home if he doesn't come to his senses soon, Elle? Please? This is getting ridiculous."

Elle sighed. "I'll come home. Serena, I just took exams. I mean, I *totally* studied. I worked harder than I've ever worked before. I'll finish this year, okay? Just trust me on this one. This interview is my last chance, and I'm giving it everything I've got." Elle cradled the phone in her shoulder and walked across the room to her closet.

"Well," Serena reconsidered, "I'll set up my crystals for you, then. Direct some good karma your way."

"You fruitcake," Elle laughed affectionately. "Thanks."

Serena squealed and splashed her Jacuzzi companion. "It's not voodoo, you geek. Naaathan! Elle, I'll catch up with you later, sweetie. Love you!"

"Miss you, Serena. Later." Elle clicked the phone off and reached into her closet to pick out an interview suit.

"I've got to look perfect tomorrow." She flung open her closet doors and began frantically searching for the perfect outfit. She paused at a navy Armani. Holding the suit up in front of her body, she glanced at Underdog's reflection behind her in the three-way mirror. "Navy?" The dog curled unenthusiastically on the floor. Elle swore she saw him yawn.

"You're right. Boring. Sarah would wear navy." She pulled out a cheerful Chanel whose gold buttons twinkled. "Better," she smiled. "Think pink, Underdog," she said. Underdog breathed a contented sigh.

CHAPTER TWENTY-NINE

JOSETTE had accommodated yet another last-minute appointment, and Elle strode in to meet Christopher Miles confident, rosy, and polished to the tips of her fingers. "Ingenue," the Italian-suited defense attorney said to her, grinning, as he sat behind a Formica table in the law lounge and watched Elle's legs cross under her narrow pink skirt.

Not to be outdone, Elle spoke back in French. "Comme il faut! As it should be."

He had his own reasons for calling her in, which were trivial. *"Mon petit bijou"*—he smiled smoothly—"I imagined you less . . . . sophisticated."

She scowled. "Indeed."

"Elle," he explained, still smiling, "I see a lot of résumés. Never a pink one."

"Stands out?" she said.

He nodded.

"It's my life there, on that page." She pointed at the résumé where it lay on the desk. "How much can you say on a page?"

"Engraved?"

"Why not? You engrave a new shipment of stationery every time your address changes, and don't think twice about it. And then people Xerox . . . Xerox!" she said, grimacing. "Their résumé, the one piece of paper that must be right!" She paused, wondering if she should be talking about stationery.

"Engraved, rose-colored résumés . . . almost a medieval script. You could send one to the House of Windsor. If the royals were hiring sociopolitical jewelry-design majors, with awards in—"

Christopher stopped in midsentence.

"Elle, under Honors and Awards"—the lawyer leaned across the table and turned the blush paper sideways so they could both read it; Elle peered cautiously at her life-on-a-page—"you have here: Homecoming Queen, '00; Greek Goddess, '99 . . ."

She smiled and traced the honors with her fingernail as he read. "President, Delta Gamma sorority, USC; Chair, Intersorority Council, USC; Spokesmodel, Perfect Tan skin products, Los Angeles." The lawyer paused. "Spokesmodel?"

Elle shrugged. "Well, as for the awards, I took some off, you know, the older crowns. Princess of this and that. Those are the most recent."

"I've never seen anything like this résumé. I had to meet you, Elle."

"Here I am, then. Let's talk about the job you're going to offer me, shall we?"

"Of course," he said, half mocking her. "What do you know about this project?"

What Elle knew she didn't want to say. She knew, thanks to Eugenia, that Christopher Miles, a Stanford Law graduate, was a famous defense attorney, and he had a quid pro quo going with the top law schools. When he had a big case, he would provide the school with name recognition and press.

In turn, the students would provide him with limitless

free research for academic credit and trial experience that would help them in later interviews.

Christopher Miles would be trying Brooke Vandermark's case in San Francisco, and when he had turned to Stanford Law for research assistants, Dean Haus had welcomed him warmly. Over forty students had become rivals for one of the four spots on the lawyer's defense team. If Dean Haus had rolled out anything but a red carpet, the halls of Stanford would soon be bloody anyway.

It was said that students weren't above telling lies about the last student they saw interviewing. "I probably shouldn't say this, but the woman you just spoke to is a manic depressive. One day without her lithium and you don't know what could happen. I think this case might be too much for her." Treachery started early in the ambitious.

Elle's interest in the job was manifold.

"I'm interested in criminal-defense work," Elle lied. "You're defending a woman who is said to have killed her husband. That's all I know. What else can you tell me?" she asked, sitting back in her chair.

"Brooke Vandermark," he began after a lengthy pause, "twenty-three, sixth wife of Heyworth Vandermark, who was in failing health at seventy-four. Heart condition. It didn't matter, though. He was shot at very close range. His health goes to motive. . . . Brooke had just married him. Multimillionaire. His will left everything to his wife."

Elle raised her eyebrows and leaned forward. "Blonde?"

"I'm sorry?"

"Nothing," she said. "Please," she said with an inviting wave of her manicured hand, "please continue."

"Brooke's been charged with the murder. There's not a lot of physical evidence: no scuffle and no murder weapon."

"What happened to the gun?"

The lawyer shrugged. "Your guess is as good as mine.

The police never found it. But an eyewitness saw Brooke at the scene."

"Eyewitness?"

Christopher nodded gravely. "Heyworth's daughter, his only child, walked in on the gory aftermath. She was in the house . . . the estate . . . and when she came downstairs she caught Brooke covered with her father's blood, bent over his body, trying to move it. She took Brooke completely by surprise."

Elle drew in her breath, cringing. "What happened then?"

"The daughter says Brooke pleaded with her, but she ran into the kitchen to call the police. Brooke chased after her, begging her to stop. When the police arrived, Brooke had fainted in the kitchen. The gun was not on the scene, and the police didn't find it in a search of the house and the grounds. So there's no evidence to dispute the eyewitness's testimony. Brooke's fingerprints were all over Heyworth's body, his blood was all over her, and she has no alibi." After a moment the lawyer shook his head with exasperation. "Well, no alibi that holds, anyway."

"What's her alibi?"

"She's a difficult one, this Brooke. When I interviewed her, she told me she was at a group meeting. A support group for Home Shopping Network addicts. Shopper Stoppers Anonymous."

"How sad!" Elle said.

"See, according to Brooke, there were a good fifteen other people who spent all afternoon with her. However, she refuses to name them because that would reveal their addiction. So her 'anonymous' alibi is as good as no alibi at all."

"Well if I, God forbid, went to a 'Shopper Stoppers' meeting, I sure wouldn't want the world to know."

Christopher Miles tapped his pen again, appearing agitated. "Well, the group members have nothing to fear. Brooke says the same thing. Apparently there are all sorts of executives, reputable types, you name it, who have this . . . problem. She won't breathe a word about who was at this meeting."

"Of course not," Elle stated with conviction.

"Everyone says it's an open-and-shut case, Elle. The murder, I mean. The prosecution faces an even greater immediate challenge though. That's what I'm working on right now, and that's what I need my defense team to help me with." He drummed his fat black Montblanc pen against his legal pad.

"Worse than *that*?" Elle marveled. Brooke's lot sounded bad enough with the murder charge.

"Heyworth's daughter has already presented his will for probate. Under California law, what's known as the Slayer Statute, a will beneficiary cannot take a legacy if that beneficiary caused the death of the donor."

"So if Brooke killed him, she's cut out."

"Right," he said, and smiled.

"Why is that worse? Losing the money . . . that's pretty bad, but I'd be worried about going to jail." Elle shuddered at the thought.

"Worse from a legal standpoint. The burden of proof in a criminal prosecution is, as you know, beyond a reasonable doubt. The burden of proof in a civil case, the burden for will probate, is lower."

"Preponderance," Elle finished. Thanks to her Secret Angel for the Civil Procedure outline.

"Preponderance," he repeated. "More likely than not. The plaintiff, Chutney, need only show that it is more likely than not that Brooke is guilty of the murder for purposes of defeating her gift . . . cutting her out of the will."

"Who is Chutney?" Elle asked, eyes innocently careful to conceal that she already knew who Chutney Vandermark was. A Delta Gamma who, according to Margot, had a terrible nose job and was probably named after a spice.

"Oh, sorry. Chutney Vandermark. That's his daughter, who, by the way, is a year older than Brooke."

"Blonde?" Elle asked the lawyer.

"I'm sorry?" Christopher Miles asked, puzzled.

"Is Chutney blonde?" Elle couldn't remember, and anyway, that could change.

"Uh, no. No. Why?" He looked at the pink homecoming queen with curiosity.

Elle knew where her sympathies lay. Smiling, she announced: "Then I am perfect for this job."

"I'm not sure I understand."

Elle beamed. "It's my ambition. That's why I'm in law school," she proclaimed momentously. "One day in Legal Ethics . . . John . . . he's very judgmental. He started this thing . . . ," Elle got sidetracked for a moment, the enthusiasm of her public-service vision taking center stage.

"Go on," Christopher encouraged with interest.

"We had to describe, you know, our idea of a public-service project in the law. So this girl Rebel, she has something for Native American alcoholics, and Cari . . . well, she just wants to send all men to the gas chamber." Elle paused.

"When my turn came around I told the class that I was going to found the BLDF. The Blonde Legal Defense Fund. My professor read my essay to the class."

Christopher Miles burst out laughing.

"Come on . . . I'm serious," Elle frowned. "There's a lot of antiblonde prejudice in the professional world. Believe me, I know. Not the jokes. I mean, that's just envy, you know? Not actionable. But I was thinking about it. Look at the world's blonde role models. Can you name a blonde president?"

He paused. "I guess not."

"Dan Quayle. He's the closest we've gotten. And look what happened to him!"

"So the Blonde Legal Defense Fund . . ."

"Will stand up for blondes everywhere!" Elle finished. "Public service! Starting with Brooke Vandermark."

Christopher Miles smiled. There had been a time when he was at Stanford and had plans to fight the system, long before he accepted that all of his clients were guilty.

Elle, a minute before effusive with the reformist zeal of youth, suddenly halted and then spoke gravely, as if telling a secret. "Anyway, Brooke didn't do it. She didn't kill Heyworth Vandermark."

He paused, surveying Elle with care, but skeptically. "Oh? How convenient. Do you also know who did it?"

"Chutney did it," Elle declared, already on the side of wholesome blonde innocence.

"His daughter? What makes you so sure, Elle?" The lawyer squinted at her. It was odd to accuse the victim's own daughter, and though Elle sounded certain, she didn't know any facts.

"Chutney did it," Elle said again.

"I've told you very little about Brooke," he said, his voice a calm contrast to her impulsiveness. "And I really couldn't tell you much of anything about Chutney. Neither of them has been deposed. Perhaps it would restrain your enthusiasm to know that witnesses are coming out of the woodwork already to testify against Brooke when the murder charge goes to trial after probate."

Elle sat sullenly without responding.

"Chutney has already given statements to the police that are very damaging. I have no doubt that she will testify against Brooke. Brooke's personal trainer, the gardener, the maid, and the interior designer, among others, are all pointing at Brooke as the murderer."

Elle didn't speak, but she looked offended. She folded her arms and glared as if the charges were against her personally.

"Remember, Elle," the lawyer pointed out, more to restate the facts to himself than to debate the matter, "Chutney is the man's daughter. She is his blood. Brooke only married Heyworth Vandermark about a year ago, and it's pretty clear she did it for the money."

"See, you take the wrong inference from that," Elle protested. "A woman my age who marries a man that old on the hope that he doesn't write her out of his will and leave it all to his daughter anyway, that's a woman who's willing to work for her money. That man had been married almost as many times as Larry King, for God's sake! He knew how to file divorce papers. But he kept Brooke around. That's honest work, hard work: keeping a rich man happy. Anyone who marries for money ends up earning it."

Christopher looked at Elle, tapped his pen, and then scribbled something on his legal pad. Now he realized that, weird as it sounded, the girl had an inkling of a defense theory. It was more than he had heard in twenty interviews during which law students had tried to sell their legal ambitions like brokers pedaling tax-deferred annuities.

"And what about Chutney?"

"Well," Elle said, "I only know a little of the facts. But from what you've told me, it's got to be Brooke or Chutney. Brooke, I tell you, was making honest money putting up with a testy old dinosaur who married and divorced on a whim. Chutney, though, the late-in-life kid: those kind think they're entitled. They never see their parents struggle, or grow up. They just see this old lump between them and their inheritance, breathing its last intolerable breaths."

"God, Elle, that's pretty cynical."

"I am from L.A.," she said, and smiled. "Have you been to California Cafe? If you'd like to test my theory, let's talk about it over dinner."

"Shall we invite the other interviewing students?" the lawyer teased.

Elle glared at him. "I have this phobia. I can't eat in company greater than two."

"You should get that checked out. Why don't I meet you there, say at five-thirty?"

"Why don't you pick me up, say at six?" Elle scribbled her address and phone number on a finely lined pink sheet of paper. "Call if you get lost." Elle crossed her fingers and turned to leave the room.

"It's casual," she called back from the doorway, impatient to change out of her suit.

The heat of the day was suspended in a sultry dusk, and the terrace tables at California Cafe, only recently open for outside dining, were lively with the appreciative buzz of shoppers enjoying the early hint of spring after Palo Alto's rainy winter. Not a few garment bags lay slung over chair backs. Elle saw a Neiman Marcus bag draped across the back of a chair at the table of a lone woman who was attacking her taco salad with too much enthusiasm.

She might have met Christopher here, instead of driving over with him, Elle thought to herself, if only she had remembered that Lancome was doing Hydradermie facials at Neiman's. A Belgian aesthetician who had pioneered the use of mild electric currents to rejuvenate the eye and neck area was visiting the store until the week's end. The

postcard that announced this event was the one piece of
unsolicited mail she had received this month that escaped
an instant trashing. It was never too early to exfoliate, Elle
believed.

Maybe another time, she thought. Elle folded her sunglasses and slipped them into their case, blinking with an
anxious smile. She noticed soft glints of gray that streaked
Christopher Miles's dark hair about the temples. She wondered if he had been divorced, thought it likely as a matter
of odds, but at the same time instinctively doubted it. He
was exceedingly graceful; his gaze rested easily wherever
he turned it; the air about him was that of a man who belonged. He was successful, welcome, and unhurried. He
had the maturity of calm knowledge without the vinegar of
hard experience. Elle had never dated an older man who
did not fancy himself a young one. She did not realize until
the waiter approached that she had been staring into his
steady hazel eyes.

Her eyes flashed when she became conscious of herself.
She looked down abruptly and busied her hands in the
folds of the silk sarong that skirted her bare legs. She
clicked her left heel in and out of her mule with apprehen-
sion. She felt entirely inappropriate.

Christopher's sleeves were rolled back and his collar
was unbuttoned at the neck under a loosened Hermès tie
whose print featured rabbits being pulled out of top hats.
He hadn't had time to change from his suit, however. Elle
remembered suggesting California Cafe specifically for its
casual atmosphere, but Christopher, in his professional for-
mality, had missed the hint. The restaurant was in the Stanford Shopping Center, for God's sake, in a mall. Nobody
wore suits in malls, she insisted to herself, gulping when
she noticed the table of happy-hour revelers who might
have been tax accountants, bankers, or lawyers . . . pin-

striped to the last. Well, nobody should be wearing suits, Elle decided. If she knew anything, she knew what to wear to the mall.

"It's a nice night to sit outside," she attempted, extending a shaky hand to her water glass.

Christopher smiled broadly. "I wish I'd had time to change out of my suit," he said. "I envy your comfort."

Elle laughed. "I'm not the least bit comfortable," she admitted. She hadn't even grabbed a snack before Christopher arrived, and now, on top of everything, she was starving. Elle had wanted to be prepared to discuss Brooke's case, so she had researched in the obsolete manner of the computer illiterate: she talked to people who knew, or knew of, Brooke Vandermark. She had spent hours on the phone with sorority sisters, gathering gossip about Brooke's USC days, making notes like a tabloid reporter of reliable, if secondhand, details. As Elle should have expected, the best rumors came from Margot, the human Internet. She had even tracked down Dookie Dean, who was president of Theta when Brooke lived in the sorority house, which was some trouble, since the recent divorcée was still living under her married name. Elle found out in the first breath that Dookie Dean didn't go by the nickname "Doo-Dee" anymore, an offending gaffe that thwarted Elle's friendly attempts to gain information.

Elle ordered a diet Coke and Christopher ordered a single-malt scotch. Elle was familiar enough with the menu to ignore the gesticulating waiter who made up for the lack of variety in the day's specials by painstakingly describing the manner in which each was prepared. Elle suspected he was a chef at heart, stuck in a second-string job. She ordered grilled mahimahi, with instructions that the fillet be accompanied by two lemon wedges and not be touched by one drop of butter. "I mean it, if I see any butter, I'll send it back," she cautioned, requesting her salad dressing on the side.

"The Trappist monk will endure her fast alone," Christopher said, and smiled. "I'd like the giant T-bone steak," he announced, "and I want enough butter on the baked potato to drown a mule."

Elle laughed. "I don't know how you manage to eat like that," she said.

"I'm from the Midwest," he answered with a shrug. "We've advanced beyond gathering nuts and berries. No ice in the scotch," he called after the departing waiter.

"Glenn Fiddich," Elle smiled, relaxing, "is what we call my Torts professor."

"Don't tell me old man Glenn is still teaching!" Christopher shook his head incredulously. "He must be a hundred years old. I thought his liver would go before the end of my first year! Still knocking them back in the afternoons, is he?"

Elle paused, wrinkling her brow. It was odd to imagine the stylish Christopher Miles at Stanford. Maybe law school was different then.

"I can't imagine you at Stanford."

Christopher smiled. "The feeling is mutual, Miss Woods."

"What, you can't imagine yourself there either? I guess it's been a while."

"Easy, young one," the lawyer cautioned. "It wasn't so long ago. I meant I can't imagine you there. Stanford must be very proud to count you in its ranks."

"Well, I doubt that it's changed very much." Elle caught herself on the verge of trotting out her grievances with law school, the bulk of which were aesthetic. "People just study mainly, and worry." She shrugged. "Stanford Law is not a proud place."

"You're right, then. It hasn't changed." Christopher winked. "There's no pride in practicing law either."

Elle shook her head vigorously. "I don't believe that. I don't believe that or I wouldn't be here. I think you should be very proud of what you're doing for Brooke. She needs someone to believe in her, and you're standing up for her. I want to help her too. That's why I want to work on her case."

"Quite noble, Miss Woods. A lawyer who wants to be of help." He cocked his head slyly, but his skeptical words were at odds with his soft eyes, looking back on a musty old feeling. He had wanted to be of help too, when he started. Students encouraged him when he felt they had not lost faith.

"Tell me, Elle," he asked mischievously, "would you take this job if I told you I would not, in any event, act as a reference? Not call around to help you get a clerkship? Not even confirm that you worked for me? Just let you . . . help?"

"Absolutely," Elle said. "If we get Brooke out of trouble, I'll just have people call her instead."

"And if we don't," Christopher sighed, "they'll have to call the warden."

Elle scowled. "That's a bad attitude."

"Realistic," the lawyer said with a shrug, nodding thanks to the waiter for his scotch. "The way it looks now, this case is the toughest of my career. Like I said, the criminal defense will be easier than the will contest. Brooke has no alibi, and if it comes down to credibility . . . " Christopher trailed off, not wanting to predict his own defeat.

"Brooke didn't do it," Elle declared firmly. "She didn't need the money. She believed in perfection. She worked very hard. She was nice to animals. She used to brush her dog every day and she gave him mints. She was . . ." Elle thought of what she had heard, and halted. It still seemed rude to mention. She blushed, taking her cocktail stirrer from the tablecloth. Christopher was in good shape. Maybe he wouldn't understand.

"She was what, Elle?" He leaned forward, setting his drink aside, staring expectantly, his hands kneading together in the manner of prayer. "What do you know about Brooke?"

"Well, I hate to say it," Elle said, grimacing, "but she was really fat."

"Fat?" Christopher settled back in his chair, breathing a heavy, disappointed sigh. "Elle, I just don't see how that makes any difference now. By the way, she's in great shape now. She's absolutely outraged that there wasn't a StairMaster in the L.A. County Jail. She was sure her rights were being violated."

Elle frowned with impatience. It was as if men never thought about the struggle women endured, daily, to stay thin. They thought about the results, all right, when they wanted the feminine trophy of their success. As if women came from cookie cutters. She would bet her life that Christopher Miles never dated a fat girl. Warner certainly hadn't, she thought in gentle reproach. It must have been hard for Brooke.

"Don't you see, she made something of herself," Elle protested. "She's worked for every pound. She's not a woman who takes the easy way."

"You talk about her as if you know her," Christopher said, puzzled but still unconvinced.

Elle nodded. "I do. She was my step-aerobics instructor at USC. It was the hardest class I ever took!"

"She taught an aerobics class in jail," Christopher said. " 'Felon-o-robics,' she called it. I'm sure there was some disappointment when she made bail. She told the ladies to keep themselves together, to use the time they had as a project to shed those few extra pounds. She said to think of it like going away to a spa and surprising your friends with the beautiful new you on your trial date. It was a pretrial confinement, so she didn't have to deal with any hopeless long-termers. She was very popular."

Elle smiled warmly, more convinced than ever by Brooke's vigorous optimism that she was on the side of truth and healthy blonde energy.

"I wasn't sure that Brooke was the same one I knew at USC when I interviewed with you this afternoon," Elle allowed, "but I made some calls. She was Brooke Rayburn then. She was a year ahead of me, but I remember the big controversy she caused at the Theta house."

Christopher raised his eyes with concern. "Controversy? That's all she needs."

"She almost moved out. See, she was a double legacy. Her mother and her grandmother were Kappa Alpha Thetas, and her mom is still really active, a chapter president or something. So when Brooke showed up at rush, she was pretty much a given. And that didn't make the Thetas real happy, since she was so fat. On top of being a legacy, her mom gives a lot of money, so there was no way they could blackball her."

"That's awful." Christopher cringed. The viciousness of pretty women never failed to take him by surprise. "So Brooke comes from money?" The lawyer grew interested. "Brooke told me that she put herself through school. Brooke seemed to say nothing to me that wasn't self-defeating. It seems as if she wants to play against the highest odds."

"Well, she did. Come from money, that is. Her dad was a real estate developer who made a fortune building strip malls, but in her sophomore year, her parents went through

a divorce. Brooke found out in the worst way that her father was having an affair. One of the guys on the swim
team was at a Theta crush party and he mentioned to
Brooke that he'd had breakfast with her father, Mr. Rayburn, just that morning. Brooke thought he must have been
interviewing for a job with her dad's real estate company,
so she asked him how the interview went. He just laughed
and said it was no interview, Mr. Rayburn just liked his
mother's blueberry pancakes. It turned out that this guy's
mother lived down the street from the Rayburns in Pasa-
dena. She was divorced, living off of a generous settle-
ment, and spending most of her time with her horses,
playing tennis at the Valley Hunt Club, and being a friendly
neighbor."

Elle took a sip of her diet Coke and looked around the
restaurant.

"Anyway, she met Brooke's dad because she got some
of his mail by mistake, and she brought it over to the
house. Brooke's mom was away on business. She was a
fashion photographer and was in Paris photographing the
spring collections. I guess Mr. Rayburn was lonely."

"Don't tell me." Christopher swatted the air with his hand.

"You guessed it," Elle sighed. "The rat started sleeping
with his neighbor. Brooke's mother said she was a photographer because of her love of art, but she must have
known something about her husband's once lucrative so-
called real estate company. It went Chapter Eleven after the divorce."

"So I guess Brooke told her mother about the affair?"

"It was terrible. Injustice should be Brooke's middle
name."

The waiter arrived with an enormous tray, carrying the
salads and dinner together, evidently to hurry the meal

along. How mercenary, Elle thought with a scowl, resolving to eat her rice grain by grain and occupy the table all night. If she could get to it without knocking something over, she thought, surveying the cluttered table for the best angle from which to approach her salad. The waiter placed Elle's dish in front of her with a grand, affected bow. "The lady will find not one ounce of butter to displease her," he said.

Elle rolled her eyes. "How grand," she answered, forcing a smile.

Christopher tapped his foot impatiently. "We would also like a bottle of Evian, please."

The lawyer grinned and stared at Elle a bit too intensely before catching himself. "I won't let that waiter rush us out of here," he said.

"I'm in no rush," she said.

She began to toss her salad in the little room that the delicate bowl allowed, forgetting in her hunger what she had been saying before.

"Well, did Brooke tell her mother?"

"Sorry," Elle smiled. "It's just unforgivable, what happened. Brooke told her mother as soon as she returned from Paris, and told her everything. Her mother called Brooke a liar and a wretched, dumpy little failure. She said all these awful things. She even said that Brooke was jealous of her mother's beauty. She wouldn't take her calls and told her to move out of the house."

"The poor thing," Christopher gasped. He was incredulous.

"Wait"—Elle held up her finger—"it gets worse. Her mother had to say something to explain Brooke's being thrown out of the house, so she told her husband of the awful rumors Brooke was spreading about his misdeeds. He denied it, of course, and they cut Brooke off. He said that the little brat tried to ruin him. He threatened to sue her for slander, but she didn't have a penny that wasn't his, so he just went about calling her a lying wretch."

"Did they divorce anyway?" Christopher asked.

"Oh," Elle said, "they did, but not for a while. Basically, they divorced Brooke instead. They held up the facade of their marriage for another year and then divorced when *W* ran a spread of the Riviera that had the indelicacy of picturing Brooke's mother asleep in the sand with her head on the chest of one of Lagerfeld's financiers. She's married him since, and she's living in France. I don't know where her father is. This happened in the fall of Brooke's sophomore year."

Christopher shook his head. He had worked in California as the natural progression of his time at Stanford, but he would never call it home. He had grown up in a small town in Iowa, where divorce was neither so common nor so ugly, and certainly not so public. His own parents, both alive, had just celebrated their golden anniversary.

"After that, she started losing weight," Elle concluded, and turned back to her plate.

After a moment Christopher halted, a question in his eyes. "So the controversy that you mentioned at her sorority . . . that was this terrible divorce?"

Elle shook her head. "No, that was about the picture. See, Brooke started on this grazing diet, and she went to the gym constantly. Her own mother called her a dumpy failure! Can you imagine?"

"Grazing? Elle, I'm surprised at you. You make Brooke sound like some kind of a cow."

"No, the grazing diet. That's just what it's called. It got really popular in L.A., but nobody I knew had heard of it before Brooke published it. The idea is to graze; to nibble now and then, but not really eat. I think it was six meals a day; tiny ones, like airplane-sized."

She glanced down at her own meal and wondered if California Cafe had trained its cook at the USC Theta house.

"Brooke lived in the sorority house at the time, and she insisted that the Theta house cook use baby food to prepare all the baked goods, and nonfat yogurt for anything with a cream base. She had this whole regimen planned out. She ate barley with skim milk every morning. She had tofu-potato mash twice a day, before her afternoon and evening aerobics. For a treat, she had strained-prune-and-carob brownies."

Christopher's steak looked more attractive to Elle when she considered the third-world alternatives fashioned by Brooke.

"So the controversy was over the house cook?"

"No, that went over really well. All of the Thetas lost a lot of weight. The controversy was over the Model Wall."

"I can hardly keep track of Brooke's troubles as it is," the lawyer said. "What's this about a Model Wall?"

"See, a lot of Thetas have been models. Not as many as the Delta Gammas, though."

"You were a Delta Gamma?"

Elle looked down at the table. "Right." With all this talk about the Thetas, she didn't feel so proud of it now. "Anyway," she continued, "it's sort of a tradition to have a wall with all the sorority sisters' best modeling shots. Keeps up the house image that they have the most beautiful girls on campus."

"You added to the Model Wall, no doubt?" Christopher said.

"Sure," Elle said, not eager to emphasize the similarity of her sorority house to Brooke's. She was sorry she had mentioned the Delta Gamma house at all.

"The Thetas have a pretty good wall, I've got to admit.

Anyway, Brooke insisted on putting this picture of herself on the wall from before she lost any weight, and Doo-Dee, the Theta president, said no way. I guess Brooke kept putting pictures up, and they kept disappearing. It caused a major conflict within the sisterhood."

"Doo-Dee?" Christopher shook his head slowly. "Are you kidding?"

"Dookie Dean, but she doesn't go by Doo-Dee anymore," Elle said. Christopher was grinning.

"It's not important," Elle said. "What matters is that Brooke finally moved out, and I think she even deactivated. She had lost enough weight by then to get a job teaching aerobics at Mega-Muscle. That's where I met her. She taught this head-banger aerobics class, with trash-metal music. The sit-ups were twice as fast as in any other class. It was one long hour!

"She was all the rage with her aerobics class. She started sponsoring competitions, and whoever did the most sit-ups got a little half T-shirt or a free tattoo on her stomach. She published her grazing diet and it went into a second printing almost immediately. Then she went membership-only with a wellness center–restaurant she set up."

Elle tried to signal the waiter for some lemon wedges, but he refused to make eye contact.

"Anyway, at the wellness center she planned all of the menus for the restaurant. It started to become a really trendy place to go. She expanded it to include a huge multiplex fitness center featuring her famous aerobics classes. All kinds of people worked out and ate there, from the trendy L.A. crowd to older people with health problems. That's how she met Heyworth. He went there under doctor's orders for her cardiac-rehab class and the food."

Christopher laughed and moved closer to the table.

"Eventually she sold forty-nine percent of the wellness

center to some investors from Texas, and it has since become a chain. I hear it's a hot stock, and she still has the controlling interest. So she did tell you the truth. She put herself through school using student loans at first, and then with the money from the wellness center."

"I wonder why she didn't tell me that," Christopher said, swirling a cut of his potato in a generous golden pool of butter.

"Please," Elle frowned, "she's gorgeous now. Why would she tell you she used to look like the Blueberry Girl in *Willy Wonka and the Chocolate Factory*?"

"Talk to her, Elle," Christopher said hurriedly. "She'll tell you things she wouldn't tell me. You've already made her a more likable witness, much less like someone who would marry or kill for money, since she already had her own."

Elle raised her water glass in a toast. "I've got a job, I take it?"

Christopher smiled. "You'll do well, my friend. I didn't realize I had made you an offer."

"Well?" Elle paused, her glass hanging uncertainly in the air.

"You've got a job," he agreed, reaching for his own glass and raising to hers. "Sealed with a toast."

Elle's heart leaped. *"Magnifique."* She smiled. "You won't regret it." She felt impulsively like making a pitch for Warner, but decided not to push her luck. Either way, she was a winner. If he got the job, she'd finally get some time with him. If he didn't, she thought impishly, who would be the "serious" lawyer then?

Christopher leaned back in his chair, folding his hands and squinting thoughtfully. "I'd like you to meet Brooke soon. She's moving up to San Francisco to be closer to my office, and to get away from L.A., from the memories."

"And the rumors," Elle added.

The lawyer nodded. "Keep up on those rumors, Elle. Rest assured I'll be mining your brain constantly between now and the trial date."

Elle gazed gratefully at Christopher Miles. She had never heard herself and her brain mentioned together in a sentence without a punch line.

CHAPTER THIRTY

EUGENIA called when she returned early from her visit home and promised Elle she had significant news that she must relay in person. Though Elle was impatient to tell Eugenia more about Christopher Miles on the phone, she accepted her friend's congratulations and agreed to meet her on Stanford's main campus with Underdog in tow.

She hung up the phone, threw on one of Warner's old sweatshirts, and put Underdog's collar on, all the while wondering what the news could be.

Underdog ran to meet Eugenia. Elle didn't recognize her friend at first. She was wearing a ribbed white mock turtle-neck sweater of a beautiful cashmere. The contrast made her blue-black bob resplendent. Her nose was chapped with a fading ski tan.

"Warholesque!" Eugenia said, and winked.

Elle gripped Eugenia in an excited hug. "You look gorgeous," she said. "Very Liv Tyler." Eugenia blushed happily. Though Elle would rather she had highlighted her ash-blonde hair, she had to admit that against Eugenia's flawless ivory complexion and her blue eyes, her newly black hair was stunning. Elle had thought many times about bringing Eugenia under the masterful painting hand of Che-Che at Savoir-Vivre, but she knew Eugenia labored under the debt of heavy student loans and avoided putting her friend in an uncomfortable position. She had found a good colorist, wherever she had gone. "You look gorgeous!" Elle repeated. "Did you get it done while you were home?"

"I did!"

"What gave you the nerve to do it?"

"I went to Vermont knowing that I was going to break up with Kenneth, and I wanted to look my best."

Elle grinned at her steely friend with admiration. "Better to drop the ax than to suffer it, I guess."

"He wanted us to get married," Eugenia said with disgust.

"Eugenia!" Elle felt the melancholy that usually afflicted her with any mention of someone else's marriage. "Why don't you want to marry him? He was your college sweetheart!"

"Elle," Eugenia chided, amused with her friend's sensitive naïveté, "we went to Yale, remember? Nobody has a college sweetheart at Yale. People don't even date. They just go out drinking in groups and sleep together at night because it's freezing cold."

"Gross." Elle wrinkled her nose, finding a new reason for distaste with the Ivy League.

"He told me I broke his heart," Eugenia said with pride, "and I told him it was never mine to break."

"Saucy," Elle said. "I thought you missed him."

"No, but MCI sure will." Eugenia shrugged. "I guess now he's neither friend nor family. No more long-distance love for me. I can't believe I spent so much time on the phone with him in the first place. All he talked about was college and our college friends. He's boring, Elle."

"We'll have to get you out on the scene," Elle began, but

she halted with the quick recollection that she had no social life in Palo Alto. "If you don't mind the trip to L.A.," she said.

"That's the other thing I need to tell you," Eugenia said. She was smiling. "Come here." She motioned to the bench of a picnic table and sat down across from Elle, gathering Underdog in her arms. "My favorite laptop," she said, stroking the dog's ears.

"Underdog missed you!"

"Remember the writer I told you about? The one that I met at the Slack and White Ball? The one who kept calling me?"

"Coerte," Elle said, intentionally drawing his name out in an affected manner. "It would be hard to forget, since you haven't stopped talking about him since."

"Changed names aside, he seems really cool. I've talked to him a lot, and now that I'm Kenneth-free, I'm going out with him tonight."

"That's great! Where are you guys going? A poetry reading or something?"

"No, you're gonna like the name of the restaurant he picked. The Elite Cafe. Maybe he's more for you!"

"Well, I can't wait to meet him, but I'm going to be pretty booked up with this internship. I was going to ask you about Nexis, that on-line thing." Elle looked embarrassed.

Eugenia arched a surprised eyebrow.

"Really," Elle continued, "I want to read all of the articles about the case. I don't want to miss a word. I'm going to help Brooke Vandermark."

"We can go over to the law library and I'll show you now," Eugenia offered, but her tone was hesitant and insincere.

"Not on your life," Elle said. "Here." She patted the picnic bench. "Put out your hand."

Wondering what her hand had to do with Nexis, Eugenia removed her hand from Underdog's head and placed it on the table with an open palm.

"Flip it over," Elle directed, fishing in her overstuffed bag. "There, Cotton Candy. I jumped the gun a bit on summer nail polish, but it'll flatter your skin tone. And pastels are all the rage this season."

"No way!" Eugenia drew her hand back to the appreciative Underdog. "The only pastel I'll wear will be the horrible bridesmaid dress you pick out when you marry Warner."

"Then you'll be wearing red-black for a while. I've got a bottle of Urban Decay Gash at my condo. Fashion is rich with alternatives."

"If you're as much help to Brooke as you are to me, she'll skate," Eugenia said. "Look, today I'm newly single and about to be manicured, with a gorgeous dinner companion for tonight. Not bad for a struggling law student."

"Struggling? I wouldn't have made it through exams if it weren't for you, forgetful," Elle said. "Let's hit the Woods Salon."

"The Woods Salon. It's got a nice ring," Eugenia said.

"*Sarah's* got the nice ring!" Elle said quickly, clipping Underdog's leash onto his collar.

Eugenia paused, folding her arms across her chest and gazing at the academic village that housed such diverse dreams. Warner was so pitifully ordinary. "If I were you"—she looked past Elle as she spoke—"nothing in the world could make me trade places with Sarah Knottingham."

Elle followed Eugenia's stare to the buildings around the empty park where they stood. "Eugenia, a month ago I would have given anything to be just like Sarah."

"And now?"

Elle sat back down on the bench and dropped her chin into her hands without speaking. After a moment, she lifted her head and tapped her fingernails briskly on the wooden table. She drew a deep breath. "Now I've finished exams, and I studied my heart out, and when I took my first breath clear of that dungeon, I felt like I had passed. I've got an internship that's worth more to me than a week in Aspen with Serena. Now I've got somebody with her fortune and her freedom in the balance and an opportunity to help her. And I'm working for a respected lawyer who listens to what I think, and spends a whole dinner keeping his hands to himself." Elle halted, surprised by her own words. "I've got a lot ahead of me," she said.

Eugenia nodded her head quietly, then broke into a grin. "I've just got a date ahead of me and I'm pretty excited."

"You'll have to tell me every detail tomorrow," Elle said. "I've forgotten what a date is like. I'll be at home, picking out my outfit for tomorrow's meeting with Christopher Miles."

Nervous and excited to see Christopher Miles again, Elle was the first to arrive the next morning. When Warner took the seat next to her, Elle blushed nervously, her heart pounding with excitement.

"Warner!" she said. "I'm so glad to see you." She gave him what he used to call her "megawatt" smile, glad she had chosen to wear her red cashmere twinset. *Marie Claire* was right, red was a "confidence color."

Sarah was Brooks Brothered from head to toe in a navy knee-length skirt-and-jacket ensemble worn with an ivory-colored high-necked silk blouse and sensible navy heels. Padding like a dog behind Warner, she entered the room, pulled a chair close to him, and linked her arm into his with a nod in Elle's direction.

"Sarah," Elle said curtly.

Cari Zellwether entered next wearing a black wool double-breasted blazer with huge square shoulder pads over a severe knee-length dress. Her short straight hair was parted at the side and pulled tightly back at the nape of her neck with a plain rubber band. After a brusque general hello, she sat and opened a huge black briefcase from which she pulled out a casebook. Placing it in her lap, she began scanning the highlighted pages with a busy air.

Elle shifted uncomfortably. The February issue of *Harper's Bazaar* had a retrospective on Bergdorf Goodman ball gowns through the ages. To keep up appearances, Elle left the magazine in her bag, removing a pink legal pad instead. She clicked her heel against the tiny chair leg, feigning inattention to the chummy conversation between Sarah and Warner.

Until Christopher Miles arrived, the couple noisily compared class schedules, Cari scribbled notes in her casebook, and Elle counted the lines on her legal pad with a vacant stare.

The lawyer swept across the tiny interview room, offering apologies for keeping them waiting and shaking hands with the four students in turn.

"You've all been notified that there are no more interviews," Christopher said, "so relax. You've made it." Elle traced a design on her paper to avoid staring at Warner, whose hand Sarah was clasping excitedly.

The lawyer continued with enthusiasm. "Out of the forty or so applicants I interviewed, I've chosen the four of you to work with me on this case. None of you have gotten your first semester grades back, so you might be wondering why you were selected. We're in confidence, so permit me to tell you exactly why."

Christopher surveyed the room. "Cari, your particular interest is criminal law, and I see that you've worked in some

clinics. This will be good experience for you if Brooke
is brought up on murder charges, which I think will happen soon.

"Sarah, I went to law school with your father. If you've
got half of his work ethic, you could try this case yourself.

"Warner, your father and I go all the way back to prep
school. And I didn't want to get accused of working with
only beautiful women!"

Warner and Christopher snickered together, Cari scowled,
and Sarah smiled sweetly, glad to be called "beautiful."

"And Elle . . ."

Everyone, including Elle, looked curiously at Christopher Miles. She wondered if he'd mention their dinner,
which she knew Sarah and Cari, at least, would regard with
suspicion. To her relief, he spoke in innocent generalities.

"You said something to me in your interview that reminded me of an axiom by Oliver Wendell Holmes . . . one
that I have always considered to be the bedrock of my
criminal defense practice. Justice Holmes said, wisely, 'To
look at the law you must look at it as a bad man.' "

Cari cleared her throat so Christopher would add "or
woman," but the lawyer didn't notice her protest. "Do you
recall what you said about my client, Elle?"

"She didn't do it," Elle said nervously. "I told you that."

Christopher nodded. "You said you felt sorry for Brooke
and you asked me if she was a blonde."

Sarah rolled her eyes and Cari looked angrily at Christopher Miles, who she thought was flirting with Elle.

"She is." Elle smiled. "I knew she was. I could tell. Any
twenty-three-year-old married to a seventy-four-year-old with
a heart condition is a blonde, I guarantee it."

Christopher Miles grinned broadly.

"Elle, I have a feeling you will be able to identify with
my client. Maybe you will understand her . . . predicament.

I'd like you to sit in on the next deposition in the case so you can meet Brooke yourself. It's next week."

The lawyer pulled a file from his soft-sided camel-colored leather briefcase.

"I have some research questions that I'd like the rest of you to get started on," Christopher said, laying several papers in a thin pile on the table. "We're on a tight schedule, so don't waste a minute. Elle, call my secretary, Mia, on Monday for the deposition schedule."

CHAPTER THIRTY-ONE

IF it weren't for that interview, Elle thought, gazing exhausted at the clock on the classroom wall, there is no way I'd be sitting here at this hour of the morning. What a waste of my only elective.

Maybe it was his eyes, or maybe his tone, which shifted from gentle to firm without being intimidating. Probably the eyes, Elle laughed to herself. The eyes have it. She trusted Christopher Miles and believed him that she could help on Brooke's case.

She thought she understood Brooke and Chutney. At the very least, she knew where they came from. Chutney was far from the only girl in Los Angeles with a stepmother younger than she was. Elle was familiar with the way these people lived, and Christopher, at least, seemed to take her perspective seriously. She laughed at the irony: it was the first time she had considered that Sarah's narrow, field-hockey world put her at a disadvantage. Elle could tap the Los Angeles rumor mills with a phone call. She could find out the name of Brooke's gardener, every ingredient of her grazing diet, every step of her aerobics regime. Could Sarah do that?

Elle watched glumly as Professor Gilbreath walked from the board up the stairs to the back of the classroom. Her hopes were momentarily raised, thinking that he might be leaving.

The gaunt professor pulled the door closed with more force than appeared natural for his frame. Turning to the class, he began his first-day intimidation routine.

"This door shuts promptly at nine. If it opens again before nine-fifty, it will be because I open it. Not you. No late arrivals; no excuses. If any of your friends are considering adding into this class, please pass the word along to them."

Elle doubted anybody who was not already present would decide on a whim to take a class about dead people at nine o'clock in the morning. Especially with Professor Gilbreath, the Grim Reaper of black humor. Elle would need her afternoons free for the internship, so she was stuck waking up to "Death with Gilbreath."

Satisfied that the door was secure, the scarecrow walked back to the podium. "Welcome." Indicating the door, he explained, "I don't like my monologue to be interrupted."

Who does he think he is, Jay Leno? Elle wondered.

"This class is about two things," Gilbreath began. "Death, number one. Death." He paused, surveying the room's quiet audience. "Number two is money. This class is about death and money."

Professor Gilbreath smiled. A brave laugh erupted somewhere behind Elle, which she guessed was probably Michael's. He would surely tell his diabolical sweetheart Cari to sign up for Death with Gilbreath. Elle suspected this class was going to turn into a bad replay of *The Munsters*.

"First, let's talk about money."

Elle did not join the excited laughs of a scattering of would-be ambulance chasers. The humor of greed was pretty well worn, considering that every class, from the spills and bills of Torts to the kills and bills of Criminal Law, could boast the same theme.

"There are three ways to make money," continued Professor Pallbearer. "You can earn it, inherit it, or marry it. I've done all three. If you're a wills lawyer, you can earn it whenever other people inherit it."

Better off marrying it, Elle mused wistfully.

"A wills lawyer sees people at their ugliest. The cases you will read in this class all concern the two things that awaken abhorrent qualities lying buried within the human spirit. Those two things, class, are . . ."

"Death and money," several students answered promptly.

"Very good. Now"—the professor smiled—"we can talk about death. This class will be your easiest class, because it is based entirely on a single rule."

Furious keyboard pecking subsided as students prepared to capture the Rule.

"Dead people can't own money."

Elle remembered Warner's grandmother and wished that she could take her whole infernal fortune to her grave.

Professor Gilbreath stepped back from the podium. "That rule is the heart and soul of the law of wills. Dead people can't own money." The room was silent as he gathered papers casually and turned to leave. "That's all I have for today."

The blunt professor walked to the door. "Any questions?"

Nobody dared.

"Very good. See you tomorrow at nine, then."

Elle glanced at the wall clock, which read 9:11. She had prejudged Gilbreath. This could turn out to be her favorite class.

* * *

Elle decided to make a rare morning appearance in both Wills and Property this morning in case Christopher asked her about law school on the way to Los Angeles.

She was uncomfortable having skipped Property class all week, concerned that a property-law issue might be important in the buzzards' fight to dish out the Vandermark estate. When she got to Property class, she seated herself in the safest back corner of the room.

All four feet eleven of Whitman Hightower, Barrister, disappeared behind the podium. "He should have stayed at Oxford," Elle muttered. In his first lecture, Hightower had directed the class to refer to him as Barrister, his proper title as a counselor admitted to the King's Court of Exchequer.

"I think they still wear powdered wigs over there," Eugenia whispered. "Maybe if he wore one here we'd be able to see him."

At least Hightower was aware of the language barrier that separated baffled students from the vocabulary of centuries-old English property law. He would often dart to the chalkboard midsentence to scribble peculiar words that formed, he insisted, the "law's living lexicography." By the end of class, the board looked like a Christmas tree decorated by children on only the low branches, an exotic language scrawled in the space within Hightower's reach.

Elle felt her head spinning as she copied down the phrase *Quicquid plantatur solo, solo cedit.*

Wizened Barrister Hightower popped suddenly from the podium and tapped his chalk on the board. "Whatsoever is affixed to the soil, belongs to the soil. An estimable maxim. Why, my apprentices, does this not end our dispute?" Elle rolled her eyes. They had been through this last week.

Larry Hesterton and Gramm Hallman were already battling with Drew for primacy with Hightower, the only professor at Stanford caught in their medieval time warp. To-day Gramm edged Larry out.

"Both the fox and the land, Barrister Hightower, are wild."

"The land, Counselor? Wild?"

"More accurately, Barrister, the land is public. As we discussed last week, the vested rights of the landowner are inapplicable to this case. At any rate, the fox being wild, it is not affixed to the soil."

"Born free," mumbled Elle, wondering what she would learn about marital property from the law of fox hunting. She was right to have skipped this class last week to get her hair highlighted. One scrawny fox was nothing to go to court about. When class ended, Elle gathered her belongings and headed for Christopher's office with nervous anticipation.

CHAPTER THIRTY-TWO

THANK God for the Tight Skirt Button in her Range Rover, Elle thought, surveying her reflection in the elevator door. This button adjusted the driver's seat to minimize skirt wrinkles, especially important during the warmer linen-wearing months.

The Vandermark case was becoming more complex every day. Witnesses and details were coming out of the woodwork. Elle felt a slight shiver, excited to be a part of it. Her parents had never pushed her toward one career or another, but the cardinal sin of the Woods family was to be "boring." Elle considered this case to be definitely cutting-edge.

The elevator door opened to the sheer moneyed luster of Miles & Slocum. The floors of the enormous grand entrance were marble of the smoothest silver-gray; the furniture was modern and beautifully crafted, and its scale was perfect. The room was bathed in light, which streamed in through an entire wall of huge vaulted windows that gave a fabulous view of the bay.

"I'm Elle Woods. I have an appointment with Christopher Miles," she said to the prim-looking receptionist.

"Elle Woods." The librarian-like receptionist repeated Elle's name with disdain as she looked Elle up and down through eyeglasses perched at the end of her long nose. "I saw your name on Mr. Miles's appointment calendar. Is this a *personal* appointment?"

"No, no," Elle protested a bit too quickly. "I'm working on the Vandermark case. I'm one of the interns from Stanford."

The secretary looked dubiously at Elle and asked her to take a seat in the waiting room while she rang through to Mia, Christopher's secretary.

Elle gazed out a vaulted window overlooking the water and remembered the spread on Miles & Slocum in *Architectural Digest.* "Best-looking firm in the country," Christopher had said in reference to it. Looking around, Elle didn't doubt it.

Christopher's secretary joined Elle moments later, greeting her with cheerleader enthusiasm.

"Sorry to have kept you waiting," Mia said. "Martha"— she glanced toward the receptionist—"is a bit of a mother hen when it comes to Christopher."

On the way to Christopher's office, Mia conducted a brief tour, dashing with Elle through halls decorated with stunning contemporary art.

The interns' office was a stark contrast to the rest of the suite. It was barren, with the exception of a Keith Haring print, four standard black desk chairs, and two heavy wooden desks, one of which was covered with documents. Elle glanced uneasily at the surroundings.

"Don't worry, that's Sarah Knottingham's pile." Mia seemed to have read her mind. "She's coming back in later for document review. Her secretary is on vacation, so I've had to walk her through her schedule."

Elle tried to maintain a poker face as she noticed a bottle of Advil on Sarah's desk, thinking of the throbbing headaches that Sarah had caused her.

"You're to wait for Mr. Miles in his office. He called from the car. He'll be here shortly. He's expecting you."

Mia led Elle into a sitting room adjoining Christopher's corner office. Elle wondered if she would get her own secretary like Sarah. She sat in a low armchair with a curving black back and leafed through a Rothko art book, the only book on an exquisite coffee table. When she heard Christopher approaching, she pulled out her Wills book and opened it to a page in the middle.

"Have important calls forwarded to my car. I'm running late for the deposition," Christopher Miles barked at Mia as he swept into the office. Elle stood up to greet the lawyer, who was busy packing thick files into an accordion litigation bag.

"Elle." He looked up, startled. "You were so quiet I didn't even know you were here. We have to leave now, so gather whatever you need and let's go."

Elle quickly shoved her Wills book inside her suede Cartier briefcase, a present from her parents, who thought that if she was going to be a lawyer she should look the part.

"I'm glad you're going to sit in on this deposition," he said, locking his briefcase. "I just wish it weren't at Henry Kohn's Los Angeles office. This is the third deposition he's taken in L.A. I think he does it just to annoy me, since his main office is only five blocks from here. I'll be glad when I'm deposing the witnesses and I can do it right here." He surveyed the office as if completing a mental checklist. "Right. Come on, Elle, we're running late."

Elle caught a glimpse of Cari looking up suspiciously from behind a paper mountain as she and Christopher flashed through the hall. Elle waited until they stepped into the elevator to mention the other interns.

"Cari seems to have a lot of documents to read," Elle said.

Christopher smiled. "I have Cari researching a venue issue. She was probably reading cases. As for you, Elle, I want to make sure you meet all of the witnesses. With your background, I think you'll have the best handle on the facts."

"I thought I went to law school to learn the law."

"You might be right, but cases are won and lost on the facts."

The elevator opened to the parking garage. Christopher opened the passenger door of his racing green Jaguar convertible and Elle slid into the low leather seat. She noticed that he was thoughtful enough to put up the top before he started the car. She felt the car lurch forward as Christopher sped out of the garage.

Christopher weaved from lane to lane, speeding toward the freeway. "I'm worried we'll miss the flight," he said, narrowly missing a car in the next lane as he forged ahead of it.

"Not with you driving," Elle said. Christopher was tracing figure eights through traffic. "If Chutney's lawyer likes to hold all of his depositions in L.A., why isn't the whole trial being held in L.A. anyway?"

"Because the old man's broker, and most of his assets including the Vandermark Vineyards, are in Northern California. They could have offered the will for probate anywhere in California, so Chutney filed suit in San Francisco. Under advice of counsel I'm sure."

"Why, is the judge better up here for her or something?"

"No, better for her lawyer. Henry Kohn, Chutney's lawyer, has a branch office in Century City, but his main office is in San Francisco. I'm sure he gave the kid sound legal advice to keep the proceedings convenient to his corner office at Kohn & Siglery. He'll bill her for all of his flights and time to and from L.A. anyway."

"Sleazy!"

"Welcome to private practice, Elle. And speaking of private," Christopher added quietly, "let me tell you about our witness, while we're still in confidence."

He sighed at the thought of the scheduled witness. "The good news first: it should be brief. The witness despises Brooke, and what's worse, he speaks flamboyantly, tends to use the word "murder" a lot, on the record. He was Brooke's interior designer, until he quit. He says she's got 'murderous' taste. According to him, she 'murdered' the sitting room, 'ravaged' the library, and 'had intent to kill' the foyer. You name the room and he'll say she killed it. Trenton Davis, the name gives me nightmares."

"Trent? *Not* Trent Davis. He is an absolute doll! I've known Trent since I was a little girl," Elle said. "My mother owns an art gallery, so she works with a lot of designers. Trent is her absolute favorite designer and mine too! Our only regret is that we don't get to see enough of him. He's not only the best designer around, he's absolutely charming! Clients are always jetting him off . . . Paris, Hong Kong . . . you name a cosmopolitan city and he's a designer and a dinner party guest in demand."

Christopher leaned over to turn up the volume of the car stereo, as if he were unable to stand hearing any more. Elle just spoke louder.

"You're just lucky you're not deposing one of the new breed of designers who insist on being called 'interior dramatists.' They usually carry small dogs with them, which they use like Kleenex, crying into their fur that something is *missing* or *lacking*."

"I can't believe you *know* Trenton Davis!" Christopher shook his head as if he felt sorry for Elle.

"Know him? He is a perfect gem! He redid our house in Bel Air after the earthquake, and I thought at the time that I might be interested in becoming a designer, so he took me everywhere with him to let me get a real view of the business. I remember this one completely wild woman . . . oh, what's her name . . ." Elle frowned briefly. "Anyway, she had him on an absolute yesterday deadline to move all of her furniture out and stage the scene with theme furniture because she was giving this party. Trent, caterers, florists, artists, party and art consultants . . . you name it. Everyone was working day and night. She was having a theme party— Tequila Sunrise—so she wanted the wallpaper stripped so she could have the walls of the house painted like a sunrise. What's worse, the woman had a terrible sense of direction and insisted that the sun rose in the west. So for her party at least, it did."

Christopher stopped his chatterbox passenger. "Art consultants?"

Perplexed, Elle wrinkled her nose at the lawyer. "Of *course* she had art consultants! What a weird question to ask. Anyway, this lady told everyone working on the house to bring their swimsuits. She *insisted*. She liked to swim, but hated to swim alone. So at exactly noon, she had everyone from Trent to the painters suit up and splash around with her for an hour."

"And I thought lawyers worked hard for their money."

"Well, on this case you certainly have," Elle said.

"Trenton Davis is going to make me work a little harder, Elle. He may have adjusted to his other clients' idiosyncrasies, but not to Brooke's. Right now he is an ideal plaintiff's witness."

"Chutney is the plaintiff, right?" Elle wanted to make sure.

"Well, she's attacking the will in probate, and we're arguing that the legacy to Brooke stands. Wills procedure is a little different, since the interested parties are not strictly adversarial. I've thought of her as the plaintiff out of habit."

Christopher glanced at Elle. "You keep me on my toes, Miss Woods."

He looked back at the road and his smile disappeared. "I don't know if being on my toes is going to be enough for this case," he admitted. "It was high-risk to begin with, but plaintiff's witnesses just keep coming out of the woodwork, Elle. Her entire household staff, her personal shopper, her personal trainer, even her shrink."

"Her psychiatrist," Elle gasped. "How horrible! What about doctor-patient confidentiality?"

"The court can subpoena those records," Christopher said grimly. He pulled into the valet parking lot, worriedly checking his watch. "Grab one of these files, Elle, would you?"

Elle hopped out of the car with the case file and dashed after Christopher, making a mental note never to trust a psychiatrist, much less a personal shopper.

CHAPTER THIRTY-THREE

A waiting car and driver used surface streets to whisk Elle and Christopher to the law office in record time, but Trent, arriving from Laguna Niguel, called from his car phone to complain that he was "stuck on the 405 parking lot." Even after he arrived, Henry Kohn was tied up in a conference for another twenty minutes. So as it turned out, their driver had risked the wrath of the California Highway Patrol for nothing.

Kohn & Siglery was no Miles & Slocum, Elle thought. Although the soaring modern architecture of the building was impressive, on the inside it was horrendous.

Elle overheard Trent talking to the receptionist from the waiting room, where she was sitting in an itchy Louis XIV chair covered in zebra skin. "I'll let your attorney know that you're waiting for him," she said, pointing the cherub-faced designer around the corner.

Short, pudgy Trent had gained another few pounds, Elle noticed.

"Elle Woods!" Trent was surprised to see her. His eyes crinkled at the corners as he grinned widely. "Are you in trouble, you little devil? Or maybe here to sign a prenup?"

he asked, kissing both of Elle's cheeks, a lock of nearly white blonde hair brushing his forehead.

Elle jumped up, happy to see him and anxious to get out of the itchy throne. "No, Trent, I'm actually here with the lawyers, not to see one," she said, and laughed.

"Coco Chanel would turn in her grave! Your mother told me about law school, but I simply cannot believe my eyes." He covered his lively blue eyes and peeked through his fingers like he was watching a horror movie and was too afraid to look at the full screen. "You, with all of your creativity, my darling . . . a lawyer?"

"Well, not yet. I lucked into helping a lawyer," Elle admitted humbly, indicating Christopher, who introduced himself as Brooke Vandermark's attorney. She went on, "I heard about the murder"—Christopher cleared his throat audibly—"uh, the alleged murder," she corrected herself, "over Christmas. Mr. Miles is kind enough to give us law students a little real-world experience through an internship."

"And you're still doing pinks." He eyed Elle's light pink Escada suit, noticing the details, the white collar and cuffs and chunky gold buttons. "Thank heavens you still find fashion exciting." Trent breathed a long sigh of relief. As always, he was as interested in what Elle was wearing as in what she was saying.

Elle smiled and glanced down at her narrow Manolo slingbacks, which were already killing her feet. She motioned to the black leather Roche Bobois couch, which wouldn't make her itch. "Let's sit down and get caught up. Are you working in Laguna now?" She loved Trent's stories.

Trent gave the couch a disapproving once-over and perched himself on the edge as if he didn't want the offending object to contaminate his aesthetic sensibilities. "Elle." He threw his arms skyward like a televangelist and then brought them down, hiding his face in his plump hands.

"My stars! This home is an atrocity. And what she wanted me to do . . . it was even worse." Trent rolled his eyes. "I say it should be a *crime!*"

"What did she want, Trent?"

"This woman, I kid you not, was in love with this notion of bubble-gum pink tile over black grout. Not just in the bathroom, which would have been bad enough. She led me around the house wearing a purple turban like she was something out of *The Arabian Nights* and told me that she wanted this bubble-gum explosion to cover the entire house and the garage! She wanted me to *murder* this house. Elle, I would never have decorated in this town again!"

Christopher cringed visibly at Trent's use of the m word.

"So you turned her down?" Elle said.

"Absolutely. I told her she had such vision, that she was so fabulously talented, that I would only serve to hinder her creative process."

"Trent, how do you make a living if you only design when it suits you?"

"Elle, I have my standards. With the exception of Brooke Vandermark's monstrosity, I'd have to say it was the worst idea I'd ever heard."

"Be nice," Elle chastised. "Was Brooke's place so awful? I thought it was written up."

"It was. Her house was written up under the 'Enough Already' column in *L.A. Whispers.* As she kept adding more square feet, it became a preposterous joke. The house was approaching the size of Candy Spelling's, and the only thing bigger than the Spelling house is Brooke Vandermark's ego. I *never* should have taken the job, even the walk-through. I was the sixth designer. All of the others had quit or been fired. The woman's impossible."

"Well, at least she didn't make you go swimming," Elle said.

"True." Trent cringed at the memory. "But Brooke's house was swimming in black lacquer. I could have drowned! The walls . . . I had to get rid of those *murderous* black lacquer walls. They nearly *killed* me! She said they were from her 'reflective phase.' Some little Shinto book from one of her support groups had struck her fancy so, she insisted on turning the place into *Shogun*! She butchered what could have been a lovely foyer with gargoyles and vases and horrendous bonsai trees. Oh, Elle, it's indescribable."

Henry Kohn and Chutney entered the waiting room. Elle glanced at Chutney's tight black dress with gold lettering around her waist, which read, "Waist of Money." She looked more confident than her lawyer, who in his rumpled, stained suit looked as if he had been pulling a lot of all-nighters.

"You shouldn't talk to lawyers about the case until I'm present," Henry Kohn cautioned Trent, exchanging a weary handshake with Christopher.

Chutney glared at the entire group, her arms crossed.

Trent shrugged his shoulder. "My little doll, Elle Woods, has brightened up an otherwise tiresome event," he said. Elle introduced herself to Henry Kohn and, feeling as if she had been chastised, told the lawyer that she had known Trent since childhood.

"We were just catching up," she said, blushing faintly.

"Of course," Henry said, with a second glance at Christopher that suggested he was not convinced. Elle followed the lawyers into a conference room as Trent, heading for the bathroom, promised to join them after he "freshened up."

Brooke Vandermark was sitting at a conference table long enough to span several zip codes. Across the table sat a stenographer. Christopher turned to Henry Kohn with obvious displeasure.

"Your receptionist did not tell me that my client had already arrived," he said, indicating Brooke.

Henry Kohn ignored the comment. "Perhaps Mrs. Vandermark would like another cup of coffee," Henry replied,
nodding at the white, lipstick-smudged mug in front of
Brooke on the table. "By all means, help yourself."

On another long table across the room were a tall silver
coffee service, several mugs and glasses, a row of canned
sodas, and a bucket of ice.

Christopher approached Brooke with a concerned, almost fatherly air. She stood up to greet him, and Elle saw
him grip Brooke's arm firmly at the elbow when he shook
her hand.

Brooke's head reached no higher than Christopher's
shoulder when she stood next to him, Elle noticed with
surprise. She had expected Brooke to be taller. She had always seemed so controlling at the head of aerobics class.
Now she didn't appear a head taller than a parking meter.

The neutral of Brooke's sleeveless linen Empire dress
melded almost imperceptibly into her straw-colored hair.
Elle recognized the dress, which she had considered ordering from J. Crew in a color other than this year's "grain" or
"almond," shades fit only for the suntanned. A turquoise
patent leather backpack that lay slouched by her chair and
matching patent sandals provided the only shimmer of color
until Elle caught Brooke's curious stare. Her eyes, which
mirrored Elle's own, were a keen, inquisitive aqua blue.

"Brooke, I would have offered to have my driver pick
you up, but I was running late. Almost missed the plane,"
Christopher said.

"I'm glad to hear you have a driver, Christopher. I've
driven with you before and I think I was safer in jail,"
Brooke said. She gave Christopher a quiet smile, but when
she sat back down, she was anything but relaxed. Her pos-
ture was rocket straight, her back not touching the chair
back, her hands fidgeting nervously in her lap.

Christopher smiled. "Mea culpa. Brooke, this is my assistant, Elle Woods. She's a student at Stanford Law School."

Brooke nodded at Elle without standing.

Elle blushed, clearing her throat. "Hello, Brooke. I'm very pleased to see you. I went to USC." Elle glanced at Chutney's grumpy lawyer, who stood at his seat arranging a notepad next to a manila folder and a foam coffee cup. This was the wrong time for small talk. Christopher had introduced her as his assistant, and there she went talking about college right off the bat, as if this were a punch bowl at a college reunion.

This is serious, Elle instructed herself. Act like it. Don't say anything. Nod and take notes. Brooke, apparently advised to do the same, hardly budged when Trent entered the room with a sulky glare. She acknowledged him, then set her gaze imperiously beyond him, a stiff pose she maintained throughout the designer's testimony.

Elle smiled at Trent and sat down silently next to Christopher, backing her chair from the table to balance the legal pad in her lap. While she waited for Henry Kohn's secretary to pour water into glasses from a heat-condensed silver pitcher, Elle began sketching Brooke's earrings. Dangling from each of Brooke's ears were small hoops in which two identical naked twins linked arms. Twins.

"Gemini," Elle thought to herself. "Ruled by the planet Mercury. Longs for affection and understanding." Good thing she had taken "Zodiac and You" for her planetary science requirement at school. When she had finished Brooke's earrings, she began sketching Pisces earrings and wondered how to distinguish them from Aquarius. It occurred to her that Aquarius was an air sign, but rather than puzzle over it any longer, she drew a bull, which was definitely a Taurus. She never considered Taurus a woman's sign, but figured she could market the earrings to men and women in Miami Beach or San Francisco.

The Libra scales reminded her of law school, and Elle began drawing earrings with a legal theme, which she felt was more appropriate given the circumstances. By the time the deposition ended, a model resembling Brooke was scribbled on Elle's legal pad, adorned with Libra-scale earrings, a necklace pendant in the shape of a gavel, and a bracelet with various casebooks for charms.

Christopher had been right; the deposition was brief, though it was hardly as damaging as he had feared. Trent did use the offending term "murder" to describe Brooke's assault on the interior of her house, but when asked about her personally, he only said that he found her "immature, and pitifully nouveau"; he said it almost apologetically, glancing at her Isaac Mizrahi patent leather backpack as if to prove his point.

Elle winked at Trent on the way out and promised to call him the next time she was in L.A. She followed Christopher and Brooke to the building lobby, not speaking because nobody else did. When they stepped outside into the sunlight, Brooke sighed with relief.

"You did great," Christopher answered the question in Brooke's eyes.

"Thanks." Brooke swallowed hard. "I can't believe what he said about my house. You should have heard him rave about my 'genius' when I proposed the idea. The mercenary! He even praised my velvet paintings, insisting that they were more than just kitsch, that such paintings were found by Marco Polo in Kashmir, where velvet was first woven by monks in the Middle Ages."

Elle bristled, her formal allegiance to Brooke uncomfortably set against her natural affection for flamboyant, lively Trent. "Trent did my family's house in Bel Air," Elle said.

Brooke shot a surprised look at Elle, as if she hadn't until that moment been visible.

"You're from Bel Air?"

Elle nodded. "I wanted to say something to you before, but I felt weird chatting at the deposition, in front of the lawyers and especially Chutney. I went to SC, Brooke, and I took your aerobics class at Mega-Muscle."

"And lived to tell?" Brooke said, and laughed gleefully.

"Barely," Elle said. "It was the toughest workout."

In the flurry of name exchanging that followed, Christopher stepped aside. He watched with approval as Elle and Brooke began to build a firm bridge toward each other on the mortar of common acquaintances, classes, enemies, and memories. Before he could suggest it, Elle had already promised to show Brooke around San Francisco, where Brooke would be moving for the duration of the trial.

They parted at the elevator, Brooke heading for her car in the garage and Elle and Christopher heading for their waiting car. Brooke folded Elle's phone number on a piece of paper, which she tucked into her tiny turquoise backpack. "Are you sure you don't mind my staying with you? I won't be but a day or so until I find a place, but if you don't have room or something . . ."

"Of course you can stay," Elle said firmly. "Underdog, my Chihuahua, will be thrilled to have some company."

In their car, Elle was surprised to find the driver headed in the opposite direction from the airport.

"I hope you like sushi, Elle. You've been working so hard, I thought I'd surprise you and take you to dinner away from Palo Alto, on a school night."

Elle was equally pleased by Christopher's recognition of her dedication to the internship.

When they pulled up to Ginza Sushi-Ko, a three-table, twenty-two-seat restaurant located on posh Via Rodeo just above Tiffany, Elle knew that Christopher had put some thought into where to take her.

Nervous, Elle launched into a story about Everett, a particularly unappealing entertainment lawyer she had a date with just before she started college. He had worked in the Fox Building, where the deposition was taken, so Elle figured it was a timely tale. Elle told Christopher how the boasting associate mentioned at least a dozen times that the Fox Building was where *Die Hard* was filmed.

"I met him at the office in order to preserve the freedom of having my own car, since Everett had gotten mixed reviews from friends of mine whom he had wined and dined. I didn't expect a ninety-minute office tour where my date pointed out the desk Michael Jackson danced on, the Montblanc pen Harrison Ford wrote with, the chair Fabio sat in, and other unremarkable celebrity fingerprints. The only area he didn't point out was the cubicle that served as his office. 'What do you think of the office?' he asked at dinner. I told him the office was lovely, but he should apply for a job as a tour guide at Universal Studios."

Christopher laughed at the story. "You've got some tall tales, Elle Woods!"

CHAPTER THIRTY-FOUR

WHEN her alarm clock jingled at 6:30, Elle felt as if she had just fallen asleep. The one thing she could say for property law was that it made great bedtime reading. Fretful and anxious the night before, Elle had only to glance at the phrase "livery of seisin" before she was out like a light.

Elle had plunged headlong into the sea of current events after Eugenia showed her how to search newspaper articles on LexisNexis. Her desk was a dumping ground for littered white papers with VANDERMARK highlighted in bold type. In an expanding "court corner" of her bedroom, piles of dog-eared textbooks and outlines on the will probate procedure were strewn. Whether Brooke won or lost, Elle was dead set on stealing Sarah's professional turf in the process. She attacked these courtroom manuals night after night, hoping to gain a home-field advantage.

As she got out of bed, she gazed at the court corner listlessly. Some way to spend Valentine's Day.

It was the first Valentine's Day that Elle had not looked forward to. Stanford Law School distributed first-semester grades on February 14, a practice known as the Valentine's Day Massacre. To make matters worse, Sarah would be spending the evening with Warner, and Elle hadn't even lined up a date.

"Oh, Underdog," Elle yawned, looking at her beloved pet whom the dog groomer had decorated with a red-and-white heart-trimmed bow. "Today's the horrible day." She slipped on her running shoes to take Underdog for a walk.

A short time later Elle dragged herself to class, wishing that she were somewhere . . . anywhere else. She lingered in the parking lot, gathering resolve in the safety of her Range Rover to enter the halls of Stanford Law. She checked her ruby lipstick in the vanity mirror and adjusted the red bow with white hearts that she had tied in her hair to match Underdog. At least she didn't look as if Valentine's Day filled her with dread. The giant red heart on her snug white T-shirt even made her smile.

"Got to keep up appearances," she said to herself, straightening her red velvet miniskirt as she walked inside. The halls were buzzing with students engaged in the socially ungracious activity of comparing grades. Heading for the student lounge, where law students met to gossip and caffeinate, Elle narrowly missed being blindsided by Aaron.

"I cannot believe it!" Aaron was springing up and down spastically, waving a piece of paper in the air. He blocked Elle's entrance to the lounge, thrusting the paper, his report card, in front of her face.

"Three point one four! Do you have any idea what this means?"

Elle didn't know and didn't care. "Excuse me, Aaron. I'd like to get a cup of coffee." Elle was looking for Eugenia, a coffee addict and permanent solitary fixture who read in the law lounge.

"My GPA is pi! It's an absolute mathematical phenomenon!"

"Congratulations, Aaron." Elle glanced around, seeing no pie or any other dessert offered for Valentine's Day.

"I just can't wait until Sidney finds out that I achieved pi! He will be so jealous. This gives new meaning to the Valentine's Day Massacre!"

Elle gave up on finding Eugenia in the lounge and headed to her mailbox instead.

Two bouquets of flowers had been delivered to the registrar's office in Elle's name. A note in her mailbox, stuffed amid a stack of cards, read: "Come to the Registrar! You have flowers!"

Elle beamed, and hurried to the front office. Just maybe, she hoped. At least flowers would soften the blow, since her report card was lurking at the same office.

One bright bouquet was from Trent with a card saying it was nice to see her; the other, strangely, was from Austin, the "darling" plastic surgeon she had dated only once. Yellow roses. "You will find nothing yellow about me except my roses," read the card. "Signature Texas. Fondly, Austin." He probably used the same cheesy line every year.

"What was I thinking?" Elle chastised herself. "Like Warner would send me flowers here. Or at all."

She stuck the report card unopened into her heart-shaped bag and leafed through her cards. Dr. Dan had sent an enormous red heart inscribed with the phrase "Your heart is my business." He probably had them left over from before the board yanked his license to practice.

Wearily, she glanced inside a card featuring the crew of the starship *Enterprise*, the same one Sidney sent every year. "Our enterprise awaits," wrote the Trekkie. "I sent your *reel* present to your home. Love, Sidney."

"Our enterprise? Vile." Elle shivered at the thought of what Sidney could have sent her. Probably a *Star Trek* home video for them to watch together.

A "secret admirer" card in Eugenia's handwriting promised to stalk and assassinate all professors at Stanford Law to win Elle's love. Elle giggled.

Next, she peeled open a pink envelope that contained her last card. "Have a great Valentine's Day, alone! Sarah."

"Lovely of her to think of me," Elle sniped.

Expecting to find Claire and Sarah in the hallway by the registrar's office rejoicing over their grades, Elle turned quickly in the opposite direction and headed for the phone booth. She figured that she could check her messages. Even though she had left her condo less than an hour ago, she wanted to stay occupied until it was time for class to begin. Long enough to avoid the Grade Question from any uppity law student who might dare to ask her.

To her dismay, Elle found herself walking directly behind the twosome, but when she noticed Sarah was wiping her eyes and sniffling, Elle paused with curiosity.

What could Sarah possibly have to cry about? I'm the one without a date on Valentine's Day. She leaned against the wall, partially obscured by a plant, and began fishing through her purse as if looking for something. She wanted to hear Sarah.

"*Nobody* gets kicked out of Stanford. You know that, Sarah," Claire said in the exasperated tone of one whose consoling advice was falling on deaf ears.

Sarah squeezed her report card in one hand and clutched several crumpled Kleenex in the other. Elle gasped.

"Her grades!" A rush of excitement consumed Elle. Sarah was crying over her grades. She strained her ears to hear more information with the singular concentration of an animal bent on its prey. If Sarah had failed her classes, and if Elle had managed to squeak by, then Elle would have Warner all to herself. It was as if a genie had appeared from a magic lamp and granted her most impassioned wish.

Sarah could be gone in a poof of Stanford's harsh air. Peeking at Sarah, who was blubbering in woe, it seemed too
good to be true.

Claire escorted Sarah down the bloodred carpet that had
been rolled through the hallway, a devilish tradition that
signified the blood of the grade massacre more than the
ardent flame of Valentine's Day. To Elle it was the red of
revolution, of victory. Finally, she thought with satisfaction,
imagining herself and Warner next semester, linking arms
in the very halls she had found such a torture alone. Finally
they would be together.

She padded after Sarah and Claire on her tiptoes, cran-
ing to overhear every word. With Claire's next comment,
Elle's hopes were dashed into confusion.

"You should be thrilled with your own grades, Sarah! I'm
sure you're at the top of our class," Claire gushed. "I don't
know anybody whose grades are as high as yours. Be happy
for yourself, at least. Warner will find his way."

Claire paused, and then said with hesitation, "Warner
can't be good at everything, Sarah. Maybe law school just
isn't his thing."

Sarah shook her head cheerlessly.

"What if it's just a rumor that Stanford doesn't kick anyone out? Warner's barely coping with the shock of his grades
now, but if he had to go back to Newport under a cloud like
that, the black sheep . . ." Sarah choked, "I don't know
what would happen to him. To be honest, I don't know what
would happen to us." Tears began to pour down Sarah's
blotchy cheeks.

Elle's heart plunged. This was no wish from a genie lamp.
It was the worst possible turn of events. It was *Warner* who
was in danger of failing out, and if Elle stayed in school, he
would be as far out of reach as ever. Farther. He would be
gone, and she'd be left with Sarah reveling at the top of the

class. Suddenly her mind jumped to the unopened report card in her red patent leather bag. Maybe she had done no better.

She withdrew the envelope with tentative curiosity, but changing her mind, returned it unopened into her purse. There was no reason to inflict bad news on herself so early in the day. Warner might be a failed law student, but it wouldn't console him to marry another.

"Your father will still hire him, won't he, Sarah?"

Sarah shrugged. "I don't know. He's not so sure about him. Nobody is, after he dated that mannequin for four years. This won't help anything. I mean, it's not like Warner's ruined," she said, but she spoke in a hollow voice, as if to convince herself of something she didn't believe.

"He'll recover," Sarah said, folding her arms in a cool, conclusive gesture. "I'd really have to lean on Daddy to hire him, but even if he works somewhere else, that won't rule out his running for office. He could spin it differently, like he dropped out because law school didn't serve his ideals," she said, her eyes darting as if searching for a new plan. Then she stopped walking and turned Claire by her arm to face her.

"The problem is, I can't tell him that now, Claire, and he's pressuring me for reassurance from Daddy. Warner's totally devastated. I'm just going to try to avoid the subject entirely. Nobody likes to be reminded of failure." Sarah spat the last word with venom, and Elle guessed she didn't like to be reminded of it either.

"He didn't even come to class today," Sarah babbled. "As if it'll do him any good to skip classes now. He ought to be here. I think he's acting irresponsibly."

"Definitely," Claire agreed. "He shouldn't be thinking of himself. I mean, your career looks splendid, but he is going to marry you and he ought to be thinking about how to provide for you aside from his trust fund. It's not just his failure now, it's both of yours. He should take a lesson from you and get serious about school."

Sarah scowled, but the mention of her own impressive grades seemed to mollify her. She adjusted her backpack on her shoulders and idled there in the hallway, not walking toward her classroom, but not heading home to console Warner either: just waiting, indecisive.

"I've got obligations to Warner too, I guess. Part of me says I should be with him, but I don't want to give him the idea he can just lean on me when we get married. I'll be fully supportive of him, but I *won't* carry him!"

Sarah whined and threw her hands up in frustration. "I don't know how to handle this, Claire. I didn't plan on propping up Warner, but I don't think he'd think me much of a partner if I sat in class like nothing happened when he's miserable, sitting at home. I should be with him now. That's what he would want his wife to do. That Barbie doll is just waiting for her chance," she added, her eyes narrowing. "I won't let Warner have the chance to turn to her."

Elle thought of Sarah's reference to her, plotting, waiting to move in on Warner, and smiled with the recognition that she still had the ability to threaten their relationship. Sarah didn't know her, either. She was waiting for her chance, all right, but she knew Warner well enough to let him lick his wounds in solitude.

Elle remembered when USC lost the College World Series, when Warner had been thrown out at the plate. He wanted to be left alone then. If his grades were as bad as they sounded, he'd feel like a loser and would rather be alone.

"Well, don't miss your classes," Claire said. "That won't help him, and it can only hurt you. I say we go to my apartment after school and bake him some chocolate chip cookies! You know the way to a man's heart is through his stomach," Claire said, and then gave Sarah the biggest, most insincere smile Elle thought she'd ever seen.

Elle called home to check her messages, of which there were none. She didn't notice in the relative safety of the phone booth that Sarah had parted ways with Claire. She stood alone in the hallway, gazing at the wall.

Impulsively, Elle called out Sarah's name.

The puffy-eyed girl turned with a surprise to face her. Elle noticed Sarah staring at her cheerful holiday outfit, cringing to see Elle's curves emphasized under the enormous red heart, which decorated her clingy stretch T-shirt. Elle's red velvet micromini blared the words LOVE, PEACE, and HARMONY, which reminded Elle, when she was dressing, of Warner.

Elle gave a mischievous grin and walked toward Sarah. Her white tights descended to a flash of red patent leather loafers that matched her showy purse.

"Thanks for the Valentine," Elle said, looking at Sarah's outfit, red wide-wale cords, white turtleneck with tiny red hearts around the neck, and the ever present wool cardigan, which today was red.

Elle's intense blue stare pierced Sarah, who bowed her head toward her tasseled loafers, shuffling her feet on the linoleum floor. Her shoulders drooped; she looked beaten. Elle smiled.

"I'm sorry, Elle," Sarah said peering at her. She spoke in a muffled voice. "I acted like a child. I feel so stupid."

Elle squinted, skeptical of the convenient apology from her otherwise hateful adversary. Sarah sniffled and turned her eyes back to the floor.

"Don't worry about it," Elle said. "Anyway, what makes you think I'm spending my Valentine's Day alone?" Elle laughed then, her eyes sparkling, her dimples young and soft, looking more the mischievous imp than the notorious femme fatale.

"You know what I meant by that," Sarah said, with an almost imperceptible smile. She checked the time on her sensible Seiko.

"Elle, we have ten minutes before class, can I talk to you?"

Elle accepted the invitation with a dubious shrug, wondering where Claire was lurking. She followed Sarah to a vacant room.

"We'll have some privacy here," Sarah said, holding the door to their Property classroom open for Elle to enter. "Nobody spends a minute more in Property than they have to."

Elle stared at Sarah's fingers playing nervously with her headband while she marshaled her thoughts. She braced herself for a mean-spirited speech, imagining Sarah warning her not to interfere if Warner and Sarah left for Rhode Island sooner than expected.

Adjusting her headband for the umpteenth time, Sarah finally cleared her throat to speak. Elle stretched her long legs on an adjoining chair with nonchalance, her gaze passing over Sarah with the impassive air of a shrink who's heard it all.

"Look"—Sarah choked back a sob—"I know I have no right to ask you this, but I need your help. Elle, I don't mean this condescendingly, so please, don't take it wrong."

Elle arched her eyebrows, but didn't respond.

"I see you in class . . . when you go to class, you hardly bother to show up. I see you reading those magazines or filing your nails, and you don't seem to give it any thought. But your grades," Sarah said with a tired slouch, "are probably better than Warner's."

Elle thought of her unopened report card, but didn't say a thing.

"Well, it's not about me anymore, Sarah," Elle said coolly, her eyes on the Rock that adorned Sarah's clenched hand.

"No, Elle, you're right. It's about me. I haven't told Warner, but my grades are excellent. I'll be at the top of our class."

"You must be very proud."

"Elle, Warner's grades will put him at the bottom of the barrel if he's even allowed to stay here, they're so bad," Sarah whined. "I'm afraid it will be hard for him to live with my success. But Warner's different, isn't he? He says he admires my serious attitude toward school, my dedication."

Elle cringed.

"I tell myself he'll love me even more when he finds out about my grades." Sarah halted, resting her head in her hands. "I don't know, Elle," she spoke toward the floor.

Elle wondered if Sarah was setting up to interrogate her about whether *Cosmo* might have an answer. But Sarah turned her eyes to Elle imploringly.

"You know Warner, Elle," she said. "You dated him. You know what he's like, and he always tells me how you know what he likes." She halted, blushing that she had admitted that Warner talked about Elle. "Will he be happy for my success, even if he fails at the same thing?"

With a heavy sigh, Elle decided to tell Sarah the truth. "Warner does admire your dedication, Sarah. He values your seriousness, you're right about that. And more than anything, he admires your background," she added, flashing Sarah an icy glare. "But Warner loves competition. He's not 'different' like you hope he is. He despises losing. He'd be happy for you if he had done well himself. Then, you'd be a prosperous, shining couple, the envy of your set. That hasn't happened."

"So what does that mean?"

"Warner wants accompaniment from a woman," Elle

said, raising her chin with a haughty gesture. "He doesn't want to be graced by your success."

Sarah stared at the floor and didn't respond.

"Warner won't love you because you did better than he did," Elle said. "He won't love you because you've succeeded." She paused, then added quietly, "Sarah, if he does love you, he'll love you in spite of that."

Sarah smiled, but her solace was a momentary light, obscured in the next moment by the reality of the unpleasant task that lay ahead. "What should I say to him then, Elle?" Sarah said. "What would *you* do?"

Elle sat up in her chair. "You want to know how to make him love you more?"

Sarah nodded sheepishly.

"You can't."

Sarah sat motionless, but Elle felt her rival had grown skeptical. Elle knew that what she had said about Warner was true. She sat forward, leaning her elbows on the desk, and explained.

"Sarah, don't you see that Warner loves himself as much as he has room to love anything? He won't love you one bit more for your achievement. It didn't do anything for him."

Sarah took off her wool cardigan, placing it on the chair back.

"You want Warner's love? I'll tell you how to get it. Make him believe you think the sun waits to rise until he gets up," Elle said matter-of-factly. "Unqualified admiration. That's what keeps Warner going."

She turned a steely glance to Sarah, whose eyes avoided her. Sarah adjusted her headband, and neither of them said another word.

The dense quiet was broken by the swing of the door behind them. The Trekkie Tribe of Five charged into the room, armed with PowerBooks. Sarah stared down at the desk and began aligning her Hi-Liters. Elle examined her fingernails for chips. It appeared to nobody that they had been speaking.

Property class flew by as Elle's mind whirled through the strange events that had just occurred. Sarah, making an overture to her for advice about Warner. She considered what she had told Sarah. In some measure, she regretted giving away any insight that might help Sarah smooth out a tension in their relationship, which, if played wrong, could have given Warner doubts about his bride-to-be. But part of her was laughing, imagining Sarah taking her advice. Sarah, humbly attending to Warner's almighty ego; Sarah, hiding her own success like a fault. For once, Elle didn't envy her.

Hightower's lecture left no more impression on Elle than an evanescent dream forgotten in the foggy morning. Sidney was still packing up his PowerBook when Elle tried to walk past him.

"Elle, did you get my present? It's reeeeeeely great," announced Sidney, beaming proudly.

"No, Sidney, but thank you in advance," Elle answered as she hurried away.

She went all day without checking her grades, fearing the worst. By the time she got home, her condo looked like a florist's shop. Her landlord, Mr. Hopson, had apparently used his key to let the delivery men inside. Nice of him, she thought warmly. Saved her several trips.

She cleared a place for her bag on the coffee table and fished inside nervously for her report card. "Get up here, Underdog." She patted the couch. "Let's see if we have to move again."

Elle looked at the row of Ps and breathed a tremendous

sigh of relief. She jumped to the phone to call Eugenia, who she had already heard had placed first in their class.

"Genie."

"What's the word?"

"I passed everything."

"I knew you would! What were your grades?"

Elle paused. "Well, they were all Ps."

"Ps?" Eugenia was stunned.

"Yeah," Elle admitted, laughing. "I took all my classes pass-fail."

"You took everything pass-fail? Are you serious? I didn't know you could do that!"

"All you have to do is ask."

Elle congratulated Eugenia on her grades, which came as no surprise. "You're a Eugenius, you know."

After hanging up, Elle glanced at her pet. "I made it, Underdog," she announced happily. Reaching to the table, she read a card from Serena and Margot. "We still love you, even if you do want to be a lawyer."

She flipped on the television, and Robert Redford in *The Way We Were* momentarily captured her attention. "Redford," she said. "Great blond of the strawberry variety. Well, I guess this is what people do who don't have a date for Valentine's Day." Elle pulled an Afghan blanket around herself, settling in to watch the movie. In two minutes, the opening scene changed her mind.

With every image of Robert Redford, Elle buried her face further in the pillow. Redford in dress whites. Oh, God, that looked like Billy. Redford rowing crew. The image of Charles. Redford in a letter sweater. Oh, Warner, and . . . how many times had she fallen for the BMOC, how trite. Elle felt as if she were looking into the mirror of her love life, and it was the common fare of a mushy movie. She flipped off the switch and headed to the kitchen.

A dozen shell pink roses sat on the counter. She rushed to open the card, positive that these flowers, finally, came from Warner. The card read, simply, "To remembrance of flings past." Elle jumped, clapping her hands together with glee. Clearly it wasn't in the past, or he wouldn't have sent her the same roses as always.

Elle froze when she glimpsed a huge aesthetic atrocity sitting on her kitchen table. Placed there because it was too enormous to fit anywhere else was a basket stuffed with styrofoam, fanned by twenty wooden sticks. A cookie was attached to the top of each stick; the whole bouquet reached at least three feet into the air. Each cookie was shaped like a fish, with a pink "girl" fish in the center. Elle pulled a note off the "girl" cookie, which was iced with a Stanford banner, yellow hair and blue eyes.

The note was signed by Sidney, and it read, "WAY TO REEL IN FIRST SEMESTER."

Elle didn't know whether to laugh or cry. She crumbled a fish cookie and fed it to Underdog.

She knew she wouldn't catch Margot or Serena at home on Valentine's, so Elle decided to call the next morning to thank them for their flowers. Elle thought Margot would flip when she found out that she was actually working for Brooke Vandermark. She began searching for Margot's new phone number under a mountain of "Murder in Malibu" articles printed off Lexis at law school expense.

Elle located the envelope with Margot's new number scribbled next to a note which read "current . . . Feb. 5th." Margot changed her phone number capriciously and often, her preferred means of distancing herself from men who grew tiresome. Now that she had Snuff, Elle figured this number would last at least a few more months, so she set the new number on memory to avoid future scavenger hunts, then dialed.

"House of Zen," Margot sang.

Elle groaned. "Zen again? Hey, it's the Dolly Parton Lama!"

"Elle, baby."

Elle cringed to hear that Margot was already picking up Snuff's record industry jargon. She'd make a good wife, functioning basically as a mirror for Snuff, who, if not looking in one, was looking for one. "Marg, baby," Elle mimicked. "Thanks for the roses. Even if I am in law school, it's nice to know you guys still love me."

Margot laughed. "We think you're kooky, but we love you just the same."

CHAPTER THIRTY-FIVE

AFTER hanging up with Margot, Elle decided she'd pen Serena a thank-you note for the flowers rather than listen to more thirdhand scandals associated with Snuff and the record industry. She opened her Wills textbook to the emery board that served as a bookmark, beginning where she had left off last night in her pre-nailfiling ambition to read the book cover to cover.

Studying with the fervor of a practitioner, as an advocate for a real-life blonde, Elle didn't notice just how interested she had become in at least this area of law. She was also intent on proving herself to Christopher Miles.

She even found herself getting to Wills class early, a move that didn't result in added class time. Gory Professor Gilbreath had a habit of appalling the student audience with his tactless death humor, then frightening questions out of them so he could end class prematurely, as if weary of his own voice.

The next morning Professor Gilbreath finished his lecture gruffly, snarling the rhetorical "Any questions?" as he stomped to the door.

Expecting two packages from Christopher Miles, Elle

rushed from class to her mailbox. Chutney Vandermark had been deposed by Christopher, and Christopher had sent copies of her deposition transcripts as well as the transcripts from Trent's deposition by messenger to Stanford Law School for his interns to review.

Elle assumed the transcripts would be stuck with flyers in her mailbox. She was puzzled to find a note instead, directing her to the copy center.

Elle figured out soon enough that Chutney's deposition was far lengthier than Brooke's and far too thick to fit into her law school mailbox. It ran over three hundred pages, scuttling Elle's prior plan to skim over the cumbersome deposition while sitting in her Property class. With an empty half hour thanks to Professor Gilbreath's early break, she headed for the law lounge to read what Chutney had had to say to the lawyers. Within the first few pages of Chutney's deposition, it was obvious to Elle the girl was ready for a knock-down-drag-out fight for her father's fortune.

In the short recess between Wills and Property classes, Eugenia entered the law lounge and recognized Elle's head bent over her reading. "Hey, Elle," she yelled from the line where she waited for a coffee refill. Elle looked up and smiled.

"Coming to Property class today, Princess?" Eugenia kidded, beckoning with her bag of peanut M&M's toward the hallway. "Maybe it's changed rooms since you last showed your face."

Elle felt a rush of anxiety, having missed days of classes to focus on a self-taught course in will probate practice, preparing for Brooke's trial. "It's still in the same place, isn't it?" she asked, startled.

"Yeah, silly." Eugenia smiled, shaking her head as if at a child. "I'm just giving you a hard time."

"Okay, only if you share your candy," Elle joked, standing to join Eugenia in line. "Hope you brought enough for everybody."

"Enough for everybody I like."

"Thanks." Elle accepted a handful of M&M's before walking to Property class, where she and Eugenia sat together.

Elle poked her friend when she saw Sarah enter the room. "Check out the power suit," she giggled, indicating Sarah's severe figure approaching in her navy Brooks Brothers uniform with a paisley bow strangling her neck.

"Hey, is this dress-like-your-mother day?" Eugenia whispered.

"Certainly not my mother!" Elle laughed.

Sarah made a point of walking by Elle's seat. "I was at Christopher Miles's office this morning," she said. She looked quizzically at Elle. "He's already got me doing document review," she said with an air of self-importance.

"Have *you* had a meeting at Miles & Slocum yet?" Nosy Claire said, having just joined Sarah. They were both quite unaware that Elle had been to one deposition in L.A. and out to dinner with Christopher twice. During both dinners they had discussed the case in detail, and Elle felt she was gaining an edge on Sarah and the other interns.

Elle smiled. She told them that Trent's deposition had been a great way for her to dive right into the case, that she was convinced of Brooke's innocence, and that today "her client" would be coming to stay with her.

By this point she had all but given up class reading and attendance, keeping abreast with Eugenia's notes and her two Secret Angels, the poet and Emanuel. She was devoting all of her time and tremendous effort to the case, which genuinely interested and challenged her.

"There's more to this case than document review," she added.

Elle's confidence came through in her voice, and Claire looked discouraged. Claire turned abruptly, and Sarah clomped behind her in heavy, thick heels to her seat.

Elle peered at the phrase *"Fructus perceptos villae non esse constat,"* Barrister Hightower's lexicon lesson of the day. Another worldly wise word for the collection, Elle thought despondently, remembering torturous grade-school vocabulary books as she copied the phrase into her notes. Barrister Hightower was crouched invisibly behind the podium, preparing his lecture.

The enormous deposition could not be hidden even from wee Whitman Hightower, so Elle opened *Interview* magazine under the desk and began reading an article on Stella McCartney's latest collection.

Elle's reading was rudely interrupted when Witless Hightower called her name. She looked up, surprised, as he bounded from the chalkboard back to his notes.

"Well, Ms. Woods, we are waiting for an answer." Hightower weaved back and forth, probably on his tiptoes, beady eyes peeking over the podium.

"I'm sorry, I'm afraid I didn't hear the question," Elle mumbled.

Hightower persisted. "Ms. Woods, the query posed for your comment relates, as I have said, to this maxim." He waved impatiently at the board behind him. *"Fructus naturales,* Ms. Woods. The products of nature alone," Hightower muttered. Sarah turned around, disappointed.

"Gathered fruits do not make a part of the farm," interjected Drew Drexler, the irrepressible Rhodes scholar. He was translating the bizarre phrase on the board, and the professor nodded with satisfaction.

"The question, Barrister," Drew continued, "is whether they belong to the farmer. It is my judgment that they do."

"Excellent, Counselor," Hightower said.

Grateful to be spared further humiliation, Elle returned to reading her magazine.

Brooke's one-day planned visit turned into six days, on the last of which Elle and Eugenia skipped their classes to spend the morning with Brooke at the Museum of Modern Art. Brooke was terribly homesick for her life and friends in Malibu, especially her support group. Elle and Brooke arrived that afternoon at the office of Miles & Slocum in a wave of breathless and cheerful chatter. The intern and the client had become fast friends. From the kitchen, Elle got a diet Coke and Brooke poured herself a cup of black coffee before they made their way to Elle's tiny office.

"I still think Eugenia was right about *Tied Tubes*," Brooke said, taking a seat. Her reference was to a sculpture in which the barrels of two handguns were twisted together. "It was a socially critical piece about birth control. She's right, it's a tool to limit our life force. If I had seen it a year ago, maybe I would have had Heyworth's child. He wanted to, you know." She began to cry softly.

"Well, you had his love," Elle said gently. "Better to have loved and lost," she added softly. So easy to tell somebody else. It never consoled her when she thought about Warner. "And anyway," Elle changed the subject as much to dodge her own maudlin sentiment as to avoid upsetting Brooke, "what about *Madonna and Twins in Jell-O*? How could you want to have children after seeing that?" The painting portrayed a mother dressed in an apron that read "EAT JELL-O" gazing distantly at the television while stirring a bowl of green slime. A set of twins were hanging limply by fangs implanted in her bloody neck.

"I'm telling you, it had nothing to do with children," Brooke said. "It was an exposé on the use of animal gelatin in Jell-O products. People think it's a family food, but it gets its consistency from animal fat. Eating Jell-O is as cruel as eating veal!"

Brooke was a vegetarian. Elle doubted her critical analysis, but found herself increasingly confident that Brooke lacked the heart of a murderer.

"You're like the calorie Rain Man, Brooke. Do me a favor and leave my lunch quotient a mystery today. Please?"

"Knowledge is power," Brooke said.

"Then tell me who was at your Shopper Stoppers meeting, Brooke, so we can prove that you didn't kill Heyworth." Elle narrowed her eyes. "Please, Brooke, you don't have a single alibi witness," she said in a whisper.

Now it was Brooke who spoke gravely. "Shut the door," she motioned.

Elle jumped from behind her desk and pulled the door closed. How proud Christopher would be if she got the name of an alibi witness out of Brooke! Brooke trusted her, she thought; Brooke knew Elle believed she was innocent. She returned to her desk as casually as she could manage, restraining an anticipatory quiver with great effort.

"Please, Brooke, who can testify for you?"

"Elle, you don't understand," Brooke said, her voice definite. "I won't hurt the people who have helped me. I won't embarrass them, and I won't set their lives back. The only people who knew where I was when my husband was shot are in my support group in Los Angeles, and I won't expose them. Even if nobody will testify for me."

Elle's heart plunged. She cursed herself for being too forceful. Brooke had been so close to telling her something.

"Elle, I have what they call an addictive personality. That's why I had the discipline to lose all that weight. I committed all of my energy to that single goal. In that di-

rection it was useful, but when I got hooked on the Home
Shopping Network, I turned all of my commitment and energy to the power of spending. It's immediate, but it's tran-
sitory. I lost sight of the future," she said, her eyes dimming
from sharp turquoise gems to the pale, blank blue of a
faded day.

Elle drooped in her chair, and for a moment neither of
them spoke. Then suddenly, like a mood ring, Brooke's
face lit up again.

"That was before I met the life leaders," Brooke said.
"The group leaders at the Shopper Stoppers meetings . . .
they gave my future back to me. I regained what Heyworth
loved about me, and he was so happy."

"What do you mean?"

"When Heyworth met me at the wellness center, he was
trying to get in shape, and I made him my project. His whole
attitude had to change. He was almost ready to die. He was
so world-weary at first, and I couldn't blame him. Everyone
treated him like some old patriarch with all of his achievements behind him like ghosts."

Elle reached for her diet Coke while she listened intently.

"It wasn't his past that I cared about. His companies, equity shares, or vineyards weren't my interests. We started
working out together, and he was like a child, with all of
the energy that made him his millions turned toward improving his health and getting stronger. That's what I cared
about. He clung to his life after that. He felt vigorous, and
capable. Together, we had our eyes set on the future. On
our future."

"What does that have to do with your alibi, Brooke?"
Elle said with exasperation. "What would Heyworth want
you to do?" she said. "Just give up?"

"We understood loyalty and support, Elle. He'd want me

to stand by my friends. He'd want me to do just what I'm doing, which is moving forward. I'll face this trial and I'll tell the judge and jury the truth. I won't involve anyone who I'll hurt. Come what may."

Elle thought of Warner, and how hard she had tried to resurrect the love of their past days. Brooke was crazy. Loyalty was fleeting. Look what Warner had done to her, even if she had changed her entire life to match his like a newly fashionable tie. Sarah was his future, and what was hers? What was Brooke's?

"Your future doesn't look so bright, Brooke. You're going to have your entire life, not just your alleged involvement in the murder, put on trial, I can promise you that."

Brooke dropped her head into her hands. "Elle, I lost both of my parents when I dug up their business. They're like strangers to me now. Without Heyworth, the only people who care about my future"—she paused, glancing at Elle—"besides you and Christopher, who I'm *paying*, are the Shopper Stoppers. So I won't bring them down by exposing them, even to save myself. They still have families. And they're my family."

Brooke wouldn't budge. She clung to the last family she had. She wouldn't sacrifice her friends on the altar of self-preservation, and yet she had everything to lose.

Elle thought of Serena and Margot. They ridiculed her for taking this job, defending a Theta . . . an unpardonable crime, forgetting the primacy of her Greek letter label. Their paths were separating. But Elle also had the misgiving that she too had filled her college days with superficial judgments. Good fraternities, bad fraternities, whispers about sisters, china pattern dreams. Her old friends seemed so remote now.

Margot was a "we," having ceased to refer to herself in

the first person singular since she became a charm bracelet on Snuff's arm. Serena, always the same, was a scattering of crystals, drugs, dates, and diets. They were the friends of habit and memory, to which she now clung like lint. She sensed that she had lost them, coming to law school, maybe for good, but then maybe inevitably. Either way, she was left with a sense of loss.

She had strayed from her old life and had found fulfillment where she least expected it, but she still hadn't given up on getting Warner back. Law school had not changed her in Warner's eyes, so she'd found a way to get him, with Brooke's case as a front and the Elle he had loved as the bait.

She'd see Warner after class, and she'd be holding a Property textbook in one hand and a deposition in the other, but to him she might as well be holding a dog-eared copy of *Cosmo*. So *Cosmo* it would be. Elle had a plan to work out at the gym available to Miles & Slocum employees. Positive that she'd run into Warner there, she dutifully packed her gym clothes and the latest *Cosmo* to read while she was on the StairMaster.

The rest of her class looked upon her like an alien. Barbie paraphernalia still made its cowardly, anonymous assault on her school mailbox. She found herself bored in classes, which she attended with less and less frequency. She sighed, and Brooke's obstinate expression caught her eye. It reminded her of Eugenia, and she smiled. Eugenia was as stubborn as a mule.

Eugenia was a miracle who strengthened her resolve to get through law school and, as hard as it was, helped her see Warner for what he really was. A happenstance of a seating chart. Another gift was her lovelorn Angel, sending her aid and comfort in ribbon-tied outlines. There were people who wanted to see her make it.

Elle set her jaw. Brooke believed in herself and Elle be-lieved in Brooke. The underdog.

"Take me to a meeting," Elle said all of a sudden. "I won't say a word to Christopher or anyone. I want to meet your friends."

"If you'll take me to law school. I want to see what your prison is like."

CHAPTER THIRTY-SIX

THAT night Elle wondered which would be more bizarre, Brooke at law school or a Shopper Stoppers meeting. Her mind wandered from the Rule of Perpetuities. It was impossible for anything else to be this boring, Elle thought, slamming her Property book shut. The phone rang, and figuring nobody could have anything worse to say than the words printed in her casebook, she answered the phone without even screening.

"So what's up on the job scene . . . or should I say job scheme?" Eugenia asked, always amused by Elle's romantic ploys.

"The internship is great . . . and it's actually yielding a way to see Warner!" Elle exclaimed enthusiastically. "The firm is adjacent to a building that has a gym, and we're allowed to use it. Warner works out twice a day, so I'm sure he'll take advantage of it. My lit bag and my gym bag are dutifully packed for tomorrow, and I've been working out every day."

"So have you seen him there yet?"

"Not yet. It's only been two weeks, and I hadn't figured out his schedule yet, but now I've got it. I'm positive I'll see him there tomorrow. We used to work out together every day," she added in a dreamy tone.

"Well I was just calling to catch up, since I never see you anymore," Eugenia said, but Coerte beeped in on call waiting before any good gossip could be exchanged.

Elle giggled as she hung up the phone. She was genuinely happy for her friend. Exhausted from her desperate, useless attempt at trying to understand her Property reading, she fell asleep immediately.

The next day, Elle got to the gym around 4:30, figuring from the schedule she saw pinned to Mia's bulletin board that Warner would arrive around 5:00.

The usual crew of secretaries and paralegals were on the StairMasters while bankers, lawyers, and other businessmen pedaled the Lifecycles that were strategically located behind the StairMasters.

Five o'clock arrived, and as Elle looked up from a compromising position on one of the machines, the unlikeliest candidate entered the gym. Sarah. "Great, now it's *Sarah* and Warner who work out together," she muttered; but he was nowhere to be seen.

Sarah took a nervous glance around, her pale arms clutching her *Property book*! Elle couldn't believe it. Noticing that the Lifecycles were all being used, Sarah headed for a StairMaster. Elle watched her. Clearly Sarah hadn't seen her yet.

Elle stood up, and Sarah's mouth gaped open. Elle's blonde hair was still hanging perfectly, her makeup unsmudged, and her pink leotard, cut to show maximum cleavage, was clinging to all the right places.

Elle's usual stiletto-gouging walk was now a long athletic stride. All eyes shifted to watch her athletic beauty as soon as she hit the floor. "Sarah!" Elle exclaimed in mock surprise as she approached the StairMasters. "I didn't know you worked out here."

"Well, today's my first day," Sarah admitted. She was maintaining an unsteady balance as she tried to keep up with the advanced level she had set the machine on. Stair-Master ruin stared her in the face. "I'm not used to these things," Sarah said as she gasped for air.

Elle reached over and lowered the level to novice. "Maybe I can help you," she said tentatively.

"Warner wrote out a schedule for me to follow," she said, and indicated a piece of paper with Warner's unmistakable scrawly handwriting sticking out of her casebook. "He said you used to do it twice a day, but I'm so exhausted from this . . . I don't know if I can do . . . step aerobics." She glanced at the sheet dubiously.

"Step aerobics? I can't believe I ever put myself through that torture. Did Warner mention my step aerobics instructor was Brooke Vandermark?" Elle asked.

"You're kidding!" Sarah exclaimed. "Not that she doesn't look like she could have been." Sarah poked irregularly at the buttons until the machine stopped.

"I'm really glad Warner doesn't work out here. He's dying to use this gym, but he doesn't want Christopher to think he's a slacker. I would have died if Warner had seen me! But I'm even more embarrassed that you did, to be honest," Sarah said.

"There's nothing to be embarrassed about. You've seen my answers in Property," Elle joked, glancing down at Sarah's casebook. "How about we make a trade?" Elle offered.

"Well . . . what kind of trade?"

"I'll show you how to find your way around the gym and work out with you, minus the step aerobics, if you'll help me out in Property. I'll need your notes and some tutoring weekly and your outline at the end of the semester."

"It's a deal," Sarah agreed, "but only if we can start to-morrow with the gym tutoring."

Elle laughed. "No problem."

The two girls showered and then headed back to Miles & Slocum for Elle's first Property session. Although Elle had passed all of her first-semester classes and was feeling increasingly confident, Property, only a second-semester course, was still a stumbling block. Sarah helped Elle with the cases that weren't covered by the commercial outlines, and Elle even withstood briefing a case for class the following day. She was determined to succeed at the entire law school game, Property included.

CHAPTER THIRTY-SEVEN

ELLE remembered a time so distant it seemed prehistoric when the week after spring break was dedicated to the wholesome activity of comparing tan lines, piña coladas, and stories from Mexican jails.

Over the March vacation, selections for the *Stanford Law Review* had been made on the basis of first-semester grades and a writing competition that had taken place in February.

On the morning of her first day back, Elle found Eugenia by the coffee machine. Eugenia watched the excited members jump around as if they were on speed while the rejects muttered plastic congratulations. She shook her head and motioned for Elle to follow her to the dreaded law library.

On the way upstairs, it occurred to Elle that Eugenia's straight As should have earned her a spot on this *Law Review.* "Did you make it, Genie?"

Eugenia grinned. "Yeah, thanks but no thanks. If I wanted to be a librarian, I would have been." She maneuvered expertly through the bookcases to a shelf of *Stanford Law Reviews.* "Open it at random, Elle." Eugenia picked out a recent volume. "I think you'll agree that there are better ways to spend your time."

"Probably few worse," Elle laughed, cracking the heavy book open to a worn interior page. She leafed through the vacuum of time and talent.

Eugenia sighed suddenly. "You'd think with all their economic analyses, the inefficiency of spending twenty hours a week checking somebody else's homework would occur to one of these people. Oh, by the way, Sarah made it, but Warner didn't."

Sensing that everyone would be caught up in the *Law Review* excitement, Elle decided that a massage and a facial would be a better way to use the next few hours than attending class. She didn't notice that Larry had followed her out until he caught up with her in the hall.

"Elle, wait up."

She turned around surprised. Larry stared intensely at Elle, walking next to her. She fished in her purse for her car keys, nearing the parking space where her trusty Range Rover was primed for exit.

"Elle," Larry said as he placed a hand on his hip and watched her struggle through the clinking contents of her bag. "You're too sexy for law school."

"Larry, my mom's Volvo is too sexy for law school."

Larry laughed and agreed with her, but added that it didn't make Elle any less sexy.

"Jezebel, my painted Jezebel," Larry shifted lyrically into the Old Testament, extending one arm as if heralding Elle to a royal audience. " 'See to this accursed woman, and give her burial; after all, she was a king's daughter.' "

Elle glanced up from her purse, surprised. "Jezebel? What on earth are you talking about?"

Larry leaned against the Range Rover, gazing at Elle with

a dreamy, quiet calm. "A loving theft, a pilfering, a joining of the lips. A trade of moisture, warmth and breath, in soft and tiny sips." He paused, watching her mouth drop in astonishment.

"You're the Secret Angel!" Elle cried, recognizing the verse from her outlines.

"Every true romantic needs his Guinevere, Elle." Larry's gaze seemed detached, his John Lennon sunglasses hiding a world only glimpsed by his eyes.

"Oh, Larry, they're so . . . unique," she said. "Your poems . . . you're inspired!" She paused, gazing at the English professor gone wrong. "But why on earth are you wasting your talents in law school?"

"Elle," he smiled, "my talents aren't wasted." A. Lawrence Hesterton turned back toward the house of law. "A poet needs but one," he said quietly.

Elle rested her weight against the car door and watched her Secret Angel depart. The unlikeliest people, she thought to herself, confounded by this flash of Larry's private mind. Now that she knew that it was someone who was with her and saw how she had struggled in all of her classes, she decided that if she was his Guinevere, he was her Palo Alto Knight.

CHAPTER THIRTY-EIGHT

ELLE awoke the next morning feeling tense. She was feeling the pressure of finals approaching again even though they were still quite a long time away. Dragging herself out of bed, she wondered how she would fare this time. She took Underdog for a long walk, ultimately arriving to Professional Responsibility a half hour late.

Elle wondered why she ever bothered to take notes on the zany antics of Charley Client, given that Professor Pfisak's ethical conclusions were foregone and unassailable. She slid the April issue of *Vogue* under her desk. After reading the "Fitness" section, she decided to tear it out for Sarah. Although Sarah was improving at the gym, she was still having trouble with crunches. Elle hoped the article on abdominal toners, with pictures, would be helpful. She genuinely wanted so see Sarah succeed at the gym.

Elle glanced up from the magazine long enough to focus on the class and ascertain that, simply put, today's ethical duty was to withhold information from paying clients. She peered into her casebook to see what rule created this Kafkaesque bureaucratic parody.

Fran volunteered to answer a hypothetical, which involved gun-wielding Charley Client racing paranoid into his lawyer's office, asking whether the state has to find a corpse within state lines in order to bring a murder charge. Indignant, Fran repeated that the lawyer's duty was to avoid at all costs giving information that would clue Charley in to his legal rights.

Also call the police and bill him for the time, no doubt, thought Elle with increasing impatience.

Finally, on Charley's third misadventure, Elle raised her hand. "Ms. Woods," Pfisak noticed her with surprise. "I presume you've caught up with the class discussion, as most of it preceded your entrance."

Elle glowered amid her classmate's smug chuckles. "Maybe I haven't caught on," she said. "Because what I hear is that we're supposed to learn all this law so we can lock it up in our offices and decide *for* people what the 'interest of justice' will permit them to know."

"She must think Charley is a blond," Claire whispered to Sarah.

"Thank you for your contribution, Ms. Woods," Professor Pfisak said. He turned to John Matthews. "Mr. Matthews, perhaps you can tell us how a lawyer would handle the next situation and not risk *disbarment.*"

This class would bankrupt them all if it had any relevance past the exam. Elle turned back to *Vogue* to learn something that mattered. She had a scheduled date with Brooke later that day.

CHAPTER THIRTY-NINE

ELLE gazed sullenly around at the student audience of Wills and Estate Planning, cheered only by the fact that Brooke was out on bail and visiting her today after class. Another grim morning of Death with Gilbreath, then maybe she'd talk Brooke into a shopping spree, nontelevised of course.

Behind her she could hear Cari and Michael exchanging death jokes. "Did you hear the one about the lawyer who believed in reincarnation? In his will he left everything to himself!" Michael laughed uproariously.

Dr. Dan dropped his head to the desk. "What I don't know won't hurt me," he declared, justifying a morning nap.

Mr. Heigh and his wife arrived carrying Thermoses of Chinese tea made from dried figs. Mr. Heigh's gray-haired chest was bared in a tank top that read: "It took me FORTY YEARS to look this good!"

Elle pulled out *Self* just as Professor Gilbreath shut the door to begin class. While Ben ar-*tic*-u-*lat*-ed an interminable theory of "partial will republication by holographic codicil," Elle immersed herself in "The Politics of Hair." It was an interesting article, but not entirely favorable to blondes, she noted with concern.

Elle was pleased when she noticed that "The Politics of Hair" had engrossed her throughout Gilbreath's entire lecture. She knew without checking the clock that class would be over in exactly two minutes, since Claire had begun to attack her split ends. On the dot, exactly two minutes before the end of every class, Claire would start arranging her unruly hair just so, preparing to approach the law school hallway as if it were her great debut. Elle used Claire's hair-poking as the signal to pack up her books.

Elle strolled toward the front entrance, where Brooke stood waiting. She looked stunning in an emerald green slinky silk tank top and a knee-length linen skirt with a thigh-high side slit.

"So you're at large again," Elle laughed, greeting the jailbird with a happy embrace. "Congratulations."

"What a relief," Brooke gushed. "Christopher's so great, you should have heard him at the bail hearing!"

"Come on." Elle linked her arm with Brooke's. "Now you can see what *my* prison is like." Together they walked to the law lounge.

"I'll have to warn you, the caffeine syrup they call 'coffee' here might keep you up for days."

Drawing glares from law students immersed in their casebooks, Brooke rattled briskly through the events of the last few days. "I've been so busy, Elle, I wanted to come see you sooner. Everything's been so crazy, trying to get back to my normal life."

"As if you ever *had* a normal life!"

"Hey, we aren't all lucky enough to go to law school," Brooke giggled. She sipped the smoking black tar and grimaced. "Eeew, you're right about the coffee. Swamp syrup!"

Elle agreed, adding a pack of Equal to hers.

"Let's go get a latte someplace decent," Brooke offered.

"Can you skip out of class? I want you to see my new Mercedes."

"Already?" Elle choked on her coffee, laughing. "Oh, Brooke!"

"Heyworth wanted to get rid of the Jag, anyway," Brooke justified her purchase casually. "His British stocks weren't doing so hot, and he said we should boycott the queen's economy."

"Respecting his wishes," Elle said, smiling. "What loyalty. You would have made a great Delta Gamma."

"I was cut in prefs," Brooke snapped back, remembering her first social trauma. "I got a Theta bid. They didn't have a choice and neither did I, since I was a legacy. If I'd had my way, I would have been a Pi-Phi."

"Oh." Elle covered her face, embarrassed. "Oops. Theta's cool, though."

"Ancient history." Brooke dismissed it with a manicured wave. "Pi-Phi had the scariest rush, though, I'll never forget it. They made us eat this dessert of ice cream scooped in the middle of a doughnut. It's *impossible* to eat, because if you use a fork you can't shake hands, but if you lift it up the ice cream drools all over the place. That's how they weed 'em out. They cut the droolers and the forkers."

Elle rolled her eyes. "I remember that. I think I was actually a forker *and* a drooler!" She looked curiously at Brooke. "How'd you . . . approach the doughnut?"

"Oh, I just told everyone that I was on a macrobiotic diet that didn't include dairy products. I got a plain doughnut."

"Bonus!"

"Yeah, those were the days." Brooke beamed at her sorority coup. "But I've made something of myself without Pi-Phi or Delta Gamma!"

"Touché," Elle laughed. "So what are you going to do now?"

"What do you mean?" Brooke asked. "After the trial?"
Elle nodded.

"Well, if Christopher keeps me out of jail, I'll get married again." Brooke wrinkled her nose and squinted at Elle quizzically. "Of course."

"Any prospects?" said Elle, grinning.

"That's the silliest thing I ever heard." Brooke shook her head, struck by Elle's naïveté. "What else would I do? I'll be married by year's end, no question. Aren't you going to get married?"

Elle grew quiet. "Not by year's end," she admitted. "Well, anyway," she added, "probably not." Suddenly she dug into her white Kate Spade tote and produced a jewelry box, which she handed to Brooke.

"I don't want to marry you!" Brooke squealed.

"Of course not! It's a present. Open it!"

Brooke dangled a gold earring and peered at its delicate italic carving. "One, Elle?"

"It's my jewelry line!" Elle exclaimed, clapping her hands. "Brooke, you're going to flip when you hear this, but I met some people from the Home Shopping Network, you know, when we were investigating your alibi."

Brooke scowled. "Leeches."

"Listen, listen." Elle grabbed for the earring, nearly spilling her coffee. "See, I was a jewelry design major in college, before"—she glanced dubiously around the lounge—"before I gave it all up for this. Anyway, some of the Home Shopping executives met me when I had to go over some of your receipts at their offices, and they actually wanted me to audition or interview . . . whatever, to be a legal correspondent—they actually called it that. It was for a proposed show called *Fashion Crimes!*"

"So you're going to be like a fashion rehabilitator?" Brooke asked skeptically.

"Exactly! Plus, I'm going to design a whole line of legal-themed jewelry and advise people, on air, which pieces to buy! Home Shopping loves the idea and I've already gotten started."

Elle reached for a tiny velvet box and handed it to Brooke. "I designed one piece with you in mind. This fabulous diamond 'shackle' on a gold chain bracelet. You don't have to wear it around your ankle this time," Elle laughed.

Brooke unhooked the dainty bracelet still in the box. "What a riot! An artist's original! Hey, Elle, I hope you sell your jewelry in stores, because you know I can't order anything off TV." Suddenly she shot from her chair, checking her watch. "Oh, Elle, I didn't realize how late it was. You just reminded me, I've got to get to my meeting."

Elle grinned. "Shopper Stoppers Anonymous?"

"Former Home Shoppers," Brooke corrected meekly. "Addicted."

Elle followed Brooke to the parking lot, where the Mercedes' owner was obvious from its license plates alone: ISO SWM.

CHAPTER FORTY

"**H**OP into my chariot!" Suddenly Brooke vaulted into the driver's seat of her sparkling gold convertible as if she were mounting a charger.

Elle giggled, opening the passenger door. Vaulting would have been impossible given the narrow dimensions of her white piqué halter dress.

Brooke looked somewhat disappointed by Elle's conventional entrance, but that didn't slow her down as she merged into the freeway traffic, heading north toward the airport.

"The color of your car really complements our hair," Elle said, thoughtfully examining a strand of her own hair as she pulled it back into a ponytail.

Brooke nodded silently.

"I'm dying to know where these anonymous meetings are held," Elle said.

"The meetings aren't anonymous at all, Elle. It's the members' identities that must be kept anonymous."

"Right. Sorry," Elle said. She realized once again how seriously Brooke took these meetings and the group members.

"Sometimes I feel like even you make fun of my addiction, Elle."

Elle looked away from Brooke, pretending to check her makeup in the side mirror of the car. "I'm so sorry, Brooke," Elle said. "I'm not making fun of your addiction. It's just hard to imagine anyone, *especially* you, with your sense of style and elegance, ordering something like porcelain commemorative dolls of the nation's first ladies."

"Those were pretty scary," Brooke admitted as she screeched the convertible to a halt in front of the airport Hilton.

The Hilton. Elle wondered if one of the members rented a suite under a false name.

Brooke and Elle pulled out hairbrushes to fix their windblown hair and then entered the hotel. Elle followed Brooke to a second-floor suite called the Archibald Room. The only furnishings were cheap plastic chairs placed around a long Formica table and oddly mismatched paintings and prints.

Several people, the most eclectic mix Elle had ever seen, were sitting around the table. They seemed to be at ease with one another and were conversing in a casual manner. A few others were gathered around an enormous coffee machine or had taken seats in extra chairs around the edges of the room. From their wide range of looks, they seemed to be everything from housewives, to mechanics, to doctors, to CEOs.

When Brooke and Elle entered, Brooke announced that Elle was there as a guest and not a member. This had the effect of quieting the nervous murmurs and stares of the nine or ten people present. Brooke suggested that they introduce themselves to Elle, and when nobody volunteered, Elle gave a wave of her hand generally around the smoke-filled room.

"My name is Elle Woods. I'm a friend of Brooke's from college, and I wanted to meet the people who have helped her so much," she said with a smile.

"I'm Miranda," said a tiny dark-haired woman. "Welcome."

Brooke tapped Elle's arm. "She's the life leader," she whispered into Elle's ear.

Miranda stood up and closed the door behind Elle. "We're all here," she said, returning to her seat. "Yves, why don't you begin by introducing yourself to our guest."

A wrinkled man sitting closest to the door, wearing a starched, collarless denim shirt, squinted through wire-rimmed glasses, then removed them from his small face. "My name is Yves Muir," he said.

Elle, having taken a seat next to Brooke at the other end of the table, waved from her chair. "Hi, Yves."

"I'm from Citrus Heights, California," the little man continued. "Last month I was rolling my shopping debt over on five credit cards, three in my wife's name, and she's been deceased for several years." He nervously reached for a cigarette and lit it.

Elle heard a sympathetic murmur from several people in the room.

"Yves is our most recent member," Miranda said. She then turned to the woman seated by the wall next to Yves who was loudly crunching her way through a bag of Cheetos. "Veronica, why don't you introduce yourself next?"

"My name is Veronica," said the garish woman, who wore a lemon yellow bouffant. Her cheeks and lips were streaked with the same bloodred color, giving her white face the appearance of a checkered gingham cloth. She was dressed in a prune-colored sweater that exposed one shoulder like Jennifer Beals in *Flashdance*. Elle wondered if her penchant was for high-volume cosmetic purchases.

"I'm a florist, originally from Bentonville, Arkansas," she said. "That's where the original Wal-Mart store is located, you know. I always did love a bargain!" She smiled engagingly and revealed that she had ordered enough scented soaps and oils to take baths every hour for twenty years. Elle giggled, but drew a scowl from Yves and Veronica together. She straightened her face into a more appropriate look of concern.

"Nice to meet you, Veronica," she said, and was relieved when the woman returned her smile.

Without prompting from the life leader, a scruffy-haired man in a black T-shirt who was seated at the table introduced himself. "I'm Jeff," he said in a deep baritone that sounded incongruous with his youthful grin. "I play bass for the Funeral Pyre. We've got a gig tonight in the city at the Cat House. I can put you on the guest list if you want."

Brooke laughed out loud. "Jeff, you're out of luck. She's hopelessly in love!"

Elle blushed. "Brooke!"

"No secrets here," Brooke said, poking Elle in the shoulder.

The rest of the people seated around the table introduced themselves to Elle one by one. There was Walter, a CEO; Gloria, a dental hygienist; Anne, an interior designer; Carolyn, a school principal; Jean, a legal secretary; and Nicolette, whom Elle recognized as the evening anchorwoman on Channel 4.

Brooke thanked the group for allowing Elle to be there. "You all know how hard it is to find someone to understand our addiction, and even though Elle never even watched Home Shopping before she met me, she's been my greatest support outside of the group. I wanted to bring her today so that she can fully understand the importance of these meetings and what the meetings and the members mean to me."

Suddenly Miranda jumped up from her chair and called the meeting to order.

Elle pulled a compact out of her purse to make sure that

her mascara hadn't been smudged from her watering eyes. The room was dense with cigarette smoke. At least ten people in the room had replaced one addiction with another. Satisfied with her mascara, she looked doubtfully at Miranda.

"For those of you who don't know me, I'm Miranda," she began. "I'm a recovering home shopper. As your life leader, I've spent a lot of time telling you how I overcame Home Shopping and what Shopper Stoppers has done for me, but today I'd like to tell you something more important."

"Hi, Miranda. Tell us your story!" the group said warmly in a loud, unified chorus.

"I used to be lonely. Now I'm not lonely, but I know that if I do get lonely, shopping won't fill that aching void. I have to turn to you . . . my friends. That is what recovery is all about. It's about friendship, support, and *anonymity*. It's about coming to people whom I can share my worst fears and secrets with and know that they'll never, under any circumstances, be revealed. That is friendship to me, and it's why I've been Home Shopping–free for one year, two months, and three days!"

Elle looked at Brooke's tear-splotched face and knew that she would never, under any circumstances, reveal the identity of her group members in L.A.

CHAPTER FORTY-ONE

"CATCHY little tune." Elle noticed she had been humming "You must pay the rent, I can't pay the rent" as she collared Underdog for his afternoon walk. "I'll pay the rent." She opened Underdog's dainty jaws to mouth each booming word.

"My hero!" she answered gaily, fluffing her puppy's crown of wispy fur. Underdog whined and trotted around in a circle, impatient to go out.

"Poor thing, I've been neglecting you." Elle glared at the pile of deposition transcripts littered about the couch. "I'll take this afternoon off, handsome, and we'll go for a walk."

When they returned, fresh-faced from the brisk spring wind, Elle warily inspected her answering machine. She shifted Underdog where he was cradled in her arms and reached to play the tape.

"Elle." Warner still didn't bother to introduce himself, knowing his voice would always be familiar. Elle gave Underdog a hopeful squeeze.

"I'm calling from the office." He paused. "From Miles & Slocum, I mean. I, uh, hoped you'd be here today. Listen, I know this is short notice, but I've had sort of a weird cou-

ple of days, and I really wanted to talk to you. Can we
have dinner, maybe, tonight?"

Warner lowered his voice, speaking tenderly. "You're still
the only . . . the only person, I think, who understands . . .
what I want in my life. I've had so little time for what's important." Elle moved her ear closer to the machine.

"Anyway," Warner sighed after a moment of thought, "I'm
making some changes. Listen, sweetie, call me here. Sarah's
not coming in today. Maybe we can meet downtown."

Elle pounced anxiously for the phone, dropping her
contented pet with a thud. "Oh, sorry, Underdog," she
gulped, dialing rapidly. "It's Elle Woods calling. Can you
connect me with Warner, please?"

She held her breath, feeling her heart pound as she tried
to restrain the excitement in her voice.

"Elle on oh-two," Warner said in falsetto, imitating Mia.
"Just what I wanted to hear."

"Oh, Warner," Elle cooed despite her effort to act com-
posed. "It's so great to hear from you." She hadn't seen him
nearly as much as she had hoped through this internship.
"What's up?"

"Listen, Elle, I can't really talk here. I'll be downtown
working on this brief for a while, and I wanted to see you.
Not in the office, though. Can we meet for dinner? My treat.
There's something I wanted to talk over with you. You alone."

Elle jumped with delight, nearly dropping the phone.
"Warner, of course," she answered breathlessly. "Time and
place."

He paused, collecting his thoughts. "It's been too long,
Elle. Let's do this right. How about Masa's?"

"Warner, that's my favorite!"

"Perfect," he decided. "Seven-thirty, then. I'll reserve a
table, under Huntington. Table for two."

"Huntington," Elle repeated dreamily. "Table for two."

"Right." Warner was businesslike. "Looking forward to it."

"Seven-thirty," Elle smiled, charmed. She started to ask Warner for a hint, but he had already hung up. "Never mind," she thought, envisioning Warner reserving a table for two: "Huntington. Two Huntingtons." She had been so busy she had hardly thought about Warner, but his voice brought all of her dreams crashing back. She knew from his air of mystery that this sudden dinner invitation could only mean one thing.

Her next call was to Josette.

"Eet eez always a new story," Josette said, and laughed, graciously waving off Elle's repeated thank-yous for taking her without an appointment.

"Warner's taking me to dinner tonight!" Elle was beaming.

"I knew eet was Warner." The manicurist smiled, one eye fluttering into a coquette's wink. "Ees eet a special occasion?"

"You bet it is." Elle nodded. "Josette . . ." She paused. "I think . . . In spite of myself, I'm hoping he'll come back to me tonight. For good."

Josette arched her eyebrow. "Eesn't there a woman already his fiancée?"

"I think it's over," Elle admitted. "He called me and said he had to see me alone. He said he's been thinking over his life, and he's making some changes. He wants to tell me about them at dinner."

Elle's enthusiasm didn't quite convince Josette. "Are you sure that's what he means?"

Elle nodded eagerly. "He was totally mysterious, but he hinted at it, you know? He's reserving a Huntington table for two! That's exactly what he said," she gushed, launching the hand Josette had finished into a victory sign of two shining fingernails. "Two. Two Huntingtons, but not Sarah. Finally, it's Warner and Elle."

CHAPTER FORTY-TWO

ELLE idled in her parking space, pondering the mechanics of car energy. "If I turn it off but leave the CD player on, that drains the battery. But I'll probably be asphyxiated soon if I sit in here any longer." She surveyed the dark interior of the parking garage and turned the engine off.

She peeked at her watch again, annoyed at its holding pattern. It had been 7:30 last time she checked, and was only 7:32 now—7:33 if she looked down from the top of her hand at an angle, but that was cheating. Elle checked her lipstick in the vanity mirror.

"One more song," she decided, and flipped the Styx CD to "Babe," a song she loved when in love. "You know it's *you, babe,*" Elle sang blissfully, ranging far from the tune. Singing had never been her strength.

She finished her operetta and sat again in the quiet, warmly envisioning a link that defied circumstance, a reunion stronger for the separation. In her heart, she had waited for Warner, never losing faith. He was her Velveteen Rabbit, finally opening his eyes to love's constancy. She breathed deeply, dreaming of their future.

Deciding that fifteen minutes satisfied the feminine necessity of tardiness, Elle entered the low-lit restaurant. Her silver Gucci mules clicked quietly but steadily with each hasty step, an apology ready on her lips to console her waiting date. "Huntington, table for two," she beamed to the maître d'.

"Yes, madam," he crooned, leading Elle to an empty table. She was oblivious of the admiring stares taking in her beauty and her silver metal-mesh dress with plunging neckline and green rhinestone straps.

"Would you care for something to drink while you wait?" He motioned to a server.

Elle sighed, downcast. She ordered mineral water, gazing uninterestedly at the menu. Warner had beaten her at the delay game, so he started with the upper hand.

"Elle!" Warner rushed to the table just as her drink arrived. She didn't stand to greet him. "Hello, Warner," she nodded, feigning indifference. He leaned around the table to kiss her cheek.

"I'm sorry I'm late. Traffic was heavy," Warner said with a shrug. As if she hadn't driven in the same.

"I just sat down, don't worry." Elle sipped her water nonchalantly. But her eyes defied her attempt at composure, shining with delight.

"You look beautiful"—he reached for her hand—"as always."

Elle smiled. "Thanks." She stirred the ice around her drink, chasing the lime about with the red plastic straw, apprehending it finally with a poke. Winning lines she had rehearsed in the car emptied from her mind as if through a sieve. "It's been too long," she attempted.

"Definitely," Warner agreed, opening the menu. "Much too long. I'm starved."

Elle turned to her own menu and commented stupidly on the range of appetizers. She felt like cornering him, asking what this was all about. *Don't push him.*

Warner motioned to the server to bring a wine list. "It's great to see you, Elle. It's so nice to get together again."

"It's wonderful." Elle smiled eagerly. Nothing had changed after all.

Elle began chatting about the Vandermark case, asking Warner politely about his research. He frowned, waving his hand to dismiss the topic. "Elle, you never did care about that stuff."

Elle retreated. She had spent such energy on Brooke's case, thinking that she and Warner would have that, at least, in common.

"But, Warner, I care about it now. I've become totally involved in this case."

"You're full of surprises, Elle." Warner laughed. "How about this for a surprise . . . I'll have a steak tonight. And rare!" He beckoned for a waiter and ordered a red wine without consulting her.

"But you always have it rare." Elle squinted, puzzled. " 'I want something that took its last breath in the kitchen,' " she imitated Warner's old line.

"Elle, you're right," Warner smiled. "It has been too long. God, I haven't said that in ages. I forgot . . . I guess you wouldn't know. I hardly ever eat red meat anymore."

"Since when?" Elle arched one eyebrow suspiciously.

Warner hid behind the menu, playing embarrassed. "You'll laugh. . . . I've been a different man lately. Sarah says red meat is bad for my heart, you know, so when I'm with her I never eat it anymore."

"Sarah's bad for your heart," Elle said. She shook the ice in her glass, more angry than nervous.

"Ha-ha, you've got me there," said Warner, winking. When he saw her disappointment, his tone dropped and he spoke seriously.

"Okay, Elle, I've let a lot of things change me. It took me a while to notice it myself. I thought I had to grow up, you know, into this new life. But I caught myself!

"See, I took a look around," he continued, "at what I was becoming . . . no, at what I was letting myself become." At that Warner shook his head abruptly, and his grin returned. "No more, though, baby: I'm a new man. A new, steak-eating man."

"How daring," Elle muttered, not loud enough to be heard.

The server arrived and poured wine for Warner to sample. "I've had it before." He motioned for the man to keep pouring. "Anyway, Elle's the epicure. Let the lady taste it, please."

Obligingly, the server handed a sharply fluted glass to Elle, who sipped and nodded her approval. Red, as if he didn't know she would have chicken or fish. She scanned the menu hastily for tomato-based pasta.

"I think a toast is in order," Warner said as he hoisted his brimming glass.

"Allow me," Elle agreed. "To the old Warner. The old, steak-eating, USC golden boy." With his USC golden girl, she added mentally.

"I'll drink to that." Warner clinked Elle's glass. "In solidarity."

Elle smiled shyly. "To Poland?"

"To what?" Warner set his glass on the table and squinted at Elle, not sure if he had heard her right. "Oh, right," he chortled, toasting anew. "Why not? Here's to Poland."

Elle frowned, unsatisfied.

"I mean it, Elle." Warner spoke naturally, soft with instinctive charm. "Since I've seen you again, through this in-

ternship, and around school . . . it's made me think about
the things we used to do, when we were together."

Elle sighed, her tender eyes anchored to Warner. "Warner,
I think about it all the time. Things were good back then.
Why . . ." She trailed off, shook the crimson pool of wine
like brandy in her glass, wondering why Warner had left
her last spring.

" 'Why' is right," Warner agreed with a hearty nod.
"Why, just because we checked ourselves into law school,
why should anything be different?"

" 'Checked in,' " Elle repeated. "That's the way to describe it. It's a madhouse, law school. A regular cuckoo's
nest."

"Elle, that's what makes you so lovable. Your charm is
that you'll never change. You're a homecoming queen, even
among toads. I didn't know what to think when you showed
up at registration. It was so . . . unlikely." Warner smiled,
gazing at Elle's captivated face.

"Man. I couldn't bear to see you waste . . . what you've
got"—he dropped his gaze beneath her eyes—"at a dull
place like Stanford. Law school can suck the life out of you,
Elle. And you were always so full of life."

"Warner," Elle gushed, "oh, I know. I *know*. I felt the
same way about you. Your films! Remember how you directed documentaries? Remember Vegas?" She paused, tracing patterns on the tablecloth with her fork. "You had such
joie de vivre. Then one day"—her eyes narrowed—"you
just traded it all in." She imagined Warner buying Sarah a
toaster, and shuddered.

Warner reached for her hand. "Elle, you've known me
better than anyone. What you say about me . . ." He drew
back, shaking his head with self-reproach. "Elle, it's true. I
bought into this law school routine. I put other things . . .

more important things . . . on the shelf. But I'm not going to live that way anymore, and I guess I should thank you."

Elle gasped, blushing. She waited for the words she dreamed Warner would say, wondering whether he had taken the Rock back from Sarah, or maybe gotten another ring for now. She was too excited to speak.

"Maybe that doesn't make sense." Warner hesitated, releasing her hand. "I'd like to think I would have come around even if you weren't in law school, but I don't know. It doesn't matter. It was you who made the difference. Seeing you just be yourself, *my* Elle from college, the calendar girl . . . taking the same exams as anyone else." He smiled. "Elle, you've taught me a lesson."

"What do you mean?" she prodded, thinking he had gotten a little off track.

Warner laughed. "I mean you haven't changed, Elle. And you shouldn't, and neither should I, just because of law school. It's a damn degree, that's all. Everything can be just the way it was before."

"Oh, Warner," Elle cried, "I've wanted so much to hear you say that!"

"I know, Elle. I can't believe it took me this long." He reached under the table, fishing for something. "I should have realized this when I first saw you at Stanford." Warner stood up suddenly, reaching deep into his pocket.

Elle shivered, knowing what moment was at hand. "Warner, thank God, you're back!"

"Listen, Elle, the old Warner *is* back. What was important to me before law school is important to me again. No matter what Sarah says." He pulled his hand from his pocket and sat back down, resting his fist, clenched, upon the table.

Elle gasped as Warner's fist opened with a flourish. She expected the Rock! Instead, two white golf tees spilled onto the tablecloth.

"I played golf in college, and I'm going to make time for it again. Law school or no law school. I don't care *what* Sarah says," Warner stated firmly, sitting back with satisfaction.

Elle gaped in shock at the golf tees. She stared at Warner for a moment, then shot from her chair, almost upending it. "Ladies' room," she explained, forcing a smile. Warner shrugged, and was glad to see his steak arriving. Elle managed to stifle her tears only until the bathroom door closed behind her.

Elle replayed the voice mail that directed her to the office of Kohn & Siglery in San Francisco. Chutney Vandermark was to be deposed at 10:30 that morning. It was the last deposition scheduled before the will probate proceeding.

"Sorry I can't drive over with you, Elle," Christopher Miles said. "Try to meet me there a little early, around ten."

Elle looked at her watch and jumped from her seat, which was a tubular creation, more artful than cozy. She caught her knee beneath the desk and winced.

Drawing back, Elle rubbed her knee and noticed a small run in her nylons. "Great," she said, reaching for her purse. She didn't have time to change, and she didn't want Chutney to see her lugging binders around with a run in her hose, like a harried proletarian. She'd disgrace the Delta Gamma house.

In her emptied bag she found only Chanel's nearly black blue polish, an annoyingly trendy purchase that she never should have made, and "Pink Alert," which she kept in her bag to touch up her manicure. A woman should always carry clear nail polish for these blunders.

She hobbled to Mia's desk, careful not to put stress on her right leg and lengthen the run. "Mia," she pleaded, "tell me you have some clear nail polish."

Mia opened the drawer of her desk and began removing its contents. Behind the pink and green Great Lash mascara and a blue jar of Nivea moisturizing cream, Mia grabbed a nail polish and brandished it happily. "Ultra Glaze Nail Enamel," she said with a smile, but Elle's heart dropped when she saw the bottle's color.

"Mauve-black. That won't work," she sighed.

"Sorry, it's all I've got." Mia shrugged.

"That's okay," Elle said. "I guess I could dot it with mauve. At least I'd match."

"I'd just leave it," Mia advised, leaning over to assess the damage. "You don't want a big spot there." Elle's nylons were white, and either course was a bad one.

"I've got clear polish, Elle, if you want to borrow it." Elle heard Sarah's voice behind her and turned around with surprise.

"It's in my office," Sarah offered simply. She started down the hall and motioned with her hand for Elle to follow her.

She walked meekly behind Sarah into her office, where she was prepared with a bottle of nail polish in her top drawer. "I keep it in here," Sarah said. "I should keep an extra pair of nylons, too, for the really bad runs."

Elle smiled in agreement. "Those horrible ones that rip down your leg before you know what hit you," she laughed. "They're the worst." She took the nail polish from Sarah's hand and stretched her leg out across the arm rest of a chair to determine the best place to paint.

"I've had some like cartoons, I swear." Sarah smiled. "Like those cartoons where somebody catches a sweater by its thread and runs away and the whole thing unravels?"

Elle paused, tapping the bottle against her hand to shake it.

"I don't know why we have to wear these silly things,

anyway," she muttered, balancing on one heel while dotting her knee with Sarah's nail polish. "I mean, the old ladies wear them to hide their varicose veins. But when you're young, what's the point?"

"Maybe because your shoes would hurt otherwise." Sarah shrugged.

"You're right," Elle said, glancing at Sarah. "Which raises the question of these painful shoes."

"I don't wear heels that narrow," Sarah replied. "I don't know how you can even stand in them."

"Slave to fashion," Elle said, noticing Sarah's steady Ferragamo pumps and considering that she might have a point. Neither spoke for a minute as Elle waited for the polish to harden.

"I've gotta run," Elle said as she stood to leave.

"I'll say, but it's not such a bad one now."

Elle turned around to look with surprise at Warner's serious fiancée suddenly turned punster. "Yeah, thanks to you," she said and grinned, then left in a rush.

"You're welcome," Sarah said quietly.

Elle hesitated.

"Elle, will you wait a minute?" Sarah asked suddenly, gathering her papers. "I'm on my way too. Christopher asked me to go to the deposition."

Elle waited at the entrance to Sarah's office while Sarah grabbed a highlighted street map from her shiny briefcase. Unclipping from the map a sheet that had directions scribbled on it, Sarah frowned.

"I hope the office isn't too hard to find," she said, hurrying toward the hall where Elle stood.

Elle glanced down at the floor. She turned and started to walk away, then turned back as if she had remembered something.

"I know where it is," Elle said quietly, not looking at Sarah.

Sarah didn't respond.

"I'll give you a ride over." Elle shrugged her shoulders, insecure at having made the offer. "If you want." Elle bit her lip and glanced uncertainly at the brunette.

Sarah turned her attention to the Brooks Brothers button on her navy blazer, which she fastened and unfastened. "That would be nice," she said. "I don't really know my way around the city yet."

Elle tossed her hair behind her shoulders and walked ahead. "Let's go, then," she said, waving for Sarah to follow her.

On the drive over, Elle found out that not all of the interns were attending the deposition.

"Warner's preparing witness books," Sarah said, sensing Elle's silent question. "It's just you and me," she added.

"His loss," Elle said sarcastically, turning up the stereo.

Chutney Vandermark was extremely well coached, so the deposition was an exercise in futility. She would not reply to a question without first turning for a nod or motion from her lawyer, Henry Kohn, and even then she mumbled terse replies under her breath. Several times the stenographer, who was straining to hear her, had to ask Chutney to repeat herself. She balked even when Christopher Miles asked her for background facts about her education, scowling and behaving like a spoiled child. Most of the time she sat sullenly with her arms crossed.

During one of the several breaks in which Chutney asked to "be excused to the hallway to consult with counsel," Christopher Miles left to check his messages. Elle sat alone in the room with Sarah.

"She seems really upset," Sarah said, finally breaking the heavy silence. "I can't imagine what it must have been like. She actually found his body." Sarah quivered, dropping her gaze to the floor.

Elle studied her fingernails for a minute, then shook her head in a sharp motion. "She's not crying."

"No, she's not," Sarah agreed. "Poor thing, she seems bewildered. I bet she's just shocked, losing her father like that. She found his body! Can you imagine?"

"No," Elle admitted, "but still, I expected her to cry." She paused, wrinkling her face, unsatisfied. "So she was working out at the gym and then home taking a shower when it happened." Elle traced on her legal pad and spoke rather absently, repeated these facts as if to herself. "Must have happened awfully fast."

"Yeah," Sarah agreed. "God, I bet he was still bleeding. Can you picture that?"

"No," Elle said, shaking with a cold shudder. "No, I really can't. It must have been horrible."

Christopher Miles reentered the room and pulled his interns aside.

"We've got a transcript," he said, glancing at the stenographer to make sure he was off the record, "so you don't have to take everything down. Listen"—he dropped his voice to a whisper—"take note on her demeanor. Her motions, where she pauses, that sort of thing. The transcript won't pick that up. Record anything that strikes you as odd. It'll give me an idea where to go on cross-examination. Right now," he muttered, "I wouldn't know where to start."

The lawyer shook his head and returned to the table across from Chutney's seat, hunching his shoulders in a weary slouch.

Tapping heels in the hallway announced Chutney's return. Straightening, Christopher checked his watch and motioned to Henry Kohn as he stepped into the room with the solemn girl at his elbow.

"Henry." Christopher stood up, smiling with light charisma and confidence. "Thanks for your patience. We'll only be another fifteen minutes or so. I've got just about everything I need."

CHAPTER FORTY-THREE

WHEN Christopher Miles was alone with Brooke in the room set aside for witness prep, his famously calm sea of patience burst as if through a dam.

"They will crucify you with this . . . with this so-called alibi of yours," he said angrily, slamming her deposition with his open hand.

She stared at the lawyer silently.

"Jesus, Brooke, why do you have to make this so difficult? Do you know how close you came to spending your twenty-fourth birthday making license plates?"

"Thanks for getting me out on bail," Brooke sighed, eyes fixed on the floor. "I hated that place." She paused, then glanced up sorrowfully at the baffled lawyer. "I didn't do it, Christopher, I told you," she protested. "Poor Heyworth was . . ." she choked, wiping her eyes. "I found him on the floor, lying there, and blood everywhere." Brooke hid her face in her hands, shaking, unable to continue.

"Brooke," Christopher repeated with frustration, "if you could just tell me who was at that meeting, I'll move for a continuance. You don't seem to understand how serious this is. You have no witnesses, Brooke. None. Nobody can corroborate what you say. You will lose everything that's yours under his will, and unless you plead to a lesser charge, your chances—"

Brooke rose from her chair, indignant. "I *will not* plead to anything. I *did not do it*. Don't you see? I can't rat on the support group, I mean . . . we swore, you know? These people have an addiction. They were the only people who helped me get my life together. Christopher, I have an *attic* full of Norman Rockwell plates and china figurines and music boxes, synthetic rugs, juicers. . . . I spent almost one hundred thousand dollars and hours and hours of my life just to hear those gentle voices take my orders. The Home Shopping Network has turned people's lives upside down like that, and Shopper Stoppers came together for help. I can't turn on them."

"Brooke." The lawyer shook his head wearily. "We've been over this ground before. They'd understand. . . . Anyone would understand."

"No." She sat back down. "Please, why can't I just tell the truth? Why won't anyone believe me? Heyworth was the sweetest soul. I'd never lift a finger against him. He was my husband, and nobody understands that I really loved him." She stared past Christopher, crying softly. "I lost my husband. I saw him dead, horribly, viciously murdered. . . ." Her voice trailed off and the room was still.

"I believe you, Brooke," he said. "I do believe you. I was only trying to prepare you for what I know will happen if you testify. They'll string you up, Brooke. You have to understand that if you don't give more information about where you were when your husband was murdered"—he paused gravely—"I might be the only one who believes you. And your inheritance will go to Chutney, or to one of his other wives."

"Ex-wives," Brooke corrected. "But why? I don't get it. His will left everything to me. I know, he showed it to me.

He cut that daughter of his right out when he changed his will. 'Chutney will grow up,' he said, 'when she has to earn something.' "

Christopher began pacing again, going over the facts in his own mind. "He didn't do it very well, Brooke. His will leaves his fortune to his 'most beautiful wife.' Not to Brooke Vandermark."

"He called *me* that!" Brooke exclaimed. " 'Hello, my most beautiful wife,' " she impersonated. "Oh, Christopher, he just wrote it that way to be *romantic*."

"Well, there's a regular beauty contest outside of former Mrs. Vandermarks who think they fit the bill, Brooke." Christopher threw his hands up in despair.

"If Heyworth knew that, he would turn in his grave." Brooke scowled.

"This case could be the end of an illustrious career," the lawyer muttered, already imagining the headlines. He sighed with fatigue, picking up his notes to walk Brooke through her doomed testimony.

Sarah chatted nervously with Warner, glancing at the crowd of hostile ex–Mrs. Vandermarks who were primping in compact mirrors to avoid speaking to one another. "Some first case," she remarked.

"Yeah," he responded. "Looks grim." He searched the courtroom for Elle, who had not arrived yet. "Wonder where Elle is."

Sarah had noticed Warner "wondering" about Elle a lot and was not oblivious of the fact that when it wasn't Elle, he would still wonder about and wander toward other women. She felt weighted down by the Rock.

Cari shuffled papers importantly as she entered the courtroom, escorted by an especially morbid, black-suited Michael. She took her seat next to the other interns, leaving empty chairs at either end of the long table. Michael sat in the gallery amid a growing mass of Stanford law students whom the judge had allowed to sit in on the hearing. Judge Carol Morgan had closed her courtroom to the media but had permitted students to watch the proceeding for its educational value.

Mr. Heigh, characteristically sharing the experience with his wife, had arrived a full hour early to get a front seat. Mrs. Heigh had packed a lunch for them to share consisting of her famous sprout-and-pickle sandwiches, which she had reluctantly agreed to leave with the bailiff.

Fran was seated with John Matthews, complaining about the "false consciousness" that led Heyworth's lineup of ex-wives to paint "tribal sex indicators" on their cheeks and lips.

Sidney had snuck in a Nintendo Game Boy, making him the envy of Aaron and Doug, who sat on either side of him. They had to be satisfied to peer over Sidney's shoulder and participate as voyeurs, sitting behind him twitching their fingers on imaginary electronic buttons.

Claire and Ben sat together arranging a sign-up sheet for refreshments at the "Welcome to *Law Review*" party.

A. Lawrence Hesterton leafed through the *New York Review of Books*, tapping his foot idly. Gramm Hallman and Drew Drexler, seated with Larry toward the back of the courtroom, were engaged in a rapid, eager discussion of the Spanish Succession and how it compared to the English War of the Roses. Neither had the least bit of interest in what the other was saying, but both were happy to corner a willing ear for their thesis-topic expertise.

Elle surveyed the ragtag crowd of spectators, trying to decide where Eugenia could tolerably sit. She found a seat close to the front.

As Eugenia left to take a seat, Henry Kohn entered the courtroom. The confident lawyer strode to his table, opened a briefcase, and began removing stacks of files. Chutney followed her lawyer and took her seat behind him. She seemed apprehensive, nervously twisting a strand of chemically enhanced hair around her finger as she glanced at her mother sitting behind her.

"Mother," Chutney greeted stiffly.

"Please, call me Emerald. You're looking well, Chutney."

"That's not a compliment, Mother. That's a second opinion." Chutney turned her back on her mother, who sat near the end of the painted group.

Wittingly or unwittingly, the women had assembled chronologically in order of their marriages. Elle surveyed the troupe and decided they should be the first women to appear on *Fashion Crimes*, with charges ranging from reckless accessorizing to excessive use of cosmetic force.

Chutney's mother, now Emerald Vandermark-Klein-Tearston-Allen-Meyers, was an artful self-made social climber. If she remarried, Emerald could pull into a tie with six-wife Heyworth.

Like windup dolls gone wrong, Chutney and Emerald, equally high-strung and difficult, avoided looking at each other. Objectionable first names were not all that Emerald and Chutney had in common. Heyworth's third wife looked exactly like Chutney, though neither would admit it.

Beyond their achingly auburn mall-girl perms, both she and Chutney wore the signature ski-jump noses of Dr. Binky Blass, but on Emerald the pert nose of a teenager merely highlighted the taut, weary compression of the rest of her features. A fortune spent on surgeries fought years of wearying failed marriages for control of Emerald's tight-as-a-trampoline face, and science had failed comically.

Nor was Emerald the only ex-Vandermark guilty of compulsive surgical attempts to imprison her youth. It looked as if Heyworth's wives would rather repeatedly face the surgeon's knife than face gravity. Heyworth's first wife, now Dawn Vandermark-Kirkland-Schaffer-Price, stared fastidiously into her compact, caking whitish powder onto her nearly translucent skin. With jet-black hair, ghostlike skin, and bloodred lips, the woman was a dead ringer for Snow White's wicked stepmother.

Whitney Vandermark-Warren-Sands, Heyworth's second wife, had the sole distinction of a successful remarriage. "Three's a charm," Whitney sniped at Chutney's mother.

"No, dear. Bad things come in threes," Emerald responded.

Ignoring Emerald's remark, Whitney adjusted the aggressive squared shoulders of her blazer. Her silver eye shadow was ferociously applied: when combined with the flaming magenta of her cheeks and lips, Whitney was the apparition of a maniacal clown.

Heyworth's fourth wife, Sonia Vandermark, appeared to be suffering from spandorexia. Her purple spandex cat suit left nothing to the imagination. Along with her tawdry jewelry, she had clearly overplayed her hand.

Heyworth's fifth wife, Angela Vandermark, was a drastic contrast to the spandex stunner beside her. Pointedly simple in a Talbots dress and polished Ferragamo loafers, the Atherton suburbanite suggested Heyworth's rebound marriage.

Elle took the empty seat at the end of the table directly across from Brooke, who looked pale, tired, and diminutive in the oversize courtroom chairs. Elle leafed through the pink pages of her legal pad to avoid looking at Warner.

Satisfied with the layout of his paperwork, Mr. Kohn approached the bench to speak with Christopher Miles.

CHAPTER FORTY-FOUR

AFTER consulting with the lawyers, Judge Morgan pounded her gavel to call the court to order. "In the matter of Estate of Heyworth Vandermark." She peered at the stenographer, who nodded to indicate that he was ready.

"First, petitioner's motion to consolidate claims for relief is denied. The instant proceeding decides only the validity of the Vandermark will entered as Exhibit A. Without objection, so ordered." The gathering of lawyers at the bench murmured but dispersed without filing any objection.

"You aren't going to object?" Chutney said loudly enough for Henry Kohn to hear. "What am I paying you for? I could have done that for free!"

"So ordered." The judge glared at Chutney, but did not comment on her outburst. "I'll recess for five minutes or so to allow you"—she indicated the lawyers behind Henry Kohn—"to explain to your clients that they are free to leave today if they'd like. If I don't admit the will to probate, we'll evaluate their claims at that stage."

The Vandermark vultures blinked like dazzled Christmas trees, stammering, demanding explanations from their attorneys.

"A five-minute recess is ordered." With another pound of the gavel, the judge turned to depart for her chambers. Elle crowded with the other interns around Christopher Miles to find out what had happened.

"That ruling is standard," he explained to the students. "In an uncontested situation, the court may consolidate petitions for relief. The lawyers for the Mrs. Vandermark pageant over there"—Elle giggled as she glanced at a petulant few arguing with their attorneys—"made a routine motion to consolidate their claims. They wanted Judge Morgan to combine the estate administration with today's will probate proceeding."

Sarah scribbled notes as if Christopher were planning to quiz the interns on these facts at the next recess. Cari, who had researched several issues of procedure, nodded vigorously to show that she understood. "Today we're only concerned with the Slayer Statute, then," Cari announced. "Whether the will is to be enforced as written, or whether the judge will throw it out, since it leaves everything to the slayer."

Christopher scowled and glanced over his shoulder. "To the *alleged* slayer."

Cari gulped. "Didn't I say 'alleged'? I meant 'alleged.'"

"Warner, can I have that witness list?" Warner sifted through document files on the desk while Christopher returned to his explanation of the court's ruling. "Probate is a relatively informal proceeding. The judge has discretion to combine all matters of interpretation, appointment of a personal representative, and distribution of assets in one proceeding. She might still do it today, if they renew their motion after her decision on whether the will stands."

Elle glanced at an uproar that was taking place between Chutney's mother and her lawyer, who were leaving the courtroom to confer out in the hallway. "Wait, Christopher." She waved her hand to get his attention. "I'm not sure I get all this." Elle tilted her head to indicate the hubbub of quarreling women.

Sarah rolled her eyes and sighed with obvious exasperation. During the internship and their tutoring sessions she had seen how quickly Elle caught on when something was explained to her. She had gained a certain respect for Elle, watching her work, but she wasn't about to show it in front of Warner. "Elle, please, can we have the remedial class some other time?" She smiled condescendingly at Warner, who ignored her.

Frowning briefly at Sarah, Christopher turned to Elle, who, knowing exactly what Sarah was doing, ignored her completely. "What is it you don't understand, Elle?"

"Okay," Elle began. "The only question for today, in the, um, probate part . . ." She hesitated, glancing at Christopher for confirmation. He nodded. "The question is whether Brooke did it. Whether she shot him. Right? And if the judge thinks she did, then she throws out the will, and then the estate is distributed by, um, you know, by statute."

"By intestacy," Christopher clarified. "Right. If the judge finds that Brooke feloniously and intentionally killed Heyworth."

"And if the judge believes Brooke, then we have to deal with the will. Like, what it means, that he left everything to his most beautiful wife, but not exactly to Brooke by name."

Cari tapped a Bic pen on her legal pad, impatient. "Thanks for the recap, Elle," she scoffed.

"No, wait, that's not my question." Elle frowned. "Those women, the ex-wives . . . which side are they on?"

"What do you mean, which side?"

"Well, do they get anything under the intestacy statute, even though they're divorced?"

"Chutney's mother would," answered the lawyer, "by law. A one-third share goes automatically to a former spouse who had children by the decedent. The rest of the wives didn't bear Heyworth any kids, so their arguments will all be equitable claims, based on their contributions during marriage to the estate. Those are mushy, unlikely to win."

"So they're on Brooke's side, then," Elle concluded. "I mean, sort of. They want the will to be valid."

"Well, that's true, Elle, but if the will is valid then they're out of her corner. Then we have to deal with the words Heyworth used to bequeath his estate." The lawyer sighed, frustrated. "If he had just said 'wife,' that would mean Brooke, his wife at the time of his death. But thanks to Heyworth's fancy description, we've got a beauty pageant of spouses who say he meant to refer to them."

Warner handed Christopher the lengthy witness list just as Judge Morgan reentered the courtroom. "Thanks. Sarah, get those witness books in the order of names on this list, please. Right here." He pointed to the desk. "Cari, do you have that brief on the Slayer Statute?"

Judge Morgan's gavel called the court to order. Sidney's beeping Game Boy subsided as the room grew quiet. Elle turned anxiously to look for Eugenia, who gave her a thumbs-up from the third row.

The day looked to be a grim one for Brooke, judging from the testimony of Thom Romeo, the first witness called by Chutney's lawyer. Brooke's personal trainer, Thomas Romero, had dropped his first name, going only by his changed last name, Romeo, after his first victory as Mr. Muscle Beach. As much of Romeo's body as was visible was stained with a greasy surface tan so thick Elle wondered if he'd leave an orange ring on the seat. He had rolled up his sleeves to display his bulging forearms, and Elle marveled that the gym rat even owned a pair of long pants. Most likely he usually wore only an indecent Speedo.

Romeo described his regular house calls to the Vandermarks' basement spa, where he sculpted Brooke's body with exhausting weight tortures and had recently begun coaching Heyworth. When Henry Kohn asked him to describe Heyworth's workouts, Romeo's deep voice boomed low and ominous.

"Heyworth Vandermark told me Brooke was going to kill him. Like a stuck pig."

It wasn't until Christopher Miles's cross-examination that the full story was revealed. Before Heyworth took up jog-walking, more to thwart his cardiologist than for his health, the old man had agreed to undergo various tests of his body's fat content.

One such morning, while Heyworth was wrenching with fat-measurement devices poking him at every angle, Brooke popped into the weight room to check on him. Groaning, Heyworth complained to Romeo that Brooke was going to kill him like a stuck pig. So Brooke's beleaguered husband had only been chafing under Romeo's fitness tortures.

Henry Kohn insisted that Brooke's physical persecution of her husband went "to motive." Images of a contorted, miserable Heyworth begging for mercy in the weight room cut the heart out of Christopher's argument that Brooke had encouraged exercise to prolong her husband's life. A crafty move, the lawyer had to concede, crossing Romeo off the short list of witnesses he planned to call on direct.

After Henry Kohn called the mailman, Judge Morgan drew the line. The parade of doomsayers, whose collective antipathy toward Brooke had established that she was a meddlesome terror to work for, had become tedious. Henry

Kohn's repeated assurances that "it goes to motive" were growing increasingly far-fetched.

Carmen Marisca, the heavyset cook who had worked in the Vandermark home for twelve years before Brooke fired her, testified that Brooke tried to starve her husband to death with recipes from Oprah's cookbook. Insisting that a man could not survive on dishes prepared from Gerber baby food, Carmen snuck Heyworth desserts on the sly. The ruse ended when Brooke found Moon Pies in her kitchen. She replaced Carmen with a chef from Olaf's Organic Garden.

Neither the gardener, the cat trainer, nor the florist had a kind word for Brooke. Without supporting evidence, the florist claimed Brooke had been pricing funeral bouquets just prior to Heyworth's death. On cross-examination, he admitted that she hadn't exactly *priced* the RIP arrangement, merely *eyed* it, but he could tell what was on her mind. Christopher Miles didn't even get the word "speculation" out of his mouth before Judge Morgan sustained his objection.

The mailman wore his dress blues to emphasize that he was, in some manner, a representative of the United States of America. He described mountains of Heyworth's letters piling up untouched in the mailbox, a dilemma that forced him to brave the landscaper's trenches and deliver door-to-door. Brooke picked up her own catalogs, but left her husband's mail to rot, the mailman said, glowering, "as if he were already dead."

Holding that further testimony from the veterinarian who treated Chutney's Persian cat, which was in Brooke's home and care during the time she was married to Heyworth, would be "cumulative, if even conceivably relevant," Judge Morgan ordered a recess.

* * *

Elle encountered Warner alone in the hallway. "Elle, how's it going?" He waved to call her over.

"Well, terrible, if you're Brooke." She shrugged with fatigue. "She hasn't exactly *endeared* herself to the community. And the worst is yet to come. Henry still has to call Chutney." Elle groaned in dread of Chutney's eyewitness tale.

"Do you have a minute?" Warner motioned toward the witness room. Elle nodded, following him curiously. He shut the door behind them.

"What's up, Warner?"

"Elle, I don't know, it's been so weird to see you," he pointed, "all suited up like this. And asking these legal questions, these *basic* questions."

Elle frowned. "What do you mean, 'basic'?"

He approached her more delicately. "Elle, for God's sake. You're so creative, remember all the jewelry stuff you used to be into? I don't know . . . are you even keeping up?"

"What do you mean, Warner?" Elle retorted. Her stare was sharp, pointed. "What about all that you said at dinner?" She recounted his words bitterly, all to Warner's quiet acknowledgment.

"Remember?" she goaded, desperate to shake any response from his terrible silence. "Remember how you were so impressed, seeing me in law school, but not caving? Not blending into this horrible herd? 'Being *yourself*'?" Elle imitated Warner's low voice. She sneered as if swallowing something acidic. "What about that, Warner?"

"Get over yourself, Elle." Warner ended the barrage of questions. "That had to do with me, not you." He glared at her, annoyed. She suddenly realized she had had the effect of raising self-doubts within him. He hadn't asked her to come to law school, to make trouble for him. Elle lost her patience with him. With the whole situation. She had more important things and people to think about.

"Take your own advice and get over *yourself,* Warner. I certainly have." Elle turned and began walking away from him.

He grabbed her shoulder and tried what he thought was a flattering approach. "Elle, listen, this law school thing is ridiculous for you. I mean, let's face it. Who are you trying to impress? Really, women like Sarah, *they* go to law school. They *belong* in law school. Come on, do you really see yourself as a lawyer?"

"Maybe." She eyed Warner with suspicion. "Why do you think I came to law school?"

"Uh, maybe on a whim?" Warner laughed at his own joke. "Really, Elle, you came because I was here. Listen, you told me that much yourself at Halloween. Don't let your memory get so selective."

"I got the same internship as you, Warner Huntington," Elle spat. "And as your precious Sarah. What makes you think I'm not as *serious?*"

Warner smiled at Elle, who grew more and more livid with his mocking tone. "Elle, I have something to say to you."

"Say anything you want to, Warner. You're the only one who's listening."

With that, she turned toward the courtroom and followed Christopher inside.

Henry Kohn practically skipped into the courtroom, tasting blood already. The only remaining witnesses were Brooke and Chutney. "Your Honor," he began after Judge Morgan gaveled to recommence the hearing, "May it please the court, I call Brooke Vandermark to the stand."

Brooke swore her oath and sat glaring sullenly in Chutney's direction.

"Brooke"—Elle noticed Henry was licking his lips—"tell the court where you were at the approximate time of day, about four in the afternoon, when your husband was murdered."

Brooke glanced at Christopher, who pleaded desperately with his eyes. "I was out of the house. I was at a meeting. And it's Mrs. Vandermark to you," she snapped at the lawyer.

"Mrs. Vandermark." Henry smiled inappropriately. "What meeting, Mrs. Vandermark, was that?"

She tilted her head, annoyed. "You know what meeting it was. I told you already," Brooke hissed. Christopher Miles dropped his head into his hands, wondering why he bothered with witness prep.

Henry Kohn paced toward the bench. "Your Honor, for the record, there was no outside communication with the witness. She refers to her deposition, I believe."

Judge Morgan peered at Brooke. "When did you tell Mr. Kohn about this meeting, Mrs. Vandermark?"

Brooke whirled around to face the judge. "At that thing they dragged me to, with all the lawyers. They had someone taking notes," she accused the stenographer, "like him."

"At your deposition?" the judge clarified.

"Yeah, that."

Henry Kohn swooped back toward Brooke like a bird of prey. "Please tell the court, Mrs. Vandermark, about this . . . meeting."

Brooke heaved a weary sigh. "Okay, for the hundredth time, I was at my support group." She peeked furtively at the crowd of Stanford spectators. "Shopper Stoppers Anonymous."

Elle heard a yelp from the gallery that she was sure came from Sidney. Other chuckles were quickly muffled as Judge Morgan glared forward, then turned back to Brooke.

"Shopper Stoppers Anonymous," Chutney's lawyer said, surpressing his own smile with effort. "I take it, Mrs. Vandermark, that this group helped you with some sort of problem . . . associated with the Home Shopping Network."

"Not a problem, a *dependency*," Brooke corrected. "I was addicted to the thing, okay? I was totally attached to those people, the shopper-helpers, the ones who took your orders," she rambled, as if opening a twelve-step sob story. "Heyworth was always so busy, and I used to order all these things, sometimes just to talk to the shopper-helpers. They have the gentlest, sweetest way about them. . . ." She trailed off dreamily.

"This addiction filled, then, an emotional void in your life? In your marriage?"

"Objection, Your Honor." Christopher Miles rose from his chair. "Pure speculation."

"Sustained." Judge Morgan scowled at Henry Kohn. "What's the relevance of Brooke's . . . addiction, Counsel?"

"It goes to motive, Your Honor. Her commitment to the Home Shopping Network is evidence that her marriage to Heyworth was emotionally unfulfilling, and—"

"That's not true!" Brooke interrupted angrily. "Heyworth was everything to me, and first I started watching it to buy him things. But he didn't really seem to like the Norman Rockwell plates"—she paused sadly—"and I kept trying to watch to find something he'd like better. Then I was watching it all the time, and I even stopped going to malls."

Several Mrs. Vandermarks gasped, horrified. Chutney's mother hid her face, toying nervously with the leather tassels of a Chanel key chain. Elle glared at Henry Kohn's self-satisfied face, feeling Brooke's frustration.

"I am not convinced you have shown a link between Mrs. Vandermark's shopping habits, Counselor, and her marriage. Objection sustained. You may ask about the meeting, but only as it relates to Mrs. Vandermark's location at the time in question."

"Well, then. Mrs. Vandermark," Henry continued eagerly, "one final question about the meeting. Did you attend this . . . counseling alone?"

"No," Brooke sighed. "The rest of them were there, too. The other group members. About fifteen, maybe even twenty people, including the life leaders."

"The life leaders?" Brooke had not gone into this detail in her deposition, or even in conference with Christopher, who looked increasingly gloomy. Henry Kohn bristled, sensing a surprise attack.

"Who are the life leaders, Mrs. Vandermark?"

"That's what we call the group captains. They have the same rank as the psychiatrist—" She caught herself. "Oops, I mean, the, uh, person who runs the program. See, anyone can be a life leader who overcomes the power of their addiction, and takes charge of their life. The support group is very egalitarian. The meetings are, like, totally life-affirming. They made such a difference for me."

Henry Kohn didn't like talk of life-affirming from the supposed murderess and directed his line of questioning to the main point. "Mrs. Vandermark, can any of the life leaders, or any group member, corroborate the fact that you were in attendance on the day in question?" Henry asked the rhetorical question slowly, savoring every word.

"They could," Brooke began angrily, "and they would be here for me, I know it. We're so committed to helping each other. But, see"—she shrugged—"the thing is, I can't tell you who they are. It's anonymous, an anonymous group. We all promised to protect that."

"So I take it that you, Mrs. Vandermark, are the only person who will testify that you attended this . . . anonymous meeting? Although you claim there were ten, maybe twenty people in attendance? Is that correct, Mrs. Vandermark?"

Christopher slumped in his chair, not even bothering to object.

"Well, yeah," Brooke admitted. "I mean, I'm stuck. I have my loyalty to the group, and I won't turn on them."

"Answer the question, please, Mrs. Vandermark," directed Judge Morgan.

"He's right," Brooke said, and sighed. "I mean, yes. I'm the only one who will tell you that I was gone from the house, at my meeting." Christopher made a cutting motion against his neck, but Brooke continued, exasperated. "So you got me. There's not a soul here who will back me up. Okay?" she glared at Henry Kohn, standing up in a huff.

"Mrs. Vandermark, you haven't been excused." Judge Morgan motioned with her hand for Brooke to remain seated. "Are there any further questions, Mr. Kohn?"

"Just one, Your Honor." Henry Kohn turned to the witness. "Would you please tell the court what your license plate reads, Mrs. Vandermark?"

"Objection, irrelevant." Christopher Miles stood by reflex, staring puzzled at opposing counsel.

"Lay a foundation, Mr. Kohn."

"Your Honor, Mrs. Vandermark will testify that her license plate on her Mercedes, purchased only weeks after the death of her husband, solicits new male companionship. It goes to state of mind."

Judge Morgan narrowed her eyes into skeptical slits. "You may proceed," she allowed.

"Mrs. Vandermark, what are the letters on your license plate, please?"

"California: I-S-O S-W-M. California," Brooke added at the end, smiling at her spelling-bee imitation.

"Would you please tell the court what those letters signify?"

"Oh, everybody knows that," Brooke dismissed.

Henry Kohn turned his palms skyward in a great affected shrug. Lawyers always knew the answers to their questions.

"Oh, *excuse me,*" Brooke said sarcastically. "Anyone who reads the *personals*. The in-search-of pages, in the classifieds. ISO SWM stands for 'in search of single white male.' "

Henry Kohn arched one eyebrow, suggesting Brooke had retired her widow's veil too early. She took the wrong inference.

"I couldn't fit *'no lawyers'* on the tag," she sniped.

Christopher collapsed heavily into his seat.

Eyes glinting, Henry Kohn took pleasure in stating the obvious. "So you are, now, after the tragic death of your husband Heyworth Vandermark . . . on the market, so to speak? In the classifieds?"

Fran cleared her throat with a thunderous cough that echoed through the courtroom. Brooke cocked her head, staring coldly at Henry Kohn.

"Yes, in fact I am, as you say, 'on the market.' Not in the classifieds, just on my car. But I didn't plan to be!" She scowled at law students hiding their chuckling faces, feeling her feminine allure had been questioned.

"I'm doing my best, Mr. Kohn," Brooke explained, "to put together a new life thanks to some *sicko* who gunned down my husband." She glared at Chutney, who stared indifferently at the floor.

"And anyway, Heyworth would have wanted me to

remarry," the witness sniffed, eyes rolling to heaven as if imploring his ghost. "All he ever wanted was for me to be happy." Brooke's shoulders shook with a sob. She peered red-eyed at the judge, quivering.

"Thank you, Mrs. Vandermark, I have no further questions," cut in the lawyer, cursing himself for allowing Brooke to show tenderness.

"Your witness," he motioned to Christopher.

"Your Honor"—Christopher rose—"I'd like Mrs. Vandermark to describe what she saw when she came home from her meeting." He stepped gingerly toward Brooke. "Please," he invited, "if it's not too painful."

"I'll tell you," Brooke nodded, wiping tears from her streaky face. She breathed deeply, gathering strength. "Oh God"—she cringed—"it was so frightening. I came home from my meeting, and the first thing I saw when I walked through the door was Heyworth. Oh, Heyworth!" She shook with a wail, face whitening as if witnessing the sight. Christopher stood frozen in passive sympathy, waiting, patient and practiced.

"I . . . I didn't know at first. I couldn't tell what had happened." Brooke struggled to continue. "I saw him flat on the floor. I thought he might have had a stroke. When I got closer, I saw there was blood everywhere, and I knelt down. I tried to shake him but he didn't move, and his eyes just stared." Brooke halted, shuddering. She drew her breath but said no more, gazing blankly, the courtroom still.

"Brooke," Christopher spoke gently, "I know this is hard. Please try to remember. Can you tell the court if you saw anything, or anyone, else in the room."

"No." Brooke dropped her weary head. "No, Heyworth was alone. I dropped to the floor and I grabbed him." Her hands shot in front of her, cupped as if around her husband's shoulders. "I shook him, like this, I tried to bring him to." She choked, a sob gurgling in her throat. She stared blankly for a horrible, still moment.

She looked up to see Christopher nod his head, guiding her.

"Nothing worked," Brooke sighed. "He was white, his face was empty, like a shell. His eyes were open, but he was . . . he was not there."

The image before her eyes, Brooke's face screwed up into a sour grimace. "Oh God, I kept talking to him, crazy, like he was playing a joke or something. I think I sat there with him for a while, I'm not sure."

At that Brooke's eyes blinked quickly, as if opening for the first time into light. "He must have been jogging!" Brooke exclaimed, slapping her forehead. She laughed, a strange, chilling cackle that resounded through the courtroom. Christopher's jaw dropped.

"Of course! He was wearing his Adidas sweat suit. It looked so ridiculous on him. Oh, the poor thing, he was trying to stay in shape, because I was so much younger. He used to kid about it, taking up jog-walking, he said he'd outlast me. I think he did it just to spite the doctors!"

Brooke smiled warmly, the chummy joke remembered as if she sat among tennis partners or at Thanksgiving dinner. Deaf to the urgent throat clearing of her lawyer, Brooke seemed to forget it was a dead man she was kidding about, a dead man she stood accused of killing.

"Brooke. Brooke, please." Christopher tried to pull his witness back to the crime scene, where her grief spoke with such compelling sincerity. Her vague, casual smile was unbearable.

"He bought it himself," she shook her head sadly. "Oh, silly Heyworth! He thought it was cool to wear what the kids wore." Accidentally, it seemed, the thought jolted

Brooke. "Aieeee! Heyworth *never* could shop for himself!" she howled, plunging her head into her hands.

"Brooke." Christopher raised his voice.

"It's horrible!" Brooke shrieked, the crowning indignity of dying without style sending her into a spasm. "Heartless! My poor Heyworth, shot in that awful Adidas sweat suit!"

"Mrs. Vandermark!" Christopher yelled over her erupting wail.

Brooke turned to the lawyer, sobbing. "What?" she choked.

"Brooke, please, try to remember what happened *after* you saw Heyworth." If he never saw an Adidas sweat suit again, Christopher thought, mopping his own sweat, it would be too soon. "Please, I know it must have been a terrible shock. I know it was," he repeated, softening his voice with an effort. "But please, if you can remember what happened next, I'd like you to tell the court what you did. What you saw. Anything you remember."

Brooke sniffed noisily, her face blotchy, agitated. "I'll try," she promised in a weak voice.

"Take your time, Brooke. I know this is difficult."

Brooke trembled silently for a moment. "Okay"—she raised her head—"but I was so scared, after I realized . . . what happened."

"That's understandable, Brooke."

"Okay." Brooke gathered her arms around her body as if a wind blew through her.

"I guess at some point it hit me to call the police, so I went to the kitchen, where the telephone is. Chutney was in the kitchen, and she looked fine, you know, a little frizzy, but she wasn't crying or anything. She was at the sink, washing her hands. I didn't know how to tell her." Brooke swallowed hard, another sob garbling in her throat. "I . . . I tried so hard to say something, but I was shaking, I was terrified. I couldn't even make a word come out."

"What did Chutney do then?" the lawyer prodded.

At that Brooke shot upright, staring wide-eyed at Christopher. She quivered with choppy breaths.

"Everything went crazy then," Brooke gasped, still disbelieving. "Chutney started yelling things at me, she ran out of the room, and I don't know what happened. I fainted, I think, in the kitchen. The police woke me up, and the next thing I knew I was handcuffed, and there were all these people in my house, marking things around my Heyworth. . . ." Brooke's shrill lament resonated through the room: "Oh, my husband, my poor Heyworth! How could anyone hurt you? My Heyworth, Heyworth . . ." Brooke murmured Heyworth's name like a mantra.

For a long moment Christopher stood still. "Thank you, Mrs. Vandermark," he sighed finally. "I have no further questions, Your Honor."

Judge Morgan glanced uneasily at Brooke. The witness had embraced her knees like a child, swaying as if to a lullaby, repeating Heyworth's name in a distant voice. Henry Kohn approached the bench with slow steps, wary of rousing another demented vision in the fragile witness.

"I'll postpone cross," he whispered to the judge, "but I ask your permission to call Brooke again later, if I need to."

Judge Morgan looked at Christopher Miles, who nodded. "I have no problem with that, Henry," Christopher agreed collegially. "I'd like Brooke to be able to pay attention to the witnesses, though, if she'll be called again. Your Honor, can you break for a few minutes? Give Brooke a chance to pull herself together?"

Judge Morgan was more than happy to oblige, anxious to avoid another hair-trigger catharsis from Brooke. "Any objection, Counselor?"

Henry Kohn shook his head no. He intended to maintain a sympathetic appearance.

Judge Morgan's pounding gavel startled Brooke out of her eerie meditation.

"Mrs. Vandermark," Judge Morgan spoke, "you may take your seat. The court will recess for five minutes."

Brooke accepted Christopher's arm gratefully, following his steady steps past the interns to the private witness prep room outside.

CHAPTER FORTY-FIVE

CHUTNEY'S hair and eyebrows were exactly the color of Romeo's uneven burnt orange tan-in-a-can, Elle decided, staring at Chutney's frizzy halo as she took her seat in the witness stand.

"With reference to the exhibits produced by Mr. LeBlanc and Ms. Maximillian, Chutney, please describe to the court where you were on the day of your father's death."

To corroborate Chutney's activities on the day in question, Henry Kohn had called Philippe LeBlanc, the head stylist at Frize of Beverly Hills. Philippe had verified a page from the salon's appointment calendar, showing that Chutney had been scheduled to get a permanent wave that morning. He had rolled her hair himself, and he testified that Chutney acted perfectly normal, no different from any of the several times he had styled her hair over the years.

Maxine Maximillian, of Max Fitness Center, had spoken with Chutney at the gym in the afternoon. She placed the time around 3:00, since she had just finished teaching her marathon step aerobics class, which ran two hours and began at 1:00.

Chutney testified that she had returned home to an empty house after working out on the StairMaster. She went upstairs to take a shower and ran downstairs to grab a drink from the kitchen. That was when she found Brooke, who was shaking, paralyzed with fright, trying to move Heyworth's body. She surprised Brooke, who must not have heard her upstairs, and Brooke ran in a frenzy to the kitchen, where she fainted. Chutney called the police while Brooke was passed out. When she revived, they arrested her in the kitchen.

As her lawyer had advised, Chutney kept it short, leaving little territory for opposing counsel to investigate on cross.

When Christopher Miles began questioning the witness, his questions were unfocused, as if he were hoping for inspiration to strike him on his feet.

He asked Chutney to describe the layout of the massive house, a ploy to buy him time; then suddenly Christopher seized on something.

"You were surprised, you said, Ms. Vandermark, when you encountered your father downstairs."

"I'd say so!" Chutney gasped. "For God's sake, my father was . . . he was dead!"

"So you didn't notice anything unusual, then, before you came downstairs." The lawyer spoke methodically, getting the facts straight, it seemed, for himself.

"Mr. Miles, are you going anywhere with this?" Judge Morgan leaned forward with annoyance.

Absorbed, the lawyer didn't respond immediately.

"And nobody was there when you got home," he mused. "So . . . so it happened while you were upstairs." His mind raced for another question, for anything to keep Chutney on the stand. Delay beat defeat, and he was down to the final witness.

Chutney glanced at her lawyer, who shrugged. Judge

Morgan, losing patience, peered expectantly at Christopher Miles.

"Counselor?"

He held a finger in the air, motioning for the judge to wait, rubbing his chin as if deep in thought.

Elle twirled her hair, wondering if she should braid it to keep herself awake. Better not. She didn't want it to frizz like Chutney's. Glancing at Chutney, Elle remembered her first and only perm and wondered why anyone paid money to have her hair ironed into wrinkles.

Suddenly, Elle shot from her chair, knocking it backward with a crash. "Wait!" she exclaimed.

Judge Morgan glared and pounded her gavel. "Order. Order."

Christopher, thankful for any excuse to delay, made no move to restrain his intern.

"Your Honor," Elle implored the bench, "I'm an intern for Mrs. Vandermark's defense team. May I ask Chutney a question?"

Judge Morgan, glancing at the student audience, decided to play to the crowd. She wanted an article in the *Law Review*, and it was so hard to get will probate research published in the current academic climate.

"Mr. Miles?" she asked. "Will you defer to co-counsel?"

Elle clasped her hands, pleading like a child yearning for one present on Christmas Eve.

All was lost already, the lawyer figured. This way, he could chalk the defeat up to an experimental inclusion of student lawyers.

"A fine idea, Miss Woods." He smiled. Sarah gaped in horror.

"Your Honor"—Elle nodded seriously—"it's relevant, I promise."

She turned to Chutney, who grinned, more comfortable

with the Intersorority Council than with a lawyer asking her questions.

"It's about your hair," Elle began. "It looks nice."

"Thanks." Chutney stared at Elle with curiosity.

"Did you just get a perm?"

"Yeah, before the trial. Philippe did it." Chutney indicated the smug Philippe, who bowed his head to the gallery.

"I'll have to get his card," Elle commented, laughing. "He did your hair during college too, didn't he?"

"Oh, yes," Chutney answered, "he's permed my hair since the first time I went with Emerald." Chutney's mother nodded proudly from her seat. "In fact, I got Philippe to teach a hair-care class to the Kappas. Kappa Kappa Gamma. My sorority sisters," Chutney explained to the judge. "Remember, Philippe, the THM class?"

"What's THM?" Elle asked.

"Total hair management. It was my idea," bragged the witness, tugging on her hair. "See, Philippe's always done my hair, and he's the best! He goes to hair shows in Paris, and he comes back with all these tips. I never do a thing to my hair unless he tells me it's okay. And I do absolutely everything he tells me. He's a total professional," Chutney rattled on.

"And you've gotten, oh, I don't know," Elle wondered aloud, "how many perms?"

"Well, one every six months since I was about ten, when I tried out to be Little Orphan Annie in the school play." Chutney scowled, remembering she hadn't gotten the part. "Tons," she changed the subject quickly, "like twenty at least."

"And you got a perm the day that Heyworth . . . your father was murdered." Elle walked toward Philippe, her back to Chutney.

"Yes," Chutney answered. "It's in the books, I was at Frize."

"But your father was shot a little later, after you got home," Elle recapped.

Sarah poked Warner with an annoyed frown. "Do we need to go through this until Elle gets it straight?" she hissed.

Elle wheeled around, approached the witness stand with her hands on her hips.

"But you didn't hear anything, not even a *gunshot.*" Elle punctuated the word loud and sharp, like a shot.

"Yes. For God's sake, I told you. I was in the shower. I worked out after I left Frize, and when I got home, I took a shower. I'm sure I didn't hear anything, any shot, because I was washing my hair. I wash it every day." Chutney glared at Elle, her story tight. She saw no need to repeat it.

Elle walked casually toward the court gallery, smiling at Philippe. "Chutney, veteran of twenty-odd perms, graduate of total hair management"—she spun to face the witness— "it is absolutely *elementary*, absolutely the *first rule* of hair care, that you can't wash your hair for *twenty-four hours* after a perm."

Chutney gasped, raising her hand to cover her open mouth. Philippe nodded excitedly.

"Is that not a fact?" Elle demanded. "Chutney?"

"Yes," Chutney sputtered, beginning to cry. "Never. You have to wait twenty-four hours."

"And you were *washing your hair*?" Elle prodded the witness. "Three hours after you walked out of Frize?"

"No!" Chutney choked, hiding behind both hands.

Henry Kohn shot from his chair, objecting.

"You would *never* wash your hair right after getting a perm, would you, Chutney?" Elle persisted over Henry Kohn's furious shouts.

Judge Morgan pounded her gavel. "Let her answer the question, Mr. Kohn."

"No, no, no," Chutney sobbed, "never! I wasn't in the shower, of course not. *I just got a perm!*"

"You lied then, Chutney." Elle folded her arms, staring at the witness. "Tell the court again where you were when your father was shot."

Chutney spun violently in her chair, pointing at Brooke. "She is *younger* than I am!" she shrieked. "She was in my *geology* class, and she moved in with my *father*!"

Henry Kohn had begun jumping up and down, desperate to silence Chutney's outburst, but the demon of her savagery was unleashed.

Chutney attacked Brooke relentlessly: "You stole my father! You ruined him! You ruined my life!"

She stood up, rushed recklessly across the courtroom in pursuit of Brooke, who leaped from her chair. "I didn't mean to shoot him," Chutney screamed, swiping air as the bailiff seized her. *"I meant to shoot you!"*

CHAPTER FORTY-SIX

WHEN the furor subsided, the lawyer for Mrs. Whitney Vandermark-Warren-Sands renewed his motion for the court to consolidate the claim of his client, on the theory that the will was valid, and Whitney was unquestionably Heyworth's most beautiful wife.

Without the least inclination to evaluate the cosmetic merits of five Mrs. Vandermarks preening excitedly in their seats, Judge Morgan ruled swiftly.

"Motion granted. There being no competent evidence that Brooke feloniously and intentionally killed Heyworth Vandermark, the will is admitted to probate. As a matter of law, the phrase 'most beautiful wife' employed by Heyworth Vandermark refers to his wife at the time of his death. Matters of taste *aside*." She directed the comment to Whitney in particular, who had stood up furiously.

"The parties have stipulated that Brooke was married to Heyworth at the time of his death," Judge Morgan continued, "and there is no further ambiguity. Pending appointment of a personal administrator to distribute assets"—she pounded her gavel several times to be heard over Whitney's sobs—"the matter of the Estate of Heyworth Vandermark is hereby dismissed."

Henry Kohn hung his head.

Eugenia practically scaled the railing that separated the lawyers' seats from the gallery, rushing to embrace Elle amid the pandemonium of wailing wives and cheering students that erupted. Brooke, free and happy, grabbed and swung Elle's hand like a child.

"Oh, today I'm free to be me, free to be me, there goes Chutney, said it was me," Brooke sang, bouncing along with her flowery little cheer. Elle burst out laughing.

"God, Brooke, it's a miracle you weren't so goofy on the stand." Elle poked Eugenia, grinning with wide-eyed relief. "Meet Eugenius," she announced to Brooke, "the smartest girl in Stanford Law School. I wouldn't have made it here without her."

"Group hug!" announced Brooke, hauling Eugenia into a merry circle.

"*You're* the smartest girl in law school!" Eugenia declared, freeing her hand to rustle Elle's hair into a white moppy mess.

Elle shook a lock from her eyes with a grin. Sarah was involved in a heated conversation with Warner at the far end of the lawyers' table. "Not bad for a Barbie doll," she said.

"Ken should be proud," Eugenia replied, pointing at Warner's blonde head.

Elle pinched Eugenia's arm and lowered her tone. "Ken's on the shelf now, Genie. With the rest of the dolls."

Eugenia wrinkled her nose, confused.

"I'll tell you later," Elle promised.

Brooke was pulling on Elle's arm with another jingle. "Free, free, always me, always gonna be me!"

Eugenia laughed and applied her tousling hand to Brooke's hair. "You oughtta take that show on the road!"

"Hey, I can do anything now," Brooke declared happily.

Elle packed up her legal pad. Brooke turned to thank

her "other lawyer Christopher," hopping away with another chorus of "free to be me."

"I'll go get the car, Elle-o-rama," said Eugenia. "Time to party!"

Elle glanced around the clearing room and agreed. "I'll meet you out front."

She turned to look for Christopher, who was nowhere to be seen. Maybe he's out in the hall, Elle decided, picking up the closest two witness books to carry back with her. Acknowledging Dan's congratulations with a smile, she glided into the hallway, where Christopher stood surrounded by reporters. Out of the corner of his eye he caught Elle, and pulled her to his side. "Here"—he beamed at Elle—"is the real star!" Cameras were flashing, placing Elle securely in her element. The reporters had a lot of questions, many of them for Elle, which she answered beautifully. The last question, however, was directed at Christopher.

"Mr. Miles, how do you feel about being upstaged by your intern?" one of the reporters asked.

"Proud! Thanks, Elle."

At the door of the courthouse she saw Warner standing alone. "I guess this is my exit cue," Christopher said, and gave Elle a wink before heading out the door.

"Elle!" Warner reached to hug her. His open arms caught air as Elle saluted him sarcastically, ducking through the door.

She couldn't resist peeking back when she heard Warner rush out behind her. Over his shoulder, she noticed Sarah standing at the doorway with her arms folded indignantly.

"Elle, stop, please," he said as she turned to face him. "God, let a man admit his mistake. That joke was all wrong. I *underestimated* you, Elle."

Elle thought she noticed Sarah look away, pretending

she didn't hear her fiancé's confession. Making an effort not to catch Sarah's eye, Elle drew closer to Warner.

"How's that, Warner?"

"Elle, come on, you know. I thought I'd have to marry *Sarah*, because she . . . oh God, Elle, she had the *brains* and everything. You know my family. I mean, I wanted to be with you, really, but everyone . . . everyone thought you were so flaky." Warner laughed heartily with Elle, who encouraged him with a warm grasp to continue.

"A frosted flake? Me?" Elle giggled in faux humility, glancing to assure herself that Sarah heard. "Little ol' Barbie doll me?"

"Oh, Elle, come on, you *act* like the biggest bimbo around." Warner chuckled, positive that Elle shared his humor. "I mean, you should just hear what people say about you at law school!"

Confident that he had won her back, he put his arm around her shoulder and jostled her like a friend. "I'm so glad they're wrong! You showed everybody! I'm so glad I can be with you again now." Warner pulled Elle close to him.

"You want me back, Warner?" Elle peered up from her old love's embrace with sweet doe eyes, trying not to laugh.

"Elle, I'll leave Sarah," he gushed. "I don't need her anymore. You are smart! Christopher and my father go all the way back to prep school, and with the glowing description he'll give of you, my family will have to love you! You've got the brains *and* the body. Thank God! Why did it take me so long?" He smacked his head jokingly. "Right here all the time. The one woman who really knows me."

Elle saw Sarah glaring furiously at Warner, and for the first time thought she and Sarah might have something in common.

"Warner, I do know you now. I didn't know you at all

before," she pronounced in a cool, even tone, lifting his hand and dropping it from her shoulder.

His smile dropped into a confused stare.

"No, Warner. I didn't *know* you," Elle repeated. "I loved some image that you never really were. It's not your fault. 'That had to do with me, not you,'" she hissed, imitating his words from their fight in the witness room.

"But, Elle, we spent so many years together," he protested. "You'll never find anyone like me again, Elle."

"I certainly hope not!" Elle answered genuinely. "By the way, your brainy fiancée looks lonely." She pointed behind him at Sarah, who was tapping her foot in a brisk allegro.

Warner wheeled around to face Sarah, his mind racing to explain what he had just declared with such indiscretion.

"Good-bye, Warner," Elle said as she started down the steps. She paused, turning back with a smile.

"I'll see you around."

CHAPTER FORTY-SEVEN

Eugenia drove back to the office of Miles & Slocum, where Elle dropped off her witness books and Brooke jumped around like a hummingbird. After waiting fruitlessly for Christopher to return, Elle decided to leave. It was Thursday, the spring days were beginning to warm and lengthen, and already she was savoring the indulgence of a long weekend.

"You'll have a summer job waiting," Eugenia beamed.

"Heyworth's ex-wives certainly had some potential hair salon malpractice," Elle said.

Brooke quieted, and Elle gulped a quick apology. "I'm sorry to bring up Heyworth, Brooke."

"That's okay." The widow shrugged, collecting herself.

"He's been avenged!" Eugenia blurted, thumping her fist on Elle's desk. "That despicable daughter of his won't see the inside of a hair salon for a long, long time."

"Fitting," Brooke said, nodding with satisfaction. Elle glanced at her curiously.

"She's got her permanent now, the wretch," Brooke said with a smile. "A permanent prison sentence."

Elle giggled. "Hey, Brooke," she said, tugging on her client's arm. "You up for partying with us tonight? I won't promise you much in Palo Alto, but I think it's time for you to get back on the scene. In search of . . ."

"Single white male," Brooke finished, smiling. "Definitely. Do you know any cute law students?"

"No!" Elle and Eugenia exclaimed in unison.

"We'll see about that." Brooke winked, trotting out the office door.

In an hour they were toasting the future around the cactus-legged table in Elle's condo. Flushed with champagne and giggling madly, the gathering was reminiscent of "Margotitaville" days at USC. Underdog leaped toward Elle's lap, missing her slightly, a bit dizzy from the champagne that Brooke had poured into his dog dish.

Brooke gave the first toast, encouraging them both to graduate early so she could finance the Blonde Legal Defense Fund with her Vandermark fortune.

Elle raised her glass. "To being a Ken-free Barbie!" Shouts and applause went all the way around.

"I wondered about that," Eugenia said, nodding. "What's up with Warner?"

"Finishing law school, then a life in Newport with Sarah, I guess." Elle shrugged. "I'm too busy thinking about all of the things I want to do to think about him. Like getting the Barbie trademark and designing an entire jewelry line in her honor."

"To Barbie," Brooke announced, raising her glass. "Forever in pink."

"To Visa," Eugenia grinned, "living pink in the red."

"Okay," Elle acknowledged Brooke's waving invitation, "my turn. To underdogs!" The drooping eyes of her faithful Chihuahua fluttered open at the sound of his name, then dropped contentedly shut. The three girls clinked glasses, drinking the remaining champagne.

Eugenia's glass struck the table first. "Let's hit University Avenue!" she chirped.

In a minute's time, only one Underdog was left. He curled his head under his paws to sleep.

Brooke's credit card flashed as gold as the microbrewed lagers they drank, as yellow as the cab, and as blonde as the heads of Brooke and Elle, who staggered back to Elle's condo and wilted like morning glories.

Class was out of the picture on the lazy Friday when they awoke; Eugenia and Brooke headed to the city to shop, and Elle, wrapped in the warmth of her bathrobe, set to the task of cleaning her littered bedroom. She discarded piles of articles on the "Murder in Malibu," trimming the raggedy edges of a few that were scrapbook worthy. In particular, one, which had a picture of Elle and Christopher on the courthouse steps.

She filed a few *Law Review* articles with her notes from Gilbreath's Wills class, in case they would help her study for the final exam, which was approaching fast. She answered the knock at her door still swaddled in terry cloth, sure that Eugenia or Brooke had forgotten something.

When she swung the door open she froze, gasping in disbelief. Before her stood Sarah Knottingham, redolent with the fragrance of salon products; smiling, blushing, and nervously tugging at a strand of her newly styled and highlighted hair, finally free from a headband.

"Oh my God," Elle stuttered, supporting herself with one hand against the wall. She stared without speaking, and Sarah grinned mischievously.

"Does it look that bad?" The preppie laughed anxiously and stared down at her espadrilles.

"Oh my God, Sarah. You're . . . you're . . ."

"Mind if I come in?" Sarah asked.

Underdog stared at Sarah suspiciously, and Elle took an unsteady hungover step backward.

"No, come in," she managed. "Sarah, you got rid of your bob and that . . . that headband," Elle said in victorious shock.

"Yeah, I pulled an Elle Woods," Sarah laughed. "I skipped class and went to the beauty salon. It seemed to work okay for you," she added. "Manicured and winning in court, I figured you had a secret."

Elle regained some measure of composure when she sat down on the couch. "No secret," she said. "Just habit, I guess. Manicures relax me."

Sarah was still standing, and Elle stared noticeably at her visitor's empty left hand.

"I gave the ring back." Sarah shrugged her shoulders. "Now Warner has two ex-girlfriends making the law school curve worse for him. What do you think of that?"

Elle gulped, then smiled. "I've finally quit thinking about Warner," she said, shaking her head as if waking from a dream. "Anyway, I think your hair looks so much better. I can't believe you even got a few highlights!"

Sarah stroked her shiny coiffure. "I think it's worth the upkeep."

"Definitely." Elle nodded with vigor. "Did you get a good conditioner?"

"Kiehls," Sarah answered. "That's what the stylist recommended."

"Perfect." Elle smiled.

Sarah handed Elle a bound outline from her shaky hand. "I'm finished with my Property outline," she said. "I'm wondering if I can mine you for the answers for the Wills final? I saw some books you brought to the office one day on your desk and it looked like you could teach the class!" Sarah was highlighted, but still brunettely sensible.

"Of course," Elle smiled, standing. "I'm almost done with my outline. Warner's out of luck, but I'll cut you in." Elle couldn't resist tugging at a strand of Sarah's highlighted hair. "After all, you're blonde at heart now."

"A *true* blonde," Sarah laughed, remembering Elle's miniessay.

"Naturally," Elle said.

The Perm

BY
AMANDA BROWN

Following is a sneak preview of
the upcoming adventures of Elle Woods

CHAPTER ONE

The Interview

Boyne Christopher wiped the construction-orange Chee-to powder from the side of his mouth and grinned.

"You're from Stanford, my alma mater," he sputtered between crunches, reaching into the bag on the interview table. Elle followed his grasping hand with her eyes, wondering if Brooke Wolf had baked all the sense out of her brain in the Phoenix sun. This was the firm where style met substance? Brooke had been too kind in her description of her new husband's law firm, Elle decided; either that, or she had a woefully underdeveloped sense of style.

Christopher, noticing Elle was eyeing his afternoon snack, took the wrong inference. He turned the bag so its open end faced Elle.

"Want one?"

"Cutting back," Elle said, wrinkling her nose with the disgust she couldn't restrain. Christopher laughed, spraying Chee-to mist into the air.

Elle forced a smile in the direction of Norman Stiles, the second interviewer, a decidedly quiet and well-groomed elder attorney, whose face reddened.

"Boyne's not on the firm's Health Committee," Norman

said, indicating the Chee-tos bag with a frown. He explained that the firm tried to match interviewing attorneys to the schools of each prospective summer associate. His tone was apologetic, a fact that seemed lost on the corpulent lawyer sitting to his right.

"Best foot forward, you know," Boyne said, winking a beady eye that was submerged in his enormous, porcine face. He stretched down underneath the table and unlaced his shoe with a great, relieved sigh. Lifting a sock-clad foot across his knee, he began to massage his toes with the singular concentration of an infant whose body struck him as a novelty.

"Aaah, much better. I can't put my best foot forward in these damn wing tips." He reached under the table to unlace his other shoe.

"Wolf & Fox takes the comfort of its associates seriously," Norman said. "We don't believe our clients should run the risk of unhappy lawyers performing substandard work." Elle nodded her head, bracing herself for the resounding chomp with which Boyne attacked another fistful of Chee-tos. His large, fat hands seemed to have a compulsion to have something to do at all times. Elle wished he would reach again for his feet, since that activity at least kept itself concealed underneath the table.

Norman studied a pink paper, Elle's résumé, and turned his bespectacled gaze to the student. Until the mention of her internship on Brooke Vandermark's case in law school, not much about the rosy résumé would suggest that Elle Woods had any interest in practicing law. A sociopolitical jewelry design major from USC, her work experience included licensing a jewelry line for sale through the Home Shopping Network, summer work in the Eva Woods Art Gallery in La Brea, and activities as a spokesmodel for Perfect Tan skin products in Los Angeles.

Under "Honors and Awards," Elle had listed the dubious collegiate distinctions of homecoming queen and Intersorority Council president ahead of Phi Beta Kappa, which appeared to be mentioned as an afterthought. Her transcript from law school showed the same grade in every first-year class: a P. She had a P in Contracts; a P in Torts; Ps in Property, Legal Writing, Ethics, Constitutional Law, Wills, and Estate Planning. The grades for her second year were good without being remarkable.

A portfolio, according to the résumé, was available upon request.

"Why Phoenix?" Norman asked, brandishing the résumé as if it incriminated her, pinning her to the California of her past. Boyne glanced at the pink-suited law student and shrugged. They both knew that Charles Wolf, the name partner of Wolf & Fox, had sent this résumé down personally.

Charles's new wife, Brooke, had prevailed upon him to hire Elle for the summer. As with Brooke's redecorating impulses, which had turned the lawyer's lounge from a keg-equipped TV room into a fern-laden juice bar, Brooke's whim was immediately translated into nonnegotiable firm policy. Elle would have the job; that much was clear. The question, which perplexed both lawyers, was why she wanted it.

"What's a California girl want down here?' Boyne added with a sharp, accusing stare. "It's six hours to the beach."

Elle caught a glimpse of herself in the glare of the window, which reflected the scorching afternoon sun, and thought of Los Angeles. She had expected the question about Phoenix, but like any question in a job interview, it called for less than the truth. If she were brave, she'd tell them up front that the hairdresser who had done her highlights for five years had first suggested she move to the Valley of the Sun. Goro had left his position in Beverly Hills to open his own salon in Phoenix, where, he argued, the dry desert air acted as a natural frizz-restrainer. "Better than Kerastase," he had said, giving nature the high compliment of beating the best conditioner on the market.

Goro had Elle's captive ear during the hour he spent wrapping the long, narrow strips of foil around each highlighted lock of her hair, and another forty-five minutes before the timer rang and anonymous hands scrubbed the mixture from her clean, newly sunny mane. She told him about her dismal on-campus interviews, and he talked of Phoenix. Phoenix, nothing but Phoenix: the land of Canaan, the Answer. At any rate, she had no other prospects for a summer job in a law firm.

Even Christopher Miles, the lawyer for whom she had interned in her spring semester, whose firm she worked for last summer, was not an option. He had sold his partnership interest when he took off for India to find the Buddha and write a screenplay. Just her luck. If she hadn't had Brooke, she'd have had to spend another summer managing her mother's art gallery, and two years of law school training would be wasted.

They surely knew about Brooke, Elle thought. She had a guardian angel in the wife of the man to whom these attorneys owed their jobs. She was secure, protected by the Wolf of Wolf & Fox.

After she married Charles Wolf last fall, Brooke had called Elle repeatedly with dazzling tales of her husband's glamorous, lucrative law firm. She had convinced Elle to interview with Wolf & Fox, promising she had a summer job for the asking. What Brooke asked, Charles gave, and in his professional fiefdom, what Charles said went. Still, Elle thought it best not to mention her tie to the name partner of the firm. She would have to see these attorneys at the office, and it was best to blend in.

Despite her impression that the firm lacked panache,

Elle had to admit that the money they offered was incredible. Wolf & Fox paid twice what any other firm in the Phoenix area paid its summer associates. The salaries of its lawyers exceeded those of even the most abundant cash cows of Wall Street. Living in Phoenix on five thousand dollars a week would be worth a try even if she never returned. She could line her pockets to launch a new jewelry line, or travel.

She thought of her jewelry line and smiled broadly, confident she would sail in and out of Phoenix on gilded wings. Why Phoenix? Who needed more than good hair and good friends? Why Phoenix, indeed.

Turning to Norman, Elle spoke as she had rehearsed. "I interned for an attorney who represented Brooke Vandermark in a complex will probate case last spring." Elle hesitated, adding softly, "You know her as Brooke Wolf."

The lawyers nodded in unison.

Elle continued. "The case involved criminal law and property issues in addition to the will dispute, and I know you've got several big criminal cases I could work on. Plus some property settlements in the meaner divorces."

"Divorce, Arizona's growth industry," Boyne said, punctuating his oft-repeated quip with a hearty, self-congratulatory laugh. "Sorry," he added, conscious of Norman Stiles, who sat scowling beside him. "Mormon," he said, indicating Norman with the point of his elbow. "Norman the Mormon."

Elle smiled. "How nice for you."

"Go on about your internship," Boyne prompted her. "What does it have to do with Phoenix?" Both lawyers appeared skeptical.

"Nothing, in and of itself," Elle replied. "I see my second-year summer as an opportunity to sample a new place to live and work, and I believe in testing myself at the best firm in the area. Don't forget, I'm a native of Southern California. You can assure yourselves I'm not in Phoenix for the sun, like the students you may see from Chicago or the Ivy League. I'm here for the firm."

"That's true," Norman said, nodding his agreement, "about the eager Ivy Leaguers. We call them our summer camp candidates. Many of the will go back to Boston or New York; we don't consider them credible candidates for permanent positions with the firm."

Boyne rolled his eyes, laughing out loud. "I wonder if some of these gunners have ever watched the Weather Channel. You'd have to be out of your mind to come to Phoenix in June as if it were some kind of spa. You know we don't change our clocks here. Don't need daylight saving time in the summer: we've got more sun than you've ever seen in one place."

Elle noticed that neither of the interviewers was even remotely tan.

"I see," she said, nodding thoughtfully. She paused, wondering if Norman the Mormon was getting ready to ask her whether she had accepted Jesus Christ as her savior. Or was that the Jehovah's Witnesses? Either way, his quiet stare made her nervous.

"Let's get to the point," Boyne declared, whisking Elle's résumé from the table in a sudden, almost violent motion, which startled her. She sat up in her chair, holding her breath.

"You're the famous Stanford Barbie. The Pentium Blonde! I've read about you in the alumni news. Dean Haus introduced you at first-year orientation as the class's only homecoming queen. Homecoming queen!" He exploded another Chee-to spout, laughing abruptly. "Get a load of that"—he poked Norman—"royalty."

Norman furrowed his pale brow and lowered his spectacles.

"There are more important matters to discuss," he said, and Boyne quieted.

"You do the honors," Boyne said, his eyes downcast as he scratched the weblike space between his toes.

"Are you married?" Norman asked, staring intently at Elle. She fought the urge to say it was none of his business.

"No," Elle said. She scowled at the somber faces of her interviewers. How dare they put her on the defensive. She felt an impulse to explain that she had some prospects, if not actually a ring, at least a few sort of likely candidates. The room was silent. Elle wondered if they had heard her. She wondered if this was a trick, an interviewing routine of some mysterious sort. She wondered what the right answer was supposed to be.

"No," she repeated sullenly. "I'm not married."

Norman grinned, leaning back, her response seeming to loosen him; Boyne's head nodded up and down vigorously, like an excited jack-in-the-box.

"The firm doesn't like its young associates to be married," Boyne said. A smile broke gratefully across Elle's face.

"Are you involved in any serious relationship, anything exclusive?"

Elle's lips parted in surprise, and she turned a startled glance toward Norman. He waited.

"Exclusive?"

Boyne nodded. "Any commitments? Any obligations? Anything that might divide your loyalty?"

Elle paused, his last comment suggesting that the lawyer had something other than a pickup line in mind.

"I'm not here to find a husband, if that is what you're getting at," Elle answered in a low, steady tone.

"No, no," Norman said, waving his arms with a laugh, "perish the thought please, let me explain. If you're not familiar with the firm, you wouldn't know about the very real danger that marriage, and with it adultery, poses to our productivity."

Elle gave Norman a quizzical glance. "I'm not familiar with the firm's thinking."

Norman folded his arms, and when he spoke, his words struck Elle as more practiced than spontaneous, as if he was repeating something he had revealed to others sitting in her chair, some idea that custom or experience had made into a rule. His voice mixed gravity and concern, like a father's. She listened curiously.

"Married young associates arrive here rather stable, but the amount of time the firm demands can be quite an imposition on family life. We can't have that in this competitive market. The firm requires all of your allegiance. The firm should be your sole loyalty."

"There's more to it than that," Boyne interrupted, Norman acknowledging his comment with a quiet nod. "We pay so much above the market for Phoenix here at Wolf & Fox. Our associates do quite well, and once they see what a hundred-dollar tip can get them, its only natural that they start playing around."

Elle blushed. She had not expected to discuss the sociology of wealthy adulterers.

Norman continued in a mild, matter-of-fact tone. "It's no secret that most attorneys haven't seen a sliver of the world on their road to the firm. They're hibernating in law school, then buried under the bar exam. This only becomes a problem with the married attorneys. The ones who married in law school married when they were poor; for love, maybe, or for convenience, but foolishly."

"They're new men when they have expense accounts," Boyne said with a lascivious grin. "I know I was."

"We've seen the same drama play out too many times to ignore the effect of marriage on our lawyers," Norman said.

"It's beyond doubt that an associate bills fewer hours when he has to take calls from his mistress or plan weekend affairs around his wife's tennis schedule. When the women kiss and tell, we have real trouble. Associates who live under the threat of blackmail are entirely unproductive. Their minds stray, and their minds must be focused on the work of our clients."

Elle blinked back her astonishment. Wasn't that what sick leave was for? "Your clients must pay handsomely," she said, remembering the firm's extravagant salaries.

"Exactly," Norman said, his eyes shining with a proud light. "And we give them our complete allegiance. We don't want our associates in any danger of blackmail: it decreases the profitability of the firm. That's why Wolf & Fox prefers to hire unmarried applicants. The fewer emotional ties you bring with you, the better. Less room for blackmail, more hours to bill. Understand?"

Elle nodded. "I think so."

"Any children?" Boyne prodded.

"God, no, no children," Elle said quickly, wondering if she had put on weight at the expensed hotel buffet.

"Good." Norman nodded, checking a line on the legal pad he held in his lap.

"In fact, I'm entirely unanchored," Elle added. She grinned. She knew the right answers now.

"Do you take antidepressants?" Norman glanced again at his legal pad.

Elle squinted at Norman. He adjusted his owl-eyed glasses and met her dubious stare.

"No, I don't," she said. She shrugged. "I'm not depressed."

Both attorneys shook their heads in criticism.

"The firm encourages monitored drug intake," Boyne announced. "Prescriptions are handled through the firm's pharmacy, on the tenth floor. It's a secured area, but that's only to keep the cleaning staff out. A Xanax takes the edge off, you know."

"But I'm not depressed."

"Not yet," Norman said. "You're also not making five thousand dollars a week for learning how to be a lawyer. Trust me, Elle, you'll work long days. The Health Committee takes a very serious view of this matter. We encourage you to calibrate a prescription regimen that flattens out any mood swings to which you might be subject. After the interview, we can take you by the physician who treats our women associates, and she'll recommend a personalized antidepressant prescription, which you should begin to take immediately."

"Immediately?" Elle looked down at the Louis Vuitton briefcase that lay at the foot of her chair, in which she had placed, in a manila file, the letters of recommendation from Christopher Miles and Professor Gilbreath. The lawyers hadn't made a routine request for references. They hadn't discussed the firm's clients, or her qualifications, or the summer associates program. More to the point, Elle realized they hadn't made her an offer.

"What do you mean, immediately? I don't remember you offering me a job." The staccato drum of her manicured nails tapping on the table was the only sound audible in the room.

Norman broke the silence. "Charles Wolf pulled your résumé himself. That's as good as an offer."

Elle flushed, her lips parting in amazement. She stared at Boyne's wry grin and Norman's owl-eyed stare; both were waiting.

The thought occurred to her that an offer was only half the deal. She had to come to Phoenix for an interview. Only an interview. If the first one went well, there should be a callback, a second interview, a period of courting, then a letter in the mail and some time to think.

"How do you know I'll take it?" she said at last.

Boyne's head wheeled so fast toward Norman that she thought it might have spun off his fleshy neck. She couldn't see his face, but Norman, after shaking his head at Boyne, turned to her with eyes that were almost angry.

"Nobody has turned down an offer from Wolf & Fox."

Elle gulped. "Nobody?"

"Nobody."

She thought of Brooke. "Can I have some time to think it over?"

"Sure you can," Norman said, standing from his chair. Boyne stood and fished under the table with a foot for his shoe. His piggy face was furrowed, questioning. Norman walked toward the door.

Elle reached for her briefcase and raised herself from her chair. She glanced at the orange powder on Boyne's hand and thought better of shaking it; Norman, who seemed to be in charge, was already in the hallway when he turned back to address her.

"I'll have my secretary call the pharmacist and tell her we're bringing you up for your test. If you accept the firm's offer, that is. I'm going to the men's room. You have five minutes."

Boyne's worried look of a moment before vanished. "I was wondering," he said, then laughed out loud. "Five minutes."

Norman nodded. "In five minutes, Ms. Woods, I'll meet you in the lobby, and you will have made your decision."

Coming Summer 2003 from Dutton

FAMILY TRUST

by

Amanda Brown

Family Trust, the second novel from the

author of *Legally Blonde,* is the

laugh-out-loud tale of what happens

when two opposites gain joint custody of

a four-year-old girl and are forced to

reevaluate the way they look at the world

…and each other.